ABOUT THE AUT

Bernard Ashley is one of the most highly regarded authors in the UK. Born in Woolwich, south London, he was evacuated during the war, and ended up attending fourteen different primary schools. After school, Bernard did National Service in the RAF, where he flew a typewriter. He then went on to become a teacher specialising in drama and later a head teacher – his two most recent schools being in east and south London, areas which have provided him with the settings for many of his books. Bernard now writes full time.

Bernard Ashley's other novels for Orchard Books include *Tiger Without Teeth*, a *Guardian* Book of the Week, *Little Soldier*, which was shortlisted for the *Guardian* Children's Book Award and the Carnegie Medal, *Revenge House*, also shortlisted for the *Guardian* Children's Book Award, and *Freedom Flight*. *Flashpoint* is the third book about Ben Maddox – the first two are *Ten Days to Zero* and *Down to the Wire*.

10633

Orchard Books
338 Euston Road
London NW1 3BH

Orchard Books Australia
Level 17/207 Kent Street
Sydney, NSW 2000

First published in Great Britain in 2007
A paperback original

ISBN 978 1 84616 060 8

1 3 5 7 9 10 8 6 4 2

Printed in Great Britain

Orchard Books is a division of Hachette Children's Books,
an Hachette Livre UK Company.
www.orchardbooks.co.uk

a BEN MADDOX assignment

FLASHPOINT

BERNARD ASHLEY

ORCHARD BOOKS

KITCHENER ROAD, LONDON E7

'This might shut your father up!' Sylvie Filey muttered as she read the e-mail. '"*Something positive*"! Well, this'll show him!' She flapped the paper at her son.

From: Jenny Tongue
[jtongue@broadway.org.uk]
Sent: 06 June 14:31
To: s.filey@tiscali.co.uk
Subject: audition

Hi Mrs Filey – please pass to Paul.

Audition for you on Thursday. The Old School Rehearsal Rooms off High Holborn, 9th June, 12:15pm. Reading for son of a pirate! Take your cutlass (only joking) and your singing voice (not joking). Shame it's half term and short notice or we could have worked on this. Ask for Martin Kent. Do your voice exercises. Get plenty of sleep, eat properly, go well!

Jenny

'Yikes!' That was more the response required, never mind showing his dad! Paul Filey read the e-mail three times while his mother stood behind him at the breakfast table. Students at the Broadway Theatre School in East London's Bridge Road didn't get many audition calls at home like this. Most of the jobs the younger students were seen for were the school-age 'soaps', and those came up regularly, coinciding with the school terms. For older kids like Paul the call-ups came 'as and when' – for black, white and Asian gang members and estate-spoilers, hoodies and druggies, whatever itch TV was scratching. Most juvenile work came through being ethnically authentic or white underclass, and Broadway specialised in both. The odd Palladium musical might come out of the blue, or a film that needed a London kid, perhaps a Dickens serial – and then the staff would twitter, because those jobs were big stuff. Either way, it was all dealt with at the school, not at home, at half term.

'What's the show?' Paul's mother asked. Sylvie Filey was an actor herself – usually only a line and a spit on *The Bill* or *Eastenders* – but if the phone in their house was ever allowed to give more than two rings it would jump off the shelf in shock.

'Don't know. Doesn't say.'

'I'll ring her.'

'You won't. She'd say if she knew. Besides, she'll only tell you who else is up for it, and I really don't want to know.' Stage school kids were like puppies at a breeder's, all barking in the same cage; whereas adult actors didn't see who else was up for a job until they got to the audition. And hope and confidence were everything – although talent helped...

'It says it's for the son of a pirate...'

'Yeah – Short John Silver.'

Sylvie did ring someone, though – the Old School Rehearsal Room manager. Why make friends if you couldn't ask a favour? 'Dougie, love, what company's auditioning on Thursday? Musical, by the sounds of it.'

'Who's speaking?'

'Sylvie Filey. The "stroppy shopper", *Eastenders*.

Spotlight number – Yes, that's me. Only, my son's up for something at your place on Thursday and we don't know what…'

Paul could hear the rustle of paper through the telephone earpiece as his mother held it away and mouthed 'Dougie's looking'. He knew why she was ringing; it was in the hope that this show could be something big – significant enough to edge him towards his father's idea of doing something with his life. Sylvie and Alex Filey were separated, Paul choosing to live with his mother, nearer to his drama school, but his father was no distant figure – in fact, he was a hell of a lot *too* involved in one way. Alex Filey was a probation officer, living in Wandsworth, over in south London. And he wanted Paul to do some sort of public service job – get a good degree and go into teaching or one of the other caring services. '*Acting?* Where's that going to take you? Look at your mother…!'

He had reluctantly agreed to Paul going to the Broadway Theatre School – but then regretted it, and until Paul was eighteen, Alex Filey was going to need constant reassurance that one day he'd see his son in the West End, at the very least. He wanted excellent reports, top-student-of-the-year stuff, or financially he could hook Paul off the boards at any time. He wrote the termly cheques as if they were in some ex-prisoner's blood. But an audition with a top company would help persuade him to get that pen out of his leather jacket for next term…

'"White Ensign Productions",' Dougie was telling Paul's mother down the phone. 'New to me.'

'What's the show?'

'Doesn't say – but they've booked the room with the best piano. The rest are all straight plays.'

'Thanks, darling.' Sylvie flipped her mobile shut and stared at her son. He was just above average height for his age – good for an actor – with his father's thick auburn hair and blue eyes. She squinted, as if to see him with an eye-patch and bandana. 'What do you know about pirates?' she asked.

'Not a lot. Skull and crossbones, walking the plank, hanging about at Execution Dock...'

'Then get on the internet and look them up.' She walked round the small table, came back to lean against the sink. 'It won't be *Peter Pan*, there's no pirate son in that – and this is June, a bit early for Christmas...'

'So?' Paul got up and moved his mother aside while he rinsed his cereal bowl. 'It's my voice they'll be interested in, and whether I can act or not. I've got my speeches and my song. It doesn't matter what show it is.'

'No? It does, Sunshine! It matters how you stand, walk, present yourself, how many buttons you have undone on your shirt. Pedro the pirate boy's going to be very different from Bertram, the half-wit baronet who's run away to sea. Get into those Wellington boots! Swish a kitchen knife! Stomp on the deck, swagger around the cabin—'

'Swarm up the curtains...'

'Now you're getting it! Think *Spanish Main!*'

'Aaaar!'

'And dry that bowl before you go upstairs.'

Paul stared at the e-mail again – and the sight of it rolled his stomach with scare, and thrill. He'd had his half term days all mapped out; a fishing trip with Brett from along the street and a midweek Bobby Moore, Cancer Fund match against Spurs at the Hammers, with a bit of revision thrown in, plus his daily voice work and singing. Now it was going to be *all* voice work and singing, and a few long bashes at his audition speeches. And he could forget West Ham because he couldn't risk his vocal chords: which was a muzzle that always flipped his stomach.

The actor's life! Well, that's where he was heading, his choice against his father's wishes, so he'd better be good. The man couldn't pull the plug if he was in work, could he? Yes, he'd better be very good, or *making a difference* loomed.

'Where's the Wellingtons?'

'In the cupboard under the stairs.'

He stared at his mother. 'Oooer!' It could just be a TV advert, *Pirate Popcorn*, or something – and derision from his dad. Or it could be the chance of a lifetime. In the acting game you never knew where anything might lead.

ZEPHON TELEVISION

INTERNAL MEMO

DATE: 5th June
FROM: Kath Lewis
TO: Ben Maddox

Please report to me as soon as you arrive.
Kath Lewis

On his first day back Ben Maddox found the memo Sellotaped over the front of his computer screen. He wasn't meant to miss it. Since returning from the assignment in Lansana he had looked for clues as to how his boss Kath Lewis would greet him. This wasn't in his own words, but he had been a bit of a hero. He'd helped to save a life, and not just any old life – he'd helped to save the life of Jonny Aaranovitch, Zephon's star cameraman, so Kath Lewis would have to be a bit grateful for that. But since flying back to London there had been no clues to her mood, no case of wine delivered to the flat, no letter, e-mail or text of any sort, no reference on Zephon TV to anything more about the Lansana story. When he had rung the newsroom to ask how Jonny was he had been told 'OK' by Kath Lewis's secretary: no 'putting you through' or 'wear your flak-jacket'. Bloom Ramsaran, his best friend at Zephon, told him that Kath had been 'incandescent' over him not obeying her orders – the real trouble being, when the press and TV interviews had been done at the end of the affair, it was the BBC's *News 24* that had scooped all the rest – and this had been supposed to be Zephon's story – so Ben hadn't expected any e-mails or texts to give him a warm glow. Kath Lewis had been unusually quiet – no, she had maintained absolute silence: it had been the personnel manager who had given Ben a few days off, with today slated for his return to work.

So, with his heart treating the occasion as if he were hearing the countdown to a live news broadcast, he went into her office, hazel eyes ready to twinkle, his six feet of athleticism ready to sit, or stand, or kneel.

She didn't look up. She didn't look at him. Her eyes were fixed on the monitor showing Zephon's live transmission. She knew he was there, he knew she knew he was there because her secretary had announced him. But she didn't look up from the broadcast. Bad start: he'd once been her favourite reporter, the one who could joke with her, who had even got to drink a glass or two of her bottom drawer Bordeaux, but today she was giving him the full 'executive and employee' routine.

He stood there: twenty-six years old, dark hair neatly cut, eyes trying not to blink. Linen summer jacket and chinos, Ecco ankle boots in mid brown. In his top pocket he sported a designer-rumpled orange handkerchief – the favourite choice of his hero Frank Sinatra. He needed to show all the bounce he could muster – but he still felt like a six-year-old in front of Mrs Pront, head of infants.

The news item was routine stuff. Faisal Chandrah was reporting live on the arrival at court in Leeds of two young white men in expensive-looking suits, their eyes blazing straight ahead, their arms swinging like soldiers as they ignored the shouts of a knot of bystanders carrying Anti

Racist League banners. Escorted by bodyguards, the two men marched in through the doors of the Crown Court while Faisal, for Zephon, spoke quickly and fluently.

FAISAL CHANDRAH (TO CAMERA)
Into Leeds Crown Court go Jake Whitstead and Brian Roberts, the White Supremacy members charged by the Crown Prosecution Service with the alleged murder of a young Asian footballer in a local park. Sixteen-year-old Abu Iqbal was found dead in the toilets of a changing room when he failed to appear for the second half of a local amateur league match. We have yet to learn what evidence the police will be presenting, but I spoke earlier to the accused men's solicitor, who claims that her clients are innocent and that there is no case for them to answer.
FAISAL CHANDRAH LOOKS DOWN. THE INTERVIEW PACKAGE BEGINS

A young, white, female solicitor looked earnestly into the camera as Kath Lewis clicked the 'mute' button on her remote. 'First-rate journalism, Faisal!' she said to the monitor, and swung to face Ben.

'You disobeyed me.' She stared at him, icicle voice to go with the glacier look.

'Kath, I had to…'

'*Had to* nothing! I run this operation, and I run you. When I say "Jump!" you jump, and when I say "Piddle!" you piddle – and when I say "Return at once to London!" you return at once to London.'

'Kath— '

She waved his interruption aside. 'There is nothing to say.

You...disobeyed...me!' She ground the words out slowly in an angry growl.

'I couldn't—!'

'You could, and you do!'

'I couldn't piddle to order, no man can.'

He could see in her eyes that she wanted to throw something at him. She stood up, as if that might control her frustration; she laid her hands flat on the desk – the claw coming into her fingers. 'You can't resign, don't think that, not without paying a fortune in legal fees. You're contracted to Zephon, and I'm not going to sack you. You're not going anywhere else to put your mug on a TV screen.'

Ben frowned. What was she going to do with him?

'So you're going to work in the film library. You bring the tributes and obituaries up to date, from A to Z.'

Ben slumped inside, but for Kath Lewis and his own pride he stayed upright. The picture library! Stills, film, digital and video, it was the graveyard for the lively journalist. It was a backroom job, and he was a front line reporter. Of course, he knew how it worked, he'd got a degree in journalism. Whenever anybody died, if they'd been of any note in life – politicians, actors, so-called 'personalities' in every field – there had to be a picture clip ready to go out with the death story. But these clips needed constant revision – some great achievement or sleazy scandal might have happened between the last update and the final gasp. In every television company's office there was somebody with good contacts who kept the 'sick list' – those people likely to be departing this world from old age, or illness, or accident – and these 'most likely' candidates' clips were refreshed daily. For the rest, it was a plod from A to Z through the picture library, pulling out the recent footage, just in case...

'Great!' said Ben. 'I've always really wanted to do that.'

Kath eyed him across her desk. 'You've got eighteen months on your contract. You can do that until you go. Time for your love of the job to grow beyond all reward.'

'Cheers.'

She sat down again, losing eye contact for a few seconds – in which time Ben took a quick look around. He wouldn't have cause ever again to come in here, he would be working for Zephon at a very different level.

'Do I get a car allowance?' he asked.

The snap of Kath's look up nearly cricked her neck. 'Travelling back into the past?' She stared her hostility at him, a punishing sight in itself: to be on the wrong side of such a great TV operator was unbelievably sad. 'I won't sack you for impertinence, not now, and not in the next eighteen months.'

Ben knew that his contract was binding. He'd need a king's ransom to take on Zephon with a legal challenge. So she'd got him screwed to the hardwood flooring. He wanted to ask whether she'd be happier if he'd let Jonny Aaranovitch die back in Lansana; but he wasn't going to stand in here and whine.

'Thank you, Ms Lewis,' he said. He knew she hated that feminist title. And he walked out, not slamming the door but leaving it a crack open.

The STAGE

FLAME REKINDLING
New departure for rock legend

By Alistair Thomas

One-time Irish rock favourite Flame is to come out of retirement to star in a new musical. More used to a thumping arena than a conventional 'house', Sadie Baker – professionally known as Flame – will tour *She-Pirate* to European theatres interspersed with dates in Bolton, Bristol, and Cardiff, announce management Rusel Hudson Inc.

The flame-haired singer with the strongest female voice in rock history is signed to a run-of-the-tour contract, taking in Germany, Holland and France – culminating in the Phoenix Theatre, Paris, in September.

Flame has been absent from recording and concert dates for three years now, and had been described by her management as 'retired'. But now, in her forties, she says she will find the adrenaline of a tour just what she needs 'to keep my hair from turning grey'.

She-Pirate, the story of the legendary Bristol pirate Meg Macroo, is written by a new partnership, Martin Kent and Nick Cannon for White Ensign Productions. It opens at the Cambridge Theatre, Shaftesbury Avenue in late July before its European tour.

SOUTH BANK, LONDON SE1

Bloom Ramsaran put down her Thursday morning reading and looked around the Zephon newsroom. It was the look of a Trinidadian schoolgirl who'd been left out of a secret in the schoolyard. She was Zephon Television's show-business correspondent, she with her ear close to the ground – so why was she reading this story in *The Stage*? She regularly read the trade papers to see what sort of a slant other correspondents had put on stories she'd covered, but not to discover something as big as this. These sorts of stories usually came after a press conference or a press release, not out of the blue. It hadn't even been flagged-up on an actor's website or by gossip. Had Rusel Hudson Inc. given *The Stage* an exclusive – and if so, why?

She rooted in her desk drawer. Was there an invitation to a press call in here that she'd lost? No. She flicked through her book and phone calendars diaries – but she'd missed nothing so far as she could see, and there's nothing worse for a journalist than to feel 'out of the loop'. She was about to ring Rusel Hudson – because an interview set up with Flame would make a great item for Zephon – when Ben Maddox came through the newsroom, on his way back from seeing Kath Lewis.

His face said everything. He looked very close to tears.

'Naughty boy?' Bloom Ramsaran made it sound sexy.

Ben nodded, as if he couldn't trust his voice.

'Smack on bottom?'

Ben groaned. 'Punch in the face! Kick in the privates!' He came over to Bloom. He wasn't going to share his misery with all those newsroom eyes that were carefully not looking at him. A colleague's success is often to be applauded, but their downfall is always to be celebrated. Quietly, of course.

But Bloom was different. They had joined Zephon at the same time, and while Bloom hadn't received the acclaim he had, she hadn't ever done other than support him. If it was possible to have a true partner outside the home, Bloom was Ben's.

'Picture library, obits and tributes!' Ben said.

'*What?* The woman's crazy!'

'No dispute about that. And I'd need to win the lottery to walk out on my contract.'

'Get buyin' those tickets!'

'There's no problem. I can do it. And it won't be for long, she'll soon come wanting the old BM for something...'

'There speaks Mr Confident!'

'...I saw her desk.'

'You noticed? She's running a new regime – no clutter, know where everything is. You should see some of her memos while you were away.'

'Not that.' Ben leant to Bloom's ear like a man about to kiss her neck. 'No wine glass. No red rings on her papers...'

'She's on the wagon.'

'And suffering. It won't last, she'll fall off it. I've never seen her the worse for it; her glasses of red keep the machinery working. She'll soon see BM in a different light. Claret.'

Bloom shook her head. 'Don't soak your seeds for sowing, might not be this season. But, obits and tributes – is that really the strength of what you're on?' She clicked in her throat.

'Yup.'

She stared up at him, about to say something significant. 'Then do a job for me? Dig out some stuff on Flame – Sadie Baker? And some Bristol pirate, Meg Macroo...'

'Don't hold back, woman! Don't delay yourself, weeping and wailing!'

'Get your jacket off, boy! We're back together.'

'Flame the rock star?'

She held out the *Stage* piece. 'I didn't *know* about this,' she said. 'It's like it's not of British interest...'

Ben frowned. 'It says she opens at the Cambridge – there's hardly a bigger theatre in London.'

'But she's not there for long, the Cambridge has got the new Lloyd Webber going in on September the third. This *She-Pirate*'s for Europe, and a couple of provincials. It'll be all action and thumping tunes to bridge the language gap.'

'So what's the problem with that?'

'Flame, back on stage – imagine Robbie Williams or the Stones, they'd play the Cambridge for a *season*, or Wembley for three nights – Flame could do the biggest box office ever. Yet they're just playing-in the show then scuttling off to Europe. Are they mad, or what?'

'I'll dig her out,' said Ben. 'Find her latest interview.'

'It'll be a year or so back.'

'I've got time. God, have I got time!' And Ben walked past his empty desk and off through the door out of the newsroom – heading for history.

ZEPHON PICTURE LIBRARY
TELEVISION SCRIPT
TRANSCRIPT SERVICE

ITV Evening News
04/02/2003

JOHN BAILEY, NEWSREADER:

You know her face, you know her hair, you know her powerful voice. But Flame, the first lady of rock, has announced her retirement. June Lafferty reports.

Shots and sounds of a Flame concert, flashing coloured lights, a sweating rock band, and a standing, arm-waving audience.
Flame, rocker-red hair in long tresses which she flourishes like a scarf as she twists and shakes her head, belts out Rock My Socks Off!

JUNE LAFFERTY (VOICE OVER):

This is the Flame familiar to us and to millions of rock fans the world over. But that world *is* over for the woman behind the legend, Sadie Baker.

Sadie Baker, formerly 'Flame', thirtyish, in a summer dress walks towards the camera, down a garden path from the doorway of a stone cottage.

JUNE LAFFERTY (VOICE OVER):

Somerset – and gone is the long red hair, gone is the strut. What has made Sadie Baker give up her rock career?

Sadie Baker, *medium shot, sitting at a garden table, seen over the shoulder of June Lafferty:*
I wasn't on the skids, I wasn't into drugs or drink, God, no, I wasn't. I had everywhere to go, and we had stuff lined up till Doomsday. (She runs her fingers through her now short, unremarkable light auburn hair.) We hadn't had a barney, the band; they're still my best friends. Wizz Burton was round here at the weekend...

JUNE LAFFERTY (OFF-CAMERA):
But?

SADIE BAKER (CLOSE-UP, LOOKING AT JUNE LAFFERTY):
There's other things in life. We couldn't be private, and the audiences were (long pause) not always what you want. Getting... (she waves her arms dismissively and wrinkles her nose)

JUNE LAFFERTY (OFF-CAMERA):
What? Badly behaved?

SADIE BAKER:
Very mixed. Now (waves her arm at the cottage) I've got peace, and the people around me – the local folk – that I want.

CUT-AWAY TO JUNE LAFFERTY:
You're at home here?

SADIE BAKER (OFF-CAMERA):
So much so. *My* Somerset.

JUNE LAFFERTY:
You said there were other things in life. Your life, I presume. What are those things?

SADIE BAKER (EXTREME CLOSE-UP):
Personal things. But not people, not a person...

JUNE LAFFERTY (OFF-CAMERA):
Religion? (Sadie Baker shakes her head) Politics?

SADIE BAKER:
Not in a...mainstream...way. No, it's about me living a private life among people I want to live with. (Pause) Rock, and noise, and touring, and giving everything to people you might not want to give it to – it's a life of great commitment. You're public, everyone's property, and you can only give so much. Or take so much. (Looks away, comes back, smiles banally.) I'll maybe write a book...

CUT-AWAY ON JUNE LAFFERTY:
Ah. The 'Flame' story will be told...

SADIE BAKER (MEDIUM SHOT, OVER JUNE LAFFERTY'S SHOULDER):
Possibly. In God's due time.

JUNE LAFFERTY (TURNING TO CAMERA):
Well, we all wish Flame a peaceful and well-deserved retreat...

SADIE BAKER:

Retreat. You've got it, that's the word. Like a prayed-out nun, I'm on retreat...

JUNE LAFFERTY (TO CAMERA):

So... This is June Lafferty for ITN in Claverham, Somerset.

PACKAGE ENDS

THE OLD SCHOOL REHEARSAL ROOMS, LONDON WC1

Sylvie Filey had prepared Paul for what to expect. She went with him on the Underground to Holborn, and walked him to the audition venue. She kept everything business-like and focused on the day, no talk of anything except what he was about to do, and how he looked, of course. Without Jenny Tongue to advise them she had chosen what clothes he should wear – a 'grandad' white shirt with uncreased chinos, and his black 'movement' shoes. She had given his neck a shave and put a light touch of gel on his hair, which had been cut not-too-long and not-too-short by Pasqual at Stratford. Now, on an overcast June morning – typical heavy, examination weather – she pointed out the old London School Board three-decker, sold off after businesses had bought-up the area.

'Forget your father – do your best for you!'

'Yeah,' he husked. He'd have to find a better voice than that, thanks! He cleared his throat as she gave him a hug, before briskly disappearing along a busy pavement; leaving Paul to walk across a small car park and into the audition rooms' reception area.

He expected to find a desk or an office, but he was directed into a very informal space, more a cafeteria, where sealed slices of cake and muffins sat on glass shelves next to pre-packed sandwiches. There were hot and cold drinks machines, and small tables where groups and individuals sat. It could have been the Broadway canteen, Paul thought. He looked around for someone in charge – perhaps this Dougie whom his mother had phoned – but he couldn't see anyone official-looking. There, across the room, though, was a blackboard and easel – how old was this place! – and on it was today's date and a chalked list of companies and rooms.

White Ensign Productions – room 16

It was a good job his mother had phoned Dougie, or Paul would have been totally lost. But before seeking out room sixteen, he took a good look around him. And anyone could see that this place was theatrical – the droop of an arm over the back of a chair, the tilt of a head, the straightness of the backs, the ubiquitous bottles of water, the short skirts and the all-in-the-same-wash T-shirts with faded logos. You could hear theatre, too: murmurings of 'cut' and 'third speech' over a script, a brittle laugh, loudish talk of 'the tour' and 'my agent'. And the accents, either 'received' or 'London' – they didn't audition for *Coronation Street* or *Liverpool Night*s down south. In all of which, what Paul was looking for were boys of his own age, competitors for the same son-of-a-pirate part.

And his insides rolled as he saw one – a boy sitting at a table in the corner with an older woman. But why should his insides roll, he expected to see other boys here, didn't he? Only the top stars didn't have to read for a part, and then not always. All the same, sight of the competition suddenly gave him that old gripe in the bowel and he looked away.

Paul had seen straight off that the boy was everything he wasn't. Paul Filey was auburn-haired, grey-eyed, a few freckles; he was 'natural boy', 'unspoilt good sort' – but that kid there was dark-brown-silky-haired, with a slight tan, a perfect nose and big eyes. He had 'young hero' written all over him – Jim Hawkins, David Balfour, Tom Brown. Paul's heart went down to meet the turmoil below. If he and this boy were both up for 'pirate son' he knew very well who would get it on looks – matey over there, sitting sipping coffee with all the poise of Oscar Wilde.

Straight off, Paul went to find room sixteen. Seeking it out he went up brown-tiled staircases and past old classrooms. There was someone sitting at a table outside most of them, and actors were bent over scripts along the corridor. Auditions were timed, and it was bad practice to have actors lining up to read. They would only meet each other going in and coming out. There was always someone waiting outside each room. The company names were pinned on the doors, *English Touring Theatre*, *Watermill*, *Enter Left*; and at last he found *White Ensign Productions* – number sixteen the only door on the second floor, once a school hall.

A blonde woman of about fifty was seated at a small table outside. As he approached her, Paul could hear a piano playing inside, and a boy coming in on a voice entrance.

'Yes?' The woman was looking up at him. 'Are you for *She-Pirate*?'

'"*Son* of a pirate"', Paul said, showing the woman his e-mail. There had to be some mistake – he wasn't doing drag, thank you very much!

'Paul Filey?' she asked.

'That's right.'

The woman ticked his name on the list: God, it looked a list from here to Nottingham.

'What do you know about the show?'

Paul shook his head. 'Nothing, really. I'm at Broadway and it's half term. I've only had an e-mail.'

The woman shrugged.

'*She-Pirate*?' Paul prompted.

'Your part's Ardal, the son of Meg Macroo, famous female pirate. A musical. Opens in London, tours Europe. Eleven weeks. How old are you?'

'Sixteen.'

She nodded. 'Good. No tutor required,' and made a note. 'Have you brought your music?'

'Yes.'

'Ready with a speech?'

'Yes.'

'Then wait along there. I'll call you.'

Paul went to sit on one of the two chairs provided. She hadn't given him a script to read, so he guessed it was his voice that mattered most, at this stage. His mother had warned him that even if they thought he was good enough today, he wouldn't walk out with a contract in his pocket – there would be 'recalls' when other aspects of the job would be tested. So he opened his music score and looked at it, made sure of words that were already cemented.

'Oh the shark babe, has such teeth dear, and he shows them pearly white,

Just a jack-knife has old Macheath babe, and he keeps it out of sight…'

Mack the Knife by Bertholt Brecht, music by Kurt Weill. It was good, dramatic, punchy stuff, not some sixteen-year-old boy singing about missing his lover.

'Paul?' The voice shot him up straight, his music fell to the floor. 'Go in now, please.'

He gathered himself up. He had been trained for these moments – by the school, and by his mother. *Don't rush. Compose yourself. That first look at you as you walk in the door is the first look an audience will have – the director knows that. Hold yourself upright and don't sit until*

you're invited. But smile – a smile is your first audition piece – and make eye contact with everyone there, even the producer's dog. Deep breaths, and show how you can control your nerves for a first night. Which this will be like…

And taking his training with him, Paul Filey walked into the audition room.

Paul Filey, Paul Filey, Paul Filey, he said in his head, which he was holding very high…*Paul Filey, son of Sylvie Filey*…

SOUTH BANK, LONDON SE1

Ben was sitting at a table under an awning outside the National Theatre on London's South Bank. He hadn't been able to bring himself to take his Sadie Baker research through to the Zephon newsroom for Bloom. He'd have only got sympathy from some and loud talk of a breaking story from others. But Bloom often took her lunch by the Thames at this time – she was one of those need-to-swim-outside-the-rock-pool people – and that suited Ben, too, working solo in the picture library. He could take his break when and where he wanted: one thing was certain, Kath Lewis wasn't suddenly going to call him in for an assignment. And the picture library was even more stifling than the newsroom at lunchtime; a couple of men in matching cardigans who liked to share a packet of home-made sandwiches over a raspberry smoothie.

He'd bought a tuna and sweetcorn baguette with a large filter coffee, which he ate as he read the free 'lite' evening paper – he would never sit at a table staring into space, even when the words weren't going in.

Kath Lewis's reaction had been predictable – at least, her displeasure had. He was tempted to think she was the hard sort of woman who would rather Jonny Aaronovitch had died and a township been flooded than have her instructions ignored. Just a roasting, that's what he'd thought he was in for. He had come to the office smart enough to go out on any assignment anywhere, expecting a couple of weeks on local news and then reinstatement to the adrenaline rush of top broadcasting. But had he misread her! Ben Maddox had transgressed and, like some jumpy prime minister, Kath Lewis had made a showy sacrifice. Ben Maddox had become a name in the business – but she was letting the industry know that she was bigger than anyone at Zephon News.

For himself, Ben could have taken the demotion; he was still working for Zephon, friends and family could think he was working undercover on a big story if they wanted, he could be vague about that. And the picture library *was* research. But telling the truth to Meera when she got in from her publishing job, that was going to be hard. His partner of four years had told him to come back to London just as strongly as Kath Lewis had; things in Lansana had turned very ugly. But for the best of reasons – for Jonny Aaranovitch – Ben had defied them both, and now he had to face the flak. And from Meera it had been heavy already. Of course she was pleased that he'd helped to save a colleague's life; of course she was delighted that a township had been saved from destruction. The trouble was, the look in her eyes said she strongly suspected that it had been Bloom Ramsaran who had bumped him up to stay and be a hero.

This all went over and over in his mind as his lunch went down seagull-fashion. But, anyway, where was Bloom? She should have shown by now. He had sent her the transcript of the Sadie Baker interview, an internet article on Meg Macroo was in his jacket pocket, and he had said that he'd be having a bite here. The invitation was clear. And she had chosen not to come. Was he less interesting all of a sudden because he wasn't buzzing in the newsroom – the man of a previous moment? There was nothing sadder...

Suddenly his mobile phone rang.

'Hello?'

'Ben?'

'Yup.'

'Bloom.'

'Oh, hi Bloom.'

'You missing me?'

'Oh, sure!' Said with the sarcastic tone called for.

'Sorry, Superman. I'm at an old school…'

'I thought you knew your tables.'

'Auditions. For the Flame thing.'

'You'll never make it – you can't sing, and you haven't got an Equity card…'

'I found out where they're being held, and Flame's here, apparently. I'm outside, but I'm going to try for an interview.'

'Good for you.' Ben looked out wistfully over the Thames. He could feel the tingle of trying for an exclusive against the odds. 'Hold on! I've got some Meg Macroo stuff in my pocket. I'll read it over if you like; could give you a leg-up.'

'You are the best!' Ben heard the click of a pen-cap. 'Shoot, darling!'

And Ben read to her what he'd got off the internet, cutting and paraphrasing as he went.

Pirates and Privateers
The History of Maritime Piracy
MEG MACROO

Meg Macroo was born April 2, 1705, in Bristol, the illegitimate daughter of a prominent judge and his wife's maid. The disgraced judge fled to the Caribbean, where his daughter grew up.

At fifteen Meg ran off from an oppressive home with a sailor, a matelot who was later killed by a landowner who found him housebreaking, so when she discovered that she was pregnant Meg went home to her father.

Here she captured the attention of Felix Lawes, one of the wealthiest slave-owners in the Caribbean. With her young son Ardal, Meg ran off with Lawes, first having to fight (and win) a duel with his current lover, a violent Spanish beauty. But she was disgusted when Lawes paid too much attention to a negro housegirl. Meg remonstrated with him; a slave was an inferior being, and she left Lawes, taking her son Ardal with her.

She next caught the eye of Ned Smart, a pirate of renown. She lived and sailed with him, and when Smart was killed in a raid, Meg took over the leadership of the pirate band, and made her son Ardal her lieutenant. At first she dressed as a man and never gave up an opportunity to show her fighting skills, but as her crew came to respect her she reverted to women's clothing, except when engaging other vessels. Her crew was sworn to secrecy, and she sailed the seven seas, gaining a reputation as the ruthless 'Cap'n Macroo', with a crew that obeyed her implicitly because for the smallest offence – and spilling her secret was a big offence – they were put to death.

But as she dallied too long over the brutal punishment of a black pirate who had questioned a decision, the rival buccaneer Roarin' James in the *Bartholomew* crept up on her ship under cover of sea fog and attacked. In the skirmish, Roarin' James killed many of Cap'n Macroo's crew, but he spared Meg herself, who knew the whereabouts of three merchantmen laid up for storm repairs in Sierra Leone. Still seen as a man, she pleaded also for her son's life, challenging Roarin' James to a duel when he refused. By pirate code – and his powerful quartermaster knew this – James had to fight her, or grant her request.

He turned it to his advantage. Against the life of her son he forced Meg to write the location of the merchantmen on a parchment and tuck it into her shirt. If Cap'n Macroo died, the boy would be taken with Roarin' James, and die a terrible death if the ships and the booty were not found there.

The two pirate captains, with Ardal and a pirate to guard him, were rowed ashore with the quartermaster onto a deserted coastline. Armed with both cutlass and pistol, the combatants obeyed the duelling code, which was to pace from back-to-back to fire their pistols once. If necessary they then fought on with cutlasses. The first to draw blood would be the winner.

Each missed with their pistols. Now the odds were in Roarin' James's favour. He was the bigger of the two and likely to cut the first wound, but Cap'n Macroo was nimble. She retreated with Roarin' James pursuing her, when he stumbled on a tree root as he lunged. She immediately seized the opportunity – ripping open her shirt, revealing not the parchment but herself as a woman.

Roarin' James gawped in surprise for a crucial second, when Meg Macroo slashed his throat with her cutlass, first blood and last blood, killing him.

The man guarding Ardal ran off into the sea. But the ship's quartermaster took the triumphant Meg Macroo and her son off the beach.

She was now cheered as the new leader of the ship, openly female – the captain of a dreaded and dangerous band.

Cap'n Macroo lived a long and successful life at sea, but in 1740 the governor of Jamaica, hearing of her presence in his waters, sent an armed sloop to capture the *Bartholomew* and her crew.

The crew were celebrating a previous victory in rum, and the ship was easily taken.

At her trial Meg Macroo was found guilty of piracy on the high seas and sentenced to hang, but she escaped the rope by dying from fever while in jail.

Her fame lives on as an uncompromising Bristol woman in a violent men's world, one who believed in her own superiority all her adult life .

Bloom whooped down the phone. 'That's great! What a question for me to ask her at the end!'

'Why the end?'

'Because by then it won't matter if she goes all moody on me.'

'What the hell question's that?' What question would Bloom ask that was so dynamite?

'What she does at the end. Will Flame flash her boobies at the audience, when she shocks old Roarin' James?'

Ben thought about it. 'Yeah, good question,' he said: and it was, because he would really like to know the answer.

Which was what good journalism was all about. And to think Ben Maddox used to be part of all that...

WHITE ENSIGN PRODUCTIONS

AUDITION CALLS

DATE   9th June

SHOW   SHE-PIRATE

PART   Ardal, Meg Macroo's son

ACTOR   PAUL FILEY

SONG   Mack the Knife

A good crack at this, started nervous, song didn't test his upper range — but good masculine voice. Gave him some scales to do and top register is sound. Breathing needs attention, prob. nerves. Overall, gd strong voice — would need some coaching.

READING   Romeo's balcony scene

Nice interpretation, the boy in love, gd poetic delivery, a bit sing-song, but gd rapport with us as if we're friends hiding in the shrubbery. Clear voice, odd London vowel, not a problem.

NOTES

Liked him. Intelligent, wd take direction. Gd reports from Broadway.
No attitude. Mother acts. Sadie liked him.

CONCLUSION

Poss. see him again.

CALL-BACK Y / N

Wait till Friday afternoon — might see others as good or better.

Martin K

THE OLD SCHOOL REHEARSAL ROOMS, LONDON WC1

Paul came out of the audition not knowing how he felt. One of his mother's great virtues was that she was always honest about an audition. If it had gone badly, if she hadn't done herself justice, she always said so – *I won't get that, I was worse than Walter Plinge's aunt!*; which also meant that when she said she'd done well, Paul knew that she had. If she didn't get the part it would be other physical factors that failed her. So it had to be the same with him. When you kidded other people you started kidding yourself, and right now he wanted to know honestly how he felt he'd done.

But this was what he couldn't do. The song had gone OK, but he was going to have to work on some other piece that tested his higher range, they'd said that. Jenny Tongue had said *Mack the Knife* was playing to his strengths, but today, in the real, cut-and-thrust world outside Broadway it had shown up as a weakness. Which he hadn't got: he could hit top F and hold it, thanks very much, which he'd proved with the scales they'd asked him to do.

The Romeo speech he reckoned they'd liked: he'd kept their attention, and their polite smiles came off their faces as they really listened when he interrupted his musings with a teenage flick of his fingers to say, '*See how she leans her cheek upon her hand! O that I were a glove upon that hand, That I might touch that cheek!*' Yes, he was happy with that bit. The interview at the end he wasn't so sure about. They didn't seem to ask him the stuff that got them to *know* him, more just his *sort*. They were keen to know his interests, what he did in his spare time, who his friends were, did he belong to anything, like a political party? The only time that they made a note was when he said he supported West Ham. They looked at one another, and smiled. Well, a lot of theatricals are failed footballers…

And he thought about who *they* were. The director, Martin Kent, was a smallish white man with a tight England rugby shirt, corduroy trousers, and black trainers, who finished most sentences with a dominating stare. The person with him – who said nothing – was a middle-aged woman wearing granny glasses. Martin Kent did the talking while she did the staring; relentless, burning off a layer of skin.

At the end, Paul couldn't credit it: the man had actually said the dreaded words: '*We'll let you know*'. Which Paul knew from his mother's experience was a lie – they never did, unless you were getting a recall. That was one of the worst parts of the job. He'd seen it so often: she'd hype herself up for an audition, do it, come home and wait for the phone to ring from her agent – all the first day, all the second day, then a weekend usually plonked itself in, and by the third working day she knew that it wouldn't happen. And it didn't. If the telephone rang it would be an offer of a free mobile phone.

So – it was go home and wait to see what happened.

Overall, how did he feel about it, then? OK, it had gone OK, he could tell his mother. But he didn't really know. The job sounded exciting, for whoever got it – and when he spoke to his dad he'd play up the solid cred of it: a London opening in a new musical followed by a European tour! But Martin Kent hadn't asked him the crucial question his mother had told him he might get asked: whether or not he had a summer holiday booked…

He walked along the corridor; and there was matey sitting reading the *Daily Express* – 'our hero' from downstairs – but no woman with him now. And how relaxed could you be, legs crossed like Lord Languid and *reading the flipping paper*?

The boy didn't look up as Paul's heart sank: perhaps this wasn't the life for him after all.

She's nipping out for a smoke. Snappy woman, surprised by me being here, pulled a face.
Didn't want to talk but when I waved my Zephon press card she looked like she suddenly thought she ought to. Slowed, didn't stop. Unremarkable looking, small old fashioned glasses, nothing hair – where was 'Flame'?
Q: (On the hoof!) Why hasn't the production of She-Pirate been press-released? Why is only The Stage in on it?
A: New PR company, ballsed it up. Please, I'm busy. (She hurries on down the stairs, thinks that's it.)
Q: (With her) Will you come on Zephon TV for an interview at the right time?
A: Doubt it. (Goes on again, fags out.)
Q: What made you decide to come out of retirement – and why a musical, not a rock show?
A: Please – I'm very busy, dear...
(No answer, pushes on away from me.)
Q: A last question, Sadie – Meg Macroo bared her chest at the rival pirate: are you going to do that in the show?
A: (Took her unawares, stopped, stared me out.) Get real!
END OF INTERVIEW FOR SURE!
NB: KEEP TABS ON HER THROUGH HER AGENT RUSEL HUDSON – COULD MAKE A LIVELY SHOWBIZ ITEM LATER. SHE'S HIDING SOMETHING, THAT COOKIE!

'Put it behind you for now. Done. Gone. Next item, please. They'll be auditioning all tomorrow, then there's the weekend. If you get a recall you'll know next week at Broadway, not before. So for now, forget it; tell yourself you didn't get it, and move on.' Sylvie Filey was going through some files from her school bag. After seeing Paul into the audition she'd gone east to Hartley Primary that afternoon to pick up the details for three days' work the following week – supply teaching paid the bills between acting jobs.

Paul watched her. 'I've got to find a better song for auditions...'

'Sure, good, work on that. I'll give it some thought.' She slapped a heft of curriculum guidelines onto the kitchen table. 'God,' she said, 'poor souls who have to do this all the time...'

Paul looked at the uninspiring pastel of the publications, small shaded boxes of emphasis, like 'big deal'! It's another world, he thought. The eight-to-six, week-in, week-out slog – the same stuff, different kids, year on year. Or the hot courtroom, taking on some hopeless case standing there in a new suit to impress the magistrate, lying his head off that he was going to go straight if he had a bit of help. Compare those worlds with eight shows a week, teatime till midnight, hundreds of different stage doors; five a.m. till 'wrap' shooting days under arc lights; TV studios when you walk in to see the set that up to then had been white lines on a scout hut floor. And he knew which world he fancied; and it wasn't the lifetime of routine: it was the stomach-churning uncertainty of the acting game, even with cold fish like old hero-matey at the audition.

And he knew that whatever platitudes his mother came out with, he wasn't going to forget the audition until time and silence evaporated it.

Sunday saw him over in SW18. True to his mother's word there had been no call from White Ensign – but he still jumped if the phone rang – and true to his dad's promise he was invited to Wandsworth for 'a bite' at the weekend. He always went. The problems between his parents were their problems. Paul was son to both of them, and most of the time he enjoyed his dad's company. To not go because he had work to do on a new song would have been a mega mistake – the termly Broadway cheques written by his dad depended on him being seen to keep his feet on the ground and not come the *ac-tor* all over the place. Plus, on this occasion, if he *did* by some outside chance get a part in this tour, he wouldn't see the man at all for three months.

Wandsworth was always a bit of an adventure. Where the house in West Ham had been built to a traditional pattern – one of a hundred in Kitchener Road whose lay-out you knew before the front door was opened – the house his father shared with an auctioneer, George de Sousa, was a one-off. With Georgian proportioned doors and windows it was narrow at the front, but it opened out in an L shape behind, holding surprises, and was explorable. Folding doors could make one room of two this week, or two rooms of one, there were both front and back stairs to the other floors, and the basement was divided into cellars, one of which ran out under the street. And the furniture was never the same two visits running. George de Sousa and Alex Filey were never afraid to sit down and use what lords and princes had sat on before.

And the man was explorable, too. One week his dad was a bachelor, liked his own company, whipped up a meal for the two of them in the kitchen; another week he was practically 'married', with a Susan or a Wendy or a Jill doing the cooking for three in the conservatory (or four if George was in); a third week and there could be a raucous gathering of George's auction house colleagues, all linen jackets and gavel knuckles, rapping for attention on a polished refectory table in the dining room.

Over one thing Alex Filey was constant, though – his son had to see the light sooner or later, get a decent degree and do something useful with his life. *Be of service, make a difference.* It seemed to have been part of the separation deal that Sylvia Filey could indulge Paul and his acting ambitions for a bit – but there was always the feeling that the curtain was about to come down; and half the questions Paul was asked over in Wandsworth were the sort the Home Secretary had to answer in the House of Commons. Social issues: crime; race; civil liberties. Meanwhile, his top commitment was to be continually doing well at Broadway.

And today he could boast of his audition.

'*She-Pirate*, eh?' His father immediately had his own take on it. Not, *Who's directing, what's the company?* like his mother, but, 'Do you know why they hanged pirates at Execution Dock, not at Tyburn? *Hanged*, mind, people were *hanged*, pictures are *hung*…'

No, Paul didn't know.

'…Because piracy was a crime against the Lords of the Admiralty, so convicted pirates were officially hanged on Admiralty property, between the low and high tides of the foreshore at Wapping. The offenders knew the rules.'

'If not they soon got the hang of them.' But Paul was immediately ashamed; some things you didn't joke about with his dad – who could have been a pirate himself, Paul thought. Take off any pirate bandana or tricorn hat or wig, and there was the shaven head and the bony face of Alex Filey, halfway to skull already, with those grey eyes that blinked only when he let them. Paul swore some of his clients kept to the terms of their probation only because they were frightened of the stare.

Now Paul was looking into it. 'So make sure you get that part! I put on the performance of my life on Friday to keep a pregnant teenage girl out of Holloway…'

This Sunday it was a bachelor day, with a couple of grim stories over lunch that would have embarrassed Paul a year ago – but his dad's sirloin language had never allowed for words to be minced. The world was the world, you couldn't hide from it, you just had to make an improvement to it. In every way he treated Paul like an equal: except in the crucial respect that Paul was a son who depended on a father's goodwill to carry on at Broadway.

'Three month tour?' Now he came back to it. 'Would that pay your fees till Christmas?'

So no pressure, then!

'Now, I've got a Speckled Hen to go with that steak. Will your mum let you have a half?' His dad's job meant he was realistic about what sixteen-year-olds liked. 'You're not likely to need saving from yourself, are you? I was working with a kid on Monday, come out of Feltham…'

'A Coke or a Pepsi's fine, thanks.'

Meanwhile no more was said regarding the audition.

But as Paul knew from his *Text and Script* lectures, what is said is only the surface of meaning. His father going on about alcoholic boys and pregnant girls who needed saving from themselves was really all about him coming out of Broadway and doing something 'useful' with his own life.

Meera's anger was worse than the professional humiliation: anger not just at Ben, but at Kath Lewis.

'She's a witch!' she ranted. 'You helped save the life of her best cameraman!'

'Which was the only story for Zephon.' Ben sagged onto the settee. 'Reuters and the BBC got the big international scoop – on the back of our digging. *That's* why she's mad...'

'Without the decency to just sack you. You could go anywhere – though God knows why when you've got no common sense.' Meera's Anglo-Asian delivery could fire like a Gattling gun.

'That's what Bloom said.'

'Oh, Bloom!' Meera did a freezy, twitchy thing with her shoulders. She stood over Ben and her eyes narrowed. 'And where does she stand in all this? Is she demoted for encouraging you to stay out there?'

Which Bloom had. 'Not so far as I know...'

'And you *would* know?'

'Sure. Of course I would.'

'Meanwhile, you're being paid – without bonuses and without an expense account – and your career is on hold for eighteen months. In eighteen months no one else will remember you, or want you.' Meera walked off into the kitchen. 'You're an ass and Kath Lewis is a cow!'

'You can visit us on the farm...'

'I can visit a solicitor!' Meera came back. 'We'll test your contract. Sometimes there are loopholes...'

Ben got up. 'With Zephon?' He shuddered. 'I doubt it!'

Meera didn't reply, but got on with cooking a hot curry; which, sad to say, Ben could hardly taste.

STUDIO AUTOCUE

A top European drugs gang was jailed for a total of two hundred years today. The old bailey heard how the Fredericks brothers of Ilford imported fifty million pounds worth of cocaine into Britain, which they turned into crack in an east ham council flat.
Sentencing the twins – Ronald and Stephen Fredericks – to twenty years each in prison, judge Renee Bryant told them that they were a scourge to civilised society.

(CUT TO PACKAGE)

TRANSCRIPT OF PACKAGE

Shots of a smallish kitchen with what look like halved pancakes spread over the counter.

ZEPHON COURT REPORTER BRIAN LEWARD (VOICE OVER):
This is the East Ham kitchen where the Fredericks twins turned their smuggled cocaine into crack to sell on the streets of Great Britain.

(Camera pans around kitchen. Cut to a baking tray in an oven.)
And this is one of the baking trays used to purify the cocaine.

(Rostrum: map of Europe with various towns in Holland, Denmark, Germany and Belgium pinpointed.)
Vulnerable young women brought up to three kilograms of pure cocaine into Europe from the Caribbean – hidden in bottles of rum, vases, shampoo bottles and toothpaste tubes.

(Shot of a Brincastle freight lorry at dock's checkpoint.)
It was smuggled into Britain in regular shipments of European veal.

(Shot of Valerie Cordobe walking into Snaresbrook Crown Court.)
Valerie Cordobe, a Spanish immigrant, was one of those convicted today at Snaresbrook Crown Court. She will serve five years.

(Still portrait of Judge Renee Bryant in judicial wig.)
In her closing remarks, Judge Bryant told the defendants that no one, however vulnerable, could be excused this despicable trade.

CUT TO STUDIO

The third Fredericks brother, Gary, is still at large, uncharged and unconvicted, with parts of the network believed to be still intact.

Now, sport...

Ben watched the Zephon newsreader doing the job he had done a few times himself in the past two years. And for the way he felt, jealousy wasn't the word: it was impure, undistilled dislike. This little squirt was one of those who'd kept his head well down over his keyboard when Ben had come out of Kath Lewis's office – not a word of sympathy, not even a *false* word, which was perhaps to the man's credit.

But the old juices were flowing in Ben. Gary Fredericks, the younger brother of the drugs gang – where was he, what was he doing? Now *that* would be a story to break, if the right reporter could get under the skin of it! And who would that reporter have been, once upon a time – going to Kath Lewis with a wild proposal? Benjamin Maddox!

Who else?

There was the academic, and there was the vocational: Paul's timetable had 'A' against some periods, 'V' against others. The academic curriculum was what most kids had to do, even after sixteen. But the V's were what they'd all gone to Broadway for – Voice, Movement, Singing, Acting, Tap Dancing, Stage Combat, and Improvisation. There was one big miss among the many V's, though: a seminar or two on 'How to Get Over an Audition'. There was plenty of advice on going for a call-up, and help with the preparation, too, but no one on the staff had thought about 'P.A.T.' – Post Audition Trauma – and how to deal with the wait.

This Monday morning Paul's head swung round every time a door opened – classroom, canteen or studio. His ears twitched whenever he heard a telephone ring. A sudden shout somewhere in the building had him thinking it could be his vocational tutor Jenny Tongue reading an e-mail from White Ensign Productions. People coming and going meant she might appear at any time with some news – because if a recall was in her hand, Sod's Law meant that it would be for that very afternoon.

All day he pond-skated on surface tension, and right to the end of the afternoon his head turned to any clear of a throat. His heart had leapt when he'd first gone in that morning, when she'd come to find him in the canteen to ask him how it had gone on the Thursday – although he truly hadn't expected any news that early. So he'd swallowed and told her most of it, leaving out what they'd said about him needing a new audition song – he'd talk about that with the singing coach. And she had given him the same useless advice as his mother had: '*Experience. You had the experience. Now forget it, and get on with the course. What's your first period...?*'

But now Monday had gone, and after hanging around in the canteen with a warm Pepsi until the cleaner jostled his chair, Paul walked home to Kitchener Road seeing more of the pavement than the traffic, knowing that he would probably have heard by now if they were considering him for Ardal, the she-pirate's son. Tucked in his bag, though, was a book from the school library, just in case. *Pirates of the Seven Seas*. Well, you never knew, you never knew... And, waiting for his mother to get in from school after he'd peeled the potatoes, he was somehow still in the mood to leaf through it. He'd give it till Monday next week before his lips curled in dislike at the word *pirate*.

And for once he might make some excuse not to go to see his father over in Wandsworth on Sunday...

SOUTH BANK, LONDON SE1

The one good thing about Ben's new job was that he was more or less his own boss. 'Box' and 'Cox' over in cardigan bay pulled out the obituaries in the order they thought the subjects were likely to die and held a little meeting to ponder on their various states of health. Shots and packages of the condemned individuals were then passed to the two or three journalists who worked in the picture library. These were run through on desktops before the researchers went looking for the latest material among the picture files: news items, promotional events, talk show appearances – all meticulously catalogued by Box or Cox – and these were cross-referenced online with the newspaper and magazine stuff, to help with the script that had to be written.

So there was lots of moving about, up and down the rows of shelves, no way could a casual eye pick out what anyone was actually working on. If a cardigan came looking over a shoulder at a desk, it was a split second's action to kill the screen. And Ben Maddox took advantage of this. Once an on-the-road reporter, always an on-the-road reporter – and having his own investigation on the go was one way he could keep his edge. Whether or not he would ever be allowed to present Kath Lewis with another story prospect was a separate issue – he wasn't going to be buried under digital dust here in this mausoleum for the just-living.

Today he was bugged with this drugs story: the Fredericks brothers, *so* right for investigation. Two of the Fredericks, the twins, had gone down for a long time; but the youngest one, Gary, was still lying low out there somewhere, and still up to it, Ben guessed. He'd met a crook brother once, a different family, and he knew the form. If you were 'inside', you were 'inside', and you made your own bed; but if you were outside, as a brother or a brother-in-law, you looked after the other's family. You kept up the villainy for two. Wives, girlfriends, boyfriends, kids – they needed support while their men were away. The Fredericks had used an East Ham council flat for their operation – but that wasn't where they lived; they had smart houses near Colchester, their wives wanted to be able to stare people in the eye, they lived the village life, and all this needed keeping up. And there had to be no danger that their kids in private schools would be kicked out for want of fees. At least, this was the traditional East End villains' criminal code. Other cultures might operate in other ways, but Ben guessed he'd be on the right track if he found out what he could about Gary Fredericks. Where Gary went, villainy went. He wouldn't have given up just because his brothers were in prison – that was all the more reason for villaining on...

Ben took the Fredericks' DVD to his desk. This pair was nowhere near an obituary or a BAFTA tribute for him to be working on, so he kept a good eye open for a cardigan. Quietly, he ran the material through. It was what he expected – shots of courtroom appearances, a nightclub scene, and CCTV footage of Gary as a teenager doing a blag in a building society. But Gary had matured since then: prison does that. He had both matured and putrefied – grown harder than his twin brothers, dealing, like them, in cannabis, marijuana, cocaine and heroin, but treating his mules like expendable slaves. Now his brothers had been caught and convicted; and Ben knew that Gary would see it as his duty to carry on the trade, for good family values. And the TV trial report had said that parts of the drug trafficking network were still intact. Ben would bet his private pension that Gary was up to his dirty neck in it.

He fished out his mobile and got through to his own brother, Patrick, at Scotland Yard. Pat could be a good help, when he was in the mood to lose a bit of discretion. He would never compromise an investigation, but he could usually be fairly open with Ben because he knew he would never be identified as a source.

But Patrick was out somewhere on a case, so Ben texted him.

Hi Pat – help me out of the doghouse? What hve u got on G Fredericks? Is he under surveillance? If not, y not? Might lead 2 parts of the network u didn't uncover. Ben

Ben didn't have to wait long. He didn't know where Patrick was, but he could hear traffic in the background when he phoned back within ten minutes.

'Pat!'

Ben's older brother had been almost a father to him when their real father had left home. As a young uniformed constable he would take care of weekend pocket money by paying Ben well over the odds for a polish of his Saturday night shoes.

'Your man...' *No names over the phone.* 'He's gone to ground, but he's definitely still in the UK. No airport or ferry departure...'

'Eurostar?'

'Nope. He's here, we're sure of that. So if you turn him up, give us a bell, we'll put him under surveillance. But take care, Benjamin – he's a shoot-first-shake-your-hand-after character these days. And don't take your black Ramsaran girl with you – he's as racist as Adolf Hitler.'

'Right. Cheers, Pat.'

'OK.'

The two Maddox brothers led very different lives. It wasn't unnatural for them to hang up with no family talk between them, but there was always a bond; a very loving bond. 'I'll tell you one thing, though,' Pat said.

'Yup?'

'Look elsewhere. Think lateral. Forget Brincastle Transport, we've punctured all their tyres. Our man's setting up another route into the UK for his merchandise, we're sure of that.'

'Don't sniffer dogs pick up stuff coming in – wherever...?'

Ben heard Pat sigh – one of his 'join-the-real-world!' sighs. 'These guys play the percentages. Consider personal searches, say, people coming through airports...'

'Yeah...'

'Drug arrests per year? Between three and four hundred. Now, how many millions of people enter the country in that time? You couldn't count. Percentage success? Minimal. Then think lorries, vans, trucks, cars? Seen them streaming out of the ports? There aren't that number of sniffer dogs in the world…!'

Ben was nodding down the phone. 'So…'

'It's where to put your dogs' noses, that's the secret, decided on the back of intelligence. Tip-offs, surveillance – that's how we know where to point those dogs' noses. Some of the time. Meanwhile, people like the Fredericks cover themselves in legitimate activity. Run ordinary business as cover.'

'I get it…'

'Would we have a drugs problem on the streets if we'd got the resources to check every person and every vehicle coming in? We got lucky with Brinsdale Transport – lucky like an inside man. And now, Benny-boy, I've said too much!'

Ben laughed. 'Pat, you've said exactly the right amount!' And with that special excitement a journalist feels when they've just had a good lead, Ben ended the call. So what other cover might Gary Fredericks be looking for – who else came and went to the European mainland apart from a freight company?

A cough had him looking up. 'Cardigan Cox' was behind him. 'Just in,' he said, handing over a Reuters slip. 'Dear old Ducky Lavender's making his final curtain speech at St Thomas's Hospital. Be dead by six, love. Do a little bustle on it, will you?'

Ben would. Poor old Douglas Lavender – he'd been brilliant in the *House of Royals* series; it wouldn't be like work to run through some of those clips.

But Ben's mind was still a long way off show business memories. Real up-and-running journalism was hard to bury under the past.

SOUTH BANK, LONDON SE1

From: Rupert O'Grady
[rgrady@waltontheatreprods.co.uk]
Sent: 13 June 12:01
To: bloomr@zephon.co.uk
Subject: writers

Bloom – I've been through our files and asked around the office but no one has heard of Martin Kent or Nick Cannon, your musical writers. Could be two names made up to disguise a couple of well known guys under contract elsewhere – unlikely – or two genuine new boys. But they must have agents, I'll pump whoever I bump into.

Loved your piece on our Lionel Bart revival, sure it helped put some b.o.s.

Off to S. Africa to open *Stardust*.

Cheers
Rupert

Next, Bloom's office telephone rang. 'Rusel Hudson management – Bunny Fortune here.'

'Hi Bunny!' Bloom didn't know Bunny from a crate of mangos.

'Sadie Baker. Flame. I'm apologising for the poor PR. Sorry you weren't told – it wasn't meant to be a *Stage* exclusive, my God, who would that reach? You should have been in the loop…'

'You tell that to your star, Bunny! I'm used to a brush-off, but she was over-the-top rude to me—'

'Darling, I'm sorry. We *worship* Zephon. *She* worships Zephon. Your pieces are so perceptive, even when you're being beastly to us…'

Bloom felt like holding the phone away from her ear: she was being snowed on from a great height by this guy. 'So, what can you do for me, Bunny? Can I get the low-down on *She-Pirate*? I don't know the writers, I can't get my head round the concept – a retired rock star doing a musical – and only a week at the Cambridge Theatre sounds madness. What's going on for God's sake?'

'I know…sounds crazy—'

'But intriguing! So how can you help me?'

Bunny Fortune drew in his breath. 'We don't want Sadie's tired response to you to colour the way Zephon looks at *She-Pirate*. We need you people on-side. How about lunch on Wednesday…?'

'Where?' Diary out.

'Dover Street Restaurant, one o'clock?'

'I can do that.'

'Then I'll see you there. I'll be in white. The jacket.'

'I'll be in black. The skin.' *But I won't miss you, Sunshine!* Bloom thought. *You're visible a mile off!*

'Lovely. See you there and then.'

'One o'clock, Dover Street Restaurant.'

Bloom put the date in her diary. She liked the Dover Street place, it did great jazz in the evenings. Wednesday lunchtime could be very interesting, though. There had been no mistaking Sadie Flaming Baker's attitude to her at the audition rooms, but her agent Bunny was coming from somewhere else. She pulled up 'Rusel Hudson management' from her own showbusiness files. Who else had they got on their books? Were they one of those agencies with particular tastes? And if they did have, what flavours were they…?

She printed the list, with her own Bloom Ramsaran comments written alongside.

RUSEL HUDSON MANAGEMENT

Address: 294 Denmark Street London WC2 3CX
Phone: 020 7349 5785
E-mail: firstname.lastname@hudson.co.uk
Website: www.hudson.org.uk

Speciality: musical performers – bands, singers, instrumentalists
directors/producers/writers – mainly musicals – for tours, arenas, TV, film

SINGERS A - Z:

AARON, BILL   *in prison – drug excess*

AVON, SALLY   *rock and pop – own TV series*

BAKER, SADIE,   AKA 'FLAME'   *retired rock star – gone to ground, own band, The Torches – disbanded*

BOOMERS   *Rock band – hit album 'Comin' On' 2004. Extensive tours, smallish venues*

CLARK, CHARLIE   *Director, spec. in big events, charity stuff, married to 'Chicky' Trevor, singer (see below)*

DENNIS, RAY   *wrote 'Tragic Tuesday' – big hit play with music, still running West End, shifts from theatre to theatre to plug dark months*

FOR GOODNESS SAKE   *Christian singers – choir: churches and halls*

FREEDOM FOUR   *Roger Attwood, Bly Cookson, Keith Keith, P.L. Short: Retro band – mainly pensioner one-nighters*

GARY GAY   *Big hit 2005 after 'Big Brother' win. Where now?*

GISMO   *BIG, BIG, BIG ! Currently touring U.S. 15 piece rock band*

Bloom went on riffling through. Her files were good – every journalist builds their own bank of information, and guards it fiercely from colleagues. Since university Bloom had put together her own sports, political, showbusiness, royalty, city and 'human interest' files, all on the hard drive with copies on several USB sticks, which she could call up on her mobile phone.

This Rusel Hudson list was what Bloom would expect – a mix of artistes, some current and big, some small-time and half-forgotten, some lurking there quietly with a project about to hit the world between the eyes. Who knew? But there was no specialist theme about Rusel Hudson apart from the music business. It wasn't an agency that was pro this or anti that – just an ordinary set-up with a long list of clients.

So where was Mr Fortune coming from? Lunch on Wednesday? Was he giving lunch to everybody who worked on a showbusiness desk? Or was he going for an exclusive with Zephon – a major interview with his client? And how would the unpleasant star feel about that?

Well, Bloom Ramsaran would just have to unwrap that lollipop and suck it.

Paul - message for you.
See me at morning break.
J.T.

Paul felt faint when he saw the piece of paper sticking out from the crack of his locker door. A message for him! This was special, it had to be – because he'd not long kissed his mother goodbye for the day, so it was unlikely to be something about her going to be late that evening at a staff meeting. He pulled out the missive like Bomb Disposal. *See Jenny Tongue at morning break...* Could it be what he was waiting for? Had he got a recall from White Ensign? Or was it the official thumbs-down – the school had heard from them and Jenny was just letting him know?

If so, why couldn't it wait until she had an acting session with his group that afternoon? Why was she asking him to go knocking on the staff room door at morning break? Perhaps he'd kept a library book too long and the librarian was on at his tutor, something as ordinary as that. But in that case, half of Broadway would have notes stuck in their locker doors.

He folded the note neatly into his shirt pocket and tried to get on with his morning. But it was hard to graft through double French until break, and the worst of it was, today it was a short spot of explanation at the white board and then a sheet of subjunctives to work through. It was head down over a sheet, silent working, with all that space in his head to be filled by imaginings of Jenny Tongue slipping out through the staff-room door at ten forty-five.

I'm sorry, Paul – they phoned to say thank you, but they're passing on you. (Woeful shake of head.)

Bad luck! Not this time. But look on it as excellent experience. (Chirpy smile.)

They said you gave it a good shot, but you're not quite there yet. (Straight stare.)

Whatever, he knew he'd gulp, and smile, and mutter something – and go back to the canteen with his secret hopes shuffling round his ankles like dropped pants – his mind grappling with how he'd report his failure to his father.

Or she'd come to the door with her eyes alight, her smile ripping wide into her cheeks.

You've got it! Pirate son! My boy! Broadway is so proud of you! Do you want to know the salary? They need your ten-by-eight photograph A.S.A.P! (Flushed, arms wide, the entire staff room behind her waving and nodding with acclaim for this new star, born at Broadway.)

'How's it going?' 'Plage' Shaw was leaning over Paul's work. '*Allons* Paul! Others have nearly finished…'

Others haven't got to see Jenny Tongue at break for an important message! Copain!

Shaw marked the first two correct answers in his unique way – a small curly 'R' with his sharpened pencil, like annotations on a legal document – and moved on. And Paul wondered what little annotation might have been written on the top corner of his audition report. *Paul Filey – 'R' for recall – or 'R' for reject?*

She wasn't in there, of course: Jenny Tongue, in the staff room. The one Thursday in the year Paul's mother looked for a review in *The Stage* would be the one Thursday the paper wasn't in at the newsagent's. His birthday would be the one day in the year the post office decided to strike. The day he needed an emergency haircut would be early closing day. So he wasn't surprised to get, 'Come back at lunchtime,' from Paddy Swan, head of Vocational. Sod's Law once more!

Which meant he now had 'Voice' and 'Stage Combat' to get through before he knew his fate: sessions where his breathing would be all to cock, and he'd probably poke out someone's eye. But the second session hadn't finished when Jenny Tongue's silhouette could be seen framed in the window of the door. She came in. 'Sorry, Toby – can I have Paul, please?'

'Paul—' Toby Rotherson waved Paul out, too stretched in a sword thrust to be interrupted.

'I told you to see me at break – didn't you get my note?'

'You weren't in the staff room…'

'I was! I was at the photocopier. Time counts. You've got a recall, tomorrow! Same place. Two o'clock. You've got some work to do.'

Suddenly his insides weren't his own as Jenny Tongue pulled a typed script from her briefcase. 'Ardal, son of Meg Macroo – scene between the two of you on pages thirty-five and thirty-six. Read it now. Come to my studio at one o'clock, we'll go through it. Cut this class and find an empty room where you can raise your voice…' She thrust the pages of a photocopied e-mail attachment into his hands, and went.

Great! No more waiting! No more wondering! *He'd got a recall!* Straight off, Paul reached for his mobile to tell his mother – but suddenly realised that she'd be in a classroom at Hartley School. And he'd sit on everything before he phoned his father – then only if he got the part. It would be silence if he didn't.

He stowed his phone and crept back into the Stage Combat lesson, crawling between the room of static pairs, retrieved his sportsbag and trainers, and slithered out again to find an empty classroom. He leapt up the stairs like Antonio Banderas and wanted to shout, *Recall! Recall! I've got a recall!* But how unprofessional would that be!

He went to a turret room, skewed himself behind a desk, and looked at the pages of script, this final examination, to be taken tomorrow at two o'clock...

Meg approaches Ardal, who is leaning on the bulwark, head down over the side.

Meg: Blast it, don't reckon to come finding you!

Ardal: Don't reckon to be found. Being sick.

Meg: Cap'ns do what cap'ns do – or the men soon depose 'em. What happened here was called for, by God!

Ardal: You had that negro flogged till his skin was off!

Meg: Best place for a black skin, say I – floating in its own blood on the quarter deck. If you're a man of the sea, you're a man of the sea. You want landlubbing, boy, I'll cast you off at the first sandbank. Don't think this cap'n wouldn't do so!

Ardal: Your own son? Marooned?

Meg: Son? What's a word? Some man put you inside me, that's the strength of it. A dropping. That's what you are to Meg Macroo, an' you can sup on that!

Ardal jumps up onto the bulwark.

Ardal: The life of a man of the sea? With its stop? We'll all be turned off some day on the end of a hangman's rope, dancing the jig o' death. Some before, some after. Drowning's kinder. (Looks down) They say the sea gives peaceful sleep. (He stands erect as if ready for the jump – but doesn't)

Meg: So? What's your stay? You reckoning on a push to help your weak spirit?

Ardal: (Looks round at her) I'm waiting on a kind word from a mother to go off on. It was no choice of mine it was your belly I fell from. With other luck it might have been the Queen of England, and I should be saluted as a prince...

Meg: Suckled on a negro maid! Black milk!

Ardal takes in a deep breath.

Meg: But you fell to me, and I brought you to be my middy. I'm reaching out no hand – but a word, I'll reach you out a word.

Ardal: What word – jump? Go? If I'm not your son I'm nothing.

Meg: Stay. Come off of that prancing platform and think on riches. You served me well till you turned the lily. We're to the Brazil coast where schooners lay deep in the water with gold. At least you should live the life with some of that afore you go...

Sings:
Where the free waves roll and men roll free,
Where blood pride goes, and thrives
There'll be air that's pure and chests secure
And bounty-laden lives.

Seek the life, seek the life, seek the life of freedom sea
Where ivory stain and purest strain
Mean home for such as me.

Ardal: Aye, there's some hope from that.

Ardal jumps down off the bulwark and joins Meg in singing the chorus.

Seek the life, seek the life, seek the life of freedom sea
Where ivory stain and purest strain
Mean home for such as me.

Meg looks at Ardal – suddenly slaps his face.

Meg: An' that's your whipping for thinking of desertion
          to the deep.

Ardal bows, accepts it.

Kennedy enters carrying a cat o' nine tails.

Kennedy: Come to your cabin, Cap'n. Your dinner's up.
          (To Ardal) And you, sir, to your watch.

*Without looking at one another, Meg and Ardal exit
in different directions.*

*Kennedy ties the cat o' nine tails to the mast, in
its place.*

Kennedy: Sweet justice!

Bring in End of Act tabs.

Paul read it through. It was typical eighteenth century
England-rules-the-waves sort of stuff, much in line with the
tone of the pirate book he'd been looking at – where black
slaves from Africa always came last on cargo manifestos,
human beings listed in importance after linen and maize. It
was a good scene for him, up on that bulwark, a chance to
act – but he wondered about the tune of the song, which
ended in a duet. From what they'd said at the audition, it

could go high – unless they'd meant some other song he had to sing.

He had to sing? It wasn't him yet! Strewth, he'd only got a recall, not the job – there could still be twenty up for it! He rapped on his head as if his knuckles carried a bit of sense. There could be more than twenty of them fighting over Ardal! But at least it was a start, a step. You don't get the part if you don't get a recall, and he'd got a recall. So now he had to go in to the Old School again and do himself a bit of his own sweet justice!

SOUTH BANK, LONDON SE1

The door between the Zephon newsroom and Kath Lewis's office was often open, but not invitingly wide. Today Jonny Aaranovitch pushed it so far open that its handle scarred into the wall.

Kath Lewis's head shot up.

'What the hell do you think you're playing at?' Jonny demanded, striding across the office and standing over her as if only the desk prevented a serious assault.

She stood. No one in this building spoke to her like that, not even the Managing Director – and certainly not a news photographer whatever the past they'd shared, however brilliant his work was. She had gone white-angry, and words were not at her disposal.

'Ben Maddox! What are you doing with him?' Jonny Aaranovitch was shouting it into her face.

If this had been a scene in a film the director would have told Jonny to leave himself somewhere to go, but he was at the top of his anger from the off.

Her voice took a while to find itself. 'And what the hell business is it of yours?'

'My life – is that my business? Then also this is my business! That man saved my life, risked his own, went undercover into a terrorist camp, risked being blown sky high at the Sikakoko Dam. I'm here because of that man!'

'He disobeyed me!' Kath Lewis hissed, an eye on the door. 'No one disobeys me! Not on my payroll!'

'Your payroll? *Yours?* Zephon's payroll – and I've been to Zephon personnel. They've got views on what you're doing...'

She didn't blink. 'Don't tell me my boundaries. I know my boundaries. And my boundaries include hiring and firing and taking disciplinary action...'

'His right to appeal, did you tell him this? Company complaints procedure, what about that? The complaints procedure he will go through, because Jonny Aaranovitch will insist!'

Kath Lewis leant with her white-knuckled fingers taking her weight over the desk. 'Then you'd better start your own complaint.' She looked at him and sneered. 'Do you think you still work here, after this? My decisions are my decisions, backed by the board. Now get out! I will not tolerate being shouted at. You're fired, Aaranovitch! Gross insubordination!'

Jonny Aaranovitch shook his head, almost pityingly. 'My resignation is at a higher level, already. I've got a kibbutz to join.'

'Get out!' she suddenly shouted herself – as a security guard came into the room.

'I've gone!' He walked to the door, the guard not touching him, not the venerated Jonny Aaranovitch. Jonny turned. 'You want talent, then you have to support talent. Ben Maddox is a good journalist, better than I ever was, or you ever were. He's special – and special people operate their own way, they take risks, sometimes they die. Your only beef is that this story didn't pan out for Zephon, the BBC got it – but other stories will, and he knows a good story like a sniffer dog knows a hidden bomb.' He stared at her for a couple of seconds. 'It's the family silver you're throwing out...'

'Please, man,' the security guard said. 'I got to see you out the office.'

Jonny took no offence at the man's hand on his arm. 'They say prime ministers' careers always end in failure,' he told Kath Lewis, 'and the same goes for news editors – when their ego gets the drop on their judgment.' He pointed a very steady finger at her face, his voice low and controlled; he had left himself somewhere to go: a soft, emotional growl. 'A brilliant journalist whom I had never thought to see brought so low by high power...'

He went, and Kath Lewis waved her arms urgently for the security guard to shut her door. She pushed the button that lit up the red light outside – *In Conference*. She sat at her desk, shaking, her left hand trembling in that space she kept for smacking her emphasis.

And incredibly, in that high-powered room, she started to cry. Kath Lewis, the hardest being in television news, found herself sobbing. And only Jonny Aaranovitch would know what that meant; the end of a certain tenderness that had gentled the lives of two young television journalists twenty years before. The end of a long relationship, both professional and personal in its time.

'Huh!' she said.

KITCHENER ROAD, LONDON E7

Sylvie Filey didn't drink alcohol, but a bottle of something bubbly was always in the fridge, a cork waiting to be unwired when the occasion demanded. But, for a recall? Sylvie took it out, and put it back; made them both a mug of coffee instead.

Paul still had an 'up' to his mouth as he sat in the front room reading the scene.

'Who's the "she-pirate"?' Sylvie asked.

'Meg Macroo.'

'I know that. Who's playing her?'

Paul shrugged. 'There was a woman at the audition – didn't say anything, just watched, wrote stuff down...I don't know if that was her...'

'No one you knew?' Sylvie waved a hand at the television set.

'Nope.'

'Can you print that script on your scanner; give me a copy? We'll go through it.'

Paul nodded. His mother had put the coffees onto the low table, very business-like. She had marking to do, and preparation for the next day; but he knew that this bit of homework was the most important in the world to her.

His throat lumped up. Dear old mum! She would move heaven and earth for him to get this part, for him – and to show his father. If they'd both been in line for the same part – if that were possible – she would much rather he got it. He had chosen her career route, not Alex Filey's, and Paul knew she would go on slogging for ever at places like Hartley School if it meant putting food in his stomach while he finished his training. She always said Broadway gave one of the best theatre educations, and she reckoned only a place with a high reputation would have got a student the *She-Pirate* audition. 'But Broadway didn't get you the recall,' she suddenly said. 'You did that!' Otherwise, she kept her enthusiasm corked for now – every actor knows that getting a recall and *then* hearing nothing is probably the worst disappointment of all, short of your show closing at the end of a week of poisonous reviews.

So after another hug of congratulation she packed Paul off to go over Jenny Tongue's notes – to prepare himself for the next hurdle on the aspiring actor's obstacle course.

BLOOM NOTES – LUNCH WITH BUNNY FORTUNE – DOVER STREET RESTAURANT – WED 15TH JUNE

Peculiar little man. Bald and powdered, white as mountain mist. Chose the wine like he was ordering his headstone. As if, how would I remember him?

Started telling me about 'She-Pirate' – yes, new departure for 'Flame' – enticed out of retirement by the 'book' (story). Heard a couple of tunes and read the words. Liked it. She was put up to it by a couple of friends because she's some sort of icon. What?!! Icon or eye-wash?

Else Bunny's got a handle on nuthin'. White Ensign's a new company to him – knows nothing of their past – possible naval connection? Couple of ex-seamen starting something up after leaving the service? West country somewhere, Bristol area – where Sadie Baker comes from. B will be as interested as any of us in what the show's like. I could go to a rehearsal with him, he'll phone: thinks Zephon is special! Oh, yeah!

All this before the first course comes. Thinking can I pump him about other Rusel Hudson clients – got any juicy stories? – when mobile rings. Mine. Kath Lewis – me to get back to the office a.s.a.p.

Did.

Billy's was far enough away from the Zephon building not to be an unofficial office canteen. There were nearer places where people went to be seen with a 'face' – and where hopefuls came in search of a TV career. Billy's was small and dark, off The Cut at Waterloo, served as many postal and railway workers as Old Vic actors and South Bank fugitives.

Ben and Jonny had a booth at the back – a bit near the kitchen, which was both noisier and quieter for them.

'You...said...*what?*' Ben's *Leffe* beer had caught his larynx.

'I've gone, Benjamin, was going anyway, going to put my camera to good purpose in Israel. Hearing about you, though, my friend, I saw red. I saw fire! These things had to be said to that woman...'

A lump came in Ben's throat, and he had to down his head over his beer for a couple of seconds after Jonny had told him what he'd said to Kath Lewis. To be honest, he had felt very alone these past couple of days. Meera at home was supportive – angry, and supportive the way a partner would be – while Bloom had taken it as given, been helpful but moved on, and the rest of the newsroom took it like any news item: a day old and it was history. No one had reacted like Jonny.

'Meera phoned me,' Jonny was saying. 'This is unbelievable, what Lewis is trying to do to you! The lack of compassion, human spirit.' He tapped a hard fingernail on the table top. 'But if we had got the story out before the BBC, this *disobedience* of yours would have been exactly what she wanted, what she would have rewarded, her brave, lone wolf Zephon staff. A ticking off, yes, we expect this, maybe a severe one. But with the soft eyes to go with the hard mouth...'

Ben nodded. 'She meant it. I think I can tell...'

Jonny leant forward. 'I once knew her before...'

Ben's eyes opened up.

'Sure, we had a thing, two young journalists. Maybe a year.'

'I didn't know that...'

'What cause to know? It's water over the Aswan.' Jonny shrugged it away. 'But that lady has changed, Benjamin. This life has changed her: chase the story, be the first, rough up anything in the way. The hard skin, she has grown; and what nerves feel the touch through hard skin? To be a good journalist and to keep our humanity, that is what we aim for. When I shoot film, I think, what can that person in the lens see of me? What is *his* view of events? This essential she has lost – and this you must never lose...'

Ben didn't know what to say. The only thing he could think of was, *I'll try* – but that sounded too trite. So he took in a deep breath and looked up and around for a waiter.

And the waiter came. 'Today's specials...' the man started saying.

'Two set lunches, the soup and the fish,' Jonny snapped at him, and a Pinot Noir. He handed back both menus.

'Would sir...?'

'Nothing. Just bring.'

The waiter went, and Jonny leant forward, confidential. 'Sit tight,' he said.

'I've got no option.'

'In the picture library be the best they ever had. Options, they will come to you. Do nothing.' Jonny was putting his napkin into his collar in readiness for his soup. 'This is the advice of an old man.'

And that was it. Jonny was now in lunching mode – and Ben was in that sort of daze that takes more than a modest meal to bring any focus to what had been said…

Go 2 www.drugczar. gov.uk. Put out as bland public info, bt 2 us is how they work.
Pat

Ben's mobile gave a message squawk as he walked back to Zephon after his lunch with Jonny. What he'd eaten he didn't know, but he was still digesting what Jonny had said. The good old boy had gone into Kath Lewis's office and given her a row, as a result of which he was advising Ben to sit tight. Things would happen for him. And Jonny was a shrewd old bird. Kath Lewis would probably just let Ben go. Now here was brother Pat from the Flying Squad giving him a nod in the right direction for a big story. Reporters need their own stories like people have their own art or music collections: they're what they're about. A media company takes on a new journalist and they take on something else: an attitude, an address book of contacts, and a bug. Something that's bugging them. And for Ben right now that bug was Gary Fredericks, the still-free brother from the family of drug traffickers, two of whom had just gone down. To go to a job interview with a story file growing – a couple of leads, an 'in' here, a 'source' there, would greatly enhance his prospects; and that stroke could be Gary Fredericks. *So, where was the man, and how was he keeping the family business alive?* That was the key.

As soon as he could get to a computer Ben called up the page his brother had recommended.

D RUGCZAR

DRUG TRAFFICKING IN EUROPE

The most commonly known illicit drugs are cannabis, cocaine, and heroin. Heroin is used by comparatively few people – in drug-use surveys the prevalence of heroin is usually among the lowest, but it is the drug most associated with drug addiction.

Cannabis, in the form of marijuana and hash, is the most used illicit drug in Europe. There are several million cannabis users in Europe.

Today cannabis is cultivated on every continent of the world. Important American producers like Colombia, Mexico, and Jamaica export to Europe.

Spain and the Netherlands are Europe's main countries of entry for cannabis, predominantly arriving by ship. Dutch criminal organisations have attained an important international position in the cannabis trade.

ENTRY TO BRITAIN

Road transport – mainly lorries – through British ports and the Channel Tunnel, mostly driven by drivers ignorant of their illicit cargo, is a major route. Stringent checks at the British end are, however, making this a risky option. Recent high profile convictions are leading traffickers to attempt other routes.

Other frequent travellers are increasingly being used, some knowingly, some not. Sports teams travelling to and fro, holidaymakers, regular cross-Channel passengers with homes abroad, touring bands and those doing company presentations at cities within the European Union – these familiar faces at the ports can all be knowingly or unknowingly importing drugs.

MODUS OPERANDUM

The system works simply. A frequent traveller is either set up or watched by the traffickers. On the fifth or seventh trip – usually an odd number – the drugs are concealed in innocent looking containers (e.g. toiletries) in the luggage. Larger amounts of drugs are concealed in promotional material, household goods such as furniture and kitchen appliances, uniform and costume hampers, sound equipment and even musical instruments. Regular and frequent, previously clean entrants, are the least likely to be caught trafficking.

But Gary Fredericks wouldn't travel abroad without attracting attention, thought Ben. His would be one of those faces certain to be picked on for a search. Which was not to say that people involved with him wouldn't be doing the drug-running...

Pat had sent Ben to this site for a likely description of Fredericks' working methods. So what he was telling him to do was find a company or organisation where Gary Fredericks was financially involved, and follow the lead...

Cheers, Pat, but to be honest, Ben wasn't entirely sure that he wouldn't have got this far himself. It did seem a bit obvious that legitimate coming and going was the key. So, what he had to do was find Gary Fredericks' links with anything that came and went. Which would be good occupational stuff while he did what Jonny Aaranovitch recommended, and sat tight.

REUTERS UK

Zephon subscriber service

Wednesday 15th June 11:04

Buckingham Palace has confirmed that HRH Princess Leanna, the teenage royal granddaughter, has been admitted to the Hatfield British Hospital in Paris, suffering from a 'mystery virus'. Her Royal Highness was on a school visit to Paris from Heathfield School, Ascot. No other girls are reported to be ill but monitoring continues.

The princess's parents – her father second in line to the throne – have flown to Paris to be at her bedside.

Medical reports from a hospital spokesman say that the princess is 'very poorly' but 'comfortable'. It is not known whether or not she is conscious, the nature of the virus, if known, is not being released.

The hospital is in the western suburbs of Paris at 3 rue Barbès 92300 Levallois Perret – tel. 01 46 391 22 22.

No further information is being released at present. Asked if the princess will be flown to London, a Buckingham Palace spokesman said that no decision has yet been taken.

Our medical correspondent adds: 'It is rare for a member of the royal family not to be flown home from such a close destination as Paris. The Hatfield British Hospital was last used by the late Duke of Windsor while in exile in the nineteen-sixties when he was treated for a "common complaint in older men". The hospital is generally regarded in diplomatic circles as being "a safe pair of hands".'

Ends.

Kath Lewis passed the print-out to Bloom. 'Get over to Paris and doorstep the hospital. Word is, she's on a ventilator. There's a *Canal Media* sound cameraman with a car meeting you at Charles de Gaulle. You're on the 17:15 Air France flight from City Airport. Make it.'

Bloom nodded.

'You've got your passport with you?'

'Natch.' No journalist worth their salt would have to go home for essentials before shooting off on a sudden assignment: always a bag packed. Zephon was lenient on expenses on such occasions – you bought locally if you hadn't got something. *And, Paris?* Dream locality for forgetting a summer dress...

'Is this all there is?' Bloom flapped the paper.

'You know Buck House! They count their words as if they're taxable. *Canal Media* are our partners in this. They'll fix interviews whenever they can, and they'll handle your down-the-line filing. You need to file for every news slot – new and live every time, even if the story doesn't move on. How's your French?'

'*Au poil!* Just be thankful she's not in Berlin. My German's not so hot—'

'No, *you* thank God she's not in Berlin. Just get there, Bloom – don't dare miss that plane...'

'I won't.' Bloom hesitated before she ran out to pick up her stuff and call a taxi. 'What about my show-biz story? Flame and the *She-Pirate* thing...?'

Kath Lewis waved her away. 'We'll cover it. This cookie HRH Leanna's going to pull more viewers than some old rock star who misses the limelight. Anyhow, you might be back here tomorrow...'

'Prayin' she's off that machine...'

'Sure, one way or the other.'

Bloom went quickly. Like Kath Lewis she knew how Zephon viewing figures would soar if Princess Leanna died in mysterious circumstances abroad; but unlike her boss, she wouldn't will it on the poor kid. Getting out of the woman's office was suddenly essential.

THE OLD SCHOOL REHEARSAL ROOMS,
LONDON WC1

The smaller the opposition, the greater the threat. Paul Filey was at the more rarified second stage of his personal Everest, and his knuckles were white. The last time he had been here he was a hopeful, no more. Now he'd moved up to being a possible – up against other possibles – and at the end of it there would only be room for one at the summit.

It takes courage just to walk into the building. Actors face it all the time, the need to give off confidence. And as Paul walked into the Old School, his first set-back was right in front of him – Little Lord Languid, the snobby boy from before, his hands in his pockets like a cricketer in the Long Room. Wherever he was, whatever he did, this kid always looked as if he belonged. *What was it with some people?* Didn't they get the same churning inside? Didn't they have to do what he was doing – breathe deeply and imagine the head held up by a taut wire to give the look of calm and poise? But matey here, with his public school haircut flopped over his forehead and his nose held high, he could crouch for a Coke at the machine and walk stooping to a table to prevent it spilling, all the while giving off some birth-right superiority. *The sort with a father who didn't care what he did so long as he was getting on with his own life...*

'Are you up for this, too?'

'Eh?' Strewth, the boy had turned from putting his Coke on the table and was speaking to him. Paul nodded, cursing his fluster as he saw a script with *She-Pirate* on the cover held up in the boy's hands. A whole script – not the two pages Jenny had been e-mailed.

'*She-Pirate*, yeah.'

'The post-flogging scene?'

Paul patted the pocket of his casual top.

'Tune's a bummer, isn't it?' The boy was eyeing Paul as systematically as a scan.

'Haven't seen the tune…' And Paul hadn't.

'It's in here.' But the bozo wasn't going to share the music. The same as in coursework, Paul thought, why should he help someone else get a decent grade? 'Good luck!' And matey mooched off towards the lavatories – or a piano! – so superior that he had gone against theatrical tradition and use those ill-omened words.

Paul looked at the blackboard, and there it was – *White Ensign Productions – room 16*. He checked his watch. He was early, he always was. It's drilled into theatricals never to be late. He got to Upton Park before the game on Saturdays in time to see the Directors' Box completely empty. Going to a show, he was there before they opened the house. He felt physically sick if he thought he was going to be late for something. It was the same with today: he'd got to Holborn tube at one o'clock. As his mum would say, he was early enough to deliver the milk, so now he had the opportunity to use his initiative. He ran upstairs to room sixteen and bothered the same woman who'd been outside before. She opened her mouth to tell him he was early.

'I know!' He waved his watch wrist. 'But have you got the music to the song on page thirty-six – the duet. I wasn't sent it…'

She riffled. And, *that's the way to deal with these people* Paul thought. Expect! She found it in a script and handed it to him. 'Ten minutes, I must have this back.'

'Cheers.' Paul hurried off, up more stairs, and found a room at the top of the building stacked with odd bits of practical rehearsal furniture. He stood in the middle of about ten plays and looked at the music – which he could read.

Where the free waves roll and men roll free,

Where blood pride goes, and thrives

There'll be air that's pure and chests secure

And bounty-laden lives.

Seek the life, seek the life, seek the life of freedom sea

Where ivory stain and purest strain

Mean home for such as me. REPEAT

He ran it over in his head: '*home*' was where one of those high notes came, higher than he'd gone in *Mack the Knife*. But that was OK, he could hit it easily – although it was in the last line and needed holding for a bar and a half. He shut the door and tried it – sang it quietly first, then again louder, and finally gave it what he'd give it in the audition. He made a mistake in the breathing, corrected it and went for it again, noted where he would have to take in a full and sharp breath. And within a quarter of an hour he had returned downstairs and given the woman back her script.

From inside room sixteen he could hear his scene being read by two voices: a young male's and a woman's: *the opposition!* But he felt a slight sense of superiority as the boy inside had to go at one of the lines twice, having been told how to phrase it – which was the way Paul's mother had told him it should go, and which he'd learnt. That was the other trick she'd taught him: have it in your hand, but go in and do the scene from memory, 'off book'. It was his initiative over the music that pleased him, though – and it somehow took the edge off his nervousness; a small achievement, perhaps, but one that bolstered his confidence.

He was called in promptly. His experience of real auditions was limited to this one, but he was impressed with the time keeping; they seemed strict about not having a build-up of people reading for the same part.

When he went in he was greeted like an old friend. Well, he was wearing what he wore when they'd seen him before – another of his mother's tips.

'Paul Filey. Thank you for coming back!' *As if he wouldn't!* 'You've had the script?' It was the same man as before, Martin Kent, a pencil behind his ear and a vacuum flask in his hand. His eyes had that earnest, single-purpose stare of a man with no sense of humour. The same woman was with him, but she was standing to one side with a script in her hand, not sitting today. 'This is Miss Baker.'

'Hello.' Paul gave Sadie Baker a Broadway smile. 'You were here before…'

'Oh, yes!' She didn't make a move to shake hands.

'We're going straight into the scene – and end with the song.' Martin Kent replaced the cup on the flask with a twist like the wringing of a neck. For a slight man he gave off a strong sense of power.

'Fine.' Paul wasn't going to whinge about not being sent the music, not to someone so rigid. Anyway, that was probably someone else's cock-up – and tour producers like happy companies, no stones in people's shoes.

They read the scene, Paul and Sadie Baker, stopping before the song, but Paul off-book, which brought a look between the other two: no more. If Martin Kent was pleased he didn't encourage with a smile.

'OK –' And no critical comment – 'now put it on its feet.' With precision Martin Kent moved a couple of chairs to be the bulwark of the ship. Sadie Baker took centre stage and they did the scene again. Which went OK, Paul thought. To get the walking and the jumping right he tried to remember the feel of the boots he'd practised in, and that seemed to work for him. And a line or two ahead of the song Martin Kent called, 'Carry on and do the duet,' and walked over to the piano, which he played himself.

Seek the life, seek the life, seek the life of freedom sea
Where ivory stain and purest strain
Mean home for such as me.

The meaning of which Paul didn't understand, and neither had his mother, but he sang it as if he did.

'Right, OK.' Martin Kent got up from the piano, Sadie Baker retreating to a corner without making any more eye contact, and Paul was ushered out. 'We shall be making our decision today,' Martin Kent said – leaving Paul to walk away past matey waiting outside, who this time gave him an appreciative nod, and headed off for the Underground.

Never feeling flatter in all his life.

ZEPHON TELEVISION

INTERNAL MEMO

DATE: 16th June
FROM: Kath Lewis
TO: Ben Maddox

I need to see you.

Kath Lewis

Ben went into Kath Lewis's office ready to have his employment cards thrown at him across the room – probably with a few ill-chosen words to go with them. Jonny Aaranovitch was what Ben wasn't – a long-serving, established name in the television world who had clutched a few BAFTA masks in his time. If Jonny chose to speak publicly about Kath Lewis people would listen to him, so he would have had his effect on this head of Zephon News. And Jonny was known and popular now, a news item himself after being held in a Kutuliza terrorist camp – while Kath Lewis was unknown outside the business. She would cut her losses, then. If he didn't make a legal issue of it, she would get rid of Ben Maddox with the least amount of fuss; which is why he had done what Jonny advised and sat tight.

Her door was open; the secretary waved him in as if he was no one special: which he wasn't any more, until he got himself established with another broadcaster.

'Ben.'

'Kath.' *One syllable – not much to get the required coldness into.*

'Princess Leanna…'

God, they didn't want her obituary, did they? Had she died since the last news bulletin? Well, Zephon wouldn't have much footage to show, her father had kept her well out of the public gaze. Was this going to be the background job on which he worked out his notice? *Poor kid!*

'Bloom's gone to Paris—'

'I know. Has the kid died?'

'Not as far as I know – but Bloom's got her hands full whichever way the story goes.'

'That figures.'

'So you pick up on her show business brief. You're closer to her than most. Work from her desk: she's saved what she had, it's all on the machine.'

Kath Lewis was staring at him. There had been no mention of Jonny Aaranovitch, nor of suspension, nor of dismissal. Ben kept his cool. He used his TV presenter skill to ensure that no flicker of eye, twitch of mouth or flare of nostril gave any hint of surprise. He gave Kath Lewis nothing, certainly not gratitude.

'OK,' was all he said.

She turned away and he walked from the room, noting, however, that there were red wine rings on her papers again.

KITCHENER ROAD, LONDON, E7

Paul read the computer screen like taking a hungry bite.

Flame (singer)

Sadie Florence Baker (born 6 August), best known by her stage name **Flame**, is an English singer and musician.

Life and career

Born in Claverham, Somerset, Flame played both bass and lead guitar in various local bands before appearing on BBC TV's *Top of the Pops* singing the lead vocal on *Easy Street*, scoring a big hit. She formed her own band The Torches which played with her until her retirement from the music scene five years ago.

During her touring career – which took in the United Kingdom, Ireland, Australia, New Zealand, Canada and the northern states of the USA – she famously kept herself free from drink and drugs, even when members of her band and crew were prosecuted and (briefly) imprisoned for possession.

She is unmarried and little is known of her private life which she has always aimed to keep away from the public eye. Even the official Flame fan club, with a huge membership in its heyday, saw and knew little of Sadie Baker's real life, which is understood to be undramatic and unremarkable. The fan club has all but disappeared, although this 'Greta Garbo' reclusiveness, always hinting at deep secrets, became part of the mystique that fanned her huge following.

Her greatest hit *Rock My Socks Off* still sells in its thousands. But the effect on Sadie Baker of considerable fame and great wealth is unrecorded. She is a very private woman.

Paul sat back at his computer while the printer did its stuff. So – he had sung a duet today with a rock legend! Already, he had printed up a photograph from another site, a fearsome image of a flame-haired girl in gothic gear twisting her mouth at a microphone. But he could see in the picture something of the woman he'd sung with today, the same way that his mum was always there in snaps of the girl on Southend Pier in the seventies.

He hadn't gone back to Broadway that afternoon. By the time he'd got on a hot, crowded Central Line tube bound for Stratford it was a quarter to three – and the drama school packed up at four o'clock. It wasn't worth it, and although his mother wouldn't be in yet, he could wind himself down, and try to come out of this 'anyhow' mood that had wrapped itself around him. Anti-climax, he supposed: all the build-up, then doing the business and getting no reaction. What sort of life was this for a sane person to go chasing? Perhaps his dad was right, perhaps a day 'making a difference' would have left him feeling more satisfied.

The telephone rang. *Mum had been kept for a staff meeting again! More like a staff detention!*

'Seven-three-four-seven.'

'Paul?'

'Yes.' *It wasn't Mum's voice.*

'Jenny, at Broadway.'

'Hi, Jenny.' Surely she hadn't expected him to go back?

'You got it!'

'What!?'

'You got the part! White Ensign just rang. They want you!'

'*No!*' Meaning, *Yes!!*

'All the details tomorrow. Come and see me first thing. You start rehearsing yesterday. There's a ton of arrangements to make.'

'Fantastic!'

'They've got the two of you...'

'Me and Sadie Baker...' So they were building the cast around the she-pirate and her son! Which meant it could be a great part, a juvenile lead...

'No, you and the other Ardal...'

'The other Ardal?' *Oi! What was this? Was Paul Filey an understudy?*

'The other boy's from Bristol Old Vic. You'll share performances with him...'

'Oh.' *Share?* Well, fair enough...

'But great news! You'll each do another named part when you're not Ardal. It's a long tour, they're covering their backs. We'll talk tomorrow.'

'Great! I'll be the one with his eyes closed! I shan't sleep tonight!'

The front door opened, and Paul's mother came in, lugging a bag of work.

'Well done, anyway!' Jenny finished.

'Cheers!' Paul switched off the phone, held his arms out wide, and stared hard at his mother.

She stared back, her face *so* serious – which meant she understood, she knew what this was.

'Want some bad news? I got it! I'm in the show! Jenny…just…' And now he couldn't finish the sentence because suddenly his voice gave out – emotion robbed him of it, leaving him vainly trying to shift the lump in his throat – while his mother whooped, shrieked, screamed, drop-kicked her bag of work over the back of the settee and jumped up onto the coffee table for the most embarrassing goal-scorer's celebration ever seen. She jumped down, zigzagged across to throw her arms around him and hugged him tighter than he'd ever been hugged in his life. She let him breathe and ran through to the kitchen to get the bottle of bubbly she'd been keeping for just this moment, her school I.D. card bobbing on her chest.

Now they were both crying.

'Tell me, tell me, tell me everything!' She wiped her tears away and wrenched the cork out of the bottle with a single twist. 'But first, to Paul Filey!' She poured, and raised her glass. 'To a first job, and an Equity card!' She shone her huge and total pride and pleasure at him. 'To Paul Filey!'

And Paul actually heard himself repeat the toast. 'To Paul Filey!' He drank, and choked, of course.

But, *'Feeling anyhow, flat'*? What sort of an alien feeling was that for an employed actor? *'Joyful'* was the word. With bubbles pinging his nose he grabbed up the phone. 'I've got to tell Dad!'

'Tell Dad. Yes.'

He dialled Alex Filey's mobile number, the only sure way to get him.

'Alex Filey.'

'Dad. Paul.'

'Hi Paul.'

'Want you to know—'

'You got that part.'

'I got that part.'

There was a long pause, time Paul left for some congratulation. But what Paul's father said next took all the fizz out of Kitchener Road.

'Good for you, Paul. It'll round things off nicely before Christmas. You'll have done it, achieved your ambition, been on the professional stage...'

'Yeah!'

'Then you can put your mind to doing something useful in life. Well done. I'll raise a glass to you tonight.'

And I'll tramp mine under my bare feet! thought Paul – and not feel a bloody thing.

SOUTH BANK, LONDON, SE1

Ben ran through the rest of the week in Bloom's diary, which was labelled *NO BUSINESS LIKE*...in her top drawer. The title immediately brought the famous tune and lyrics into his head. There certainly was no business like show business, but then there was no business like that big business called Sport, no business like the Westminster politics scene, either. Everything had its special glamour. Fame. Money. Power. Driven people were driven people, each in their own direction.

He checked through what he might have to do this week, covering for Bloom, and found without thinking about it that he was back at work. He had come out of Kath Lewis's office, gone to Bloom's desk, nodded at a couple of faces in the newsroom, and delved for the diary – every journalist's first action. He'd get on with the job in hand. *Professional.* He reckoned that made him a real professional. *The show must go on!*

So, what was there to go on? Ben didn't have to bother with Bloom's Royal diary – there was a back-up reporter to cover the London end of the Princess Leanna story; it was only the show-business brief that Ben had to worry about. And since that brief was part of the News division it wasn't too deep or expert. Zephon had its own Culture editor backed by a team of freelance correspondents for the serious stuff – the reviews, the discussion programmes, the in-depth profiles. Bloom's role was to cover the tidbits that might make Zephon's national news. So she went to premieres and big first nights, she got to interview the stars, did a few plugs for shows and CDs and books, and made a few, light, homes-of-the-stars-style features – but all for the News division. She wasn't a critic or a pundit. So what had the rest of her week got in store?

16   THURSDAY

White Ensign – company history? Look into
Opening night: The Importance of Being Earnest Garrick 7pm
Interview Dame Rebecca Fowler 18:28 live news spot (dressing room).

17   FRIDAY

Covent Garden – 11am – street theatre festival launch.
Interview 11:15 – Denny Rochester – sword swallower – angle: legal to carry thro' streets?
15:00   HAIR!
19:00   Zephon Culture Show – live discussion of Earnest, guests t.b.c. – me on stand-by, have something to say!

18   SATURDAY

FREE!
Flicks with S.

19 SUNDAY

16:00 'Hen and Chickens' Highbury Corner. Robert Douglas acting on the pub theatre fringe – see show and try to fix interview for next week – live if poss. <u>Robert Douglas!!</u> Get Ben to dig out his Royal Shakespeare and Hollywood footage.

Tomorrow, Thursday. White Ensign – he didn't know what she wanted to 'look into' there; he might text her in Paris. But tomorrow night's opening at the Garrick was a must-do. They'd got what looked like a two minute live interview at the end of Zephon News – and thank God he knew the play – who didn't? He'd go back to Cardigan Bay and dig up some Dame Rebecca stuff for the interview. And if anyone was a no-show he might be live on the discussion the following night, so he'd better get his beauty sleep. It had been a long time since he'd crinkled a smile in front of a camera.

From Friday's news editor he'd find out how firm the Covent Garden item was likely to be – and he'd blow that one out if he could. This was for a national broadcast – and how many Liverpool viewers would be interested in a cockney sword swallower – unless he cut his gizzard?

But Sunday with Robert Douglas was a must! The man who made a million with MGM, who had all but bought the Royal Shakespeare Company; the Hamlet whom all Ben's school generation had been taken to see at Stratford – he'd find out who was on Sunday duty from the camera pool, it could be a nice little item.

He settled himself with a black coffee and looked

up 'White Ensign' on the web. It was all about a company that sold model ships, and the history of the British naval flag. Neither of those sounded very show-business. But he persevered and went through all the available pages – and there on page six it was! *White Ensign Productions*.

WHITE ENSIGN PRODUCTIONS

This new company is based at the Old Sailing Loft building in Bristol Docks. Its founders, Martin Kent and Nick Cannon, intend to write, produce and tour new British shows in Europe – playing in theatres, arenas and stadia – highlighting the best of British-born talent.

White Ensign's debut show, *She-Pirate*, the story of Bristol's Meg Macroo, will star rock legend Flame on an eleven week tour of northern Europe, Bolton, Bristol and Cardiff.

Venues include the Luxor Theatre, Rotterdam, the Staatsschauspiel at Dresden, and the Göttingen Concert Hall, culminating in a one-off show at the Phoenix Theatre, Paris on Saturday 24th September.

The Old Sailing Loft telephone number is 0117 345345. Martin Kent's mobile number is 0780 8172 9635

Nick Cannon's mobile number is (to be confirmed)
White Ensign's email address is
whitensign@tivoli.co.uk

Ben saved the page to Bloom's shared documents and printed it up. He was sure that it would become clear why she wanted this; but hadn't she blown him out for this old rocker, Flame? She'd been at an audition rooms somewhere instead of meeting him for lunch on the South Bank. He delved into her drawer again and found her spiral notebook, riffled through it – and there it was! Her notes on the Flame meeting, where from the looks of things she'd been big time cold-shouldered.

Well, who cold-shoulders a national television reporter when there's a show to publicise? Usually they move heaven and earth to get some air-time. OK, Flame may have been off the public scene – she reputedly treasured her privacy – but they all come out of doors when the TV ice-cream van plays its jingle in the street. Marketing's a huge budget-eater – so what comes free is grabbed with both hands.

Normally.

Anyhow, that was something for him to think about, and work on. But without the royal side of Bloom's brief to worry about, this was a light workload for an energetic young man! And he was partially solving his own what-to-do quandary when it struck him that he could cover Bloom's commitments – and also pursue his own investigations into Gary Fredericks and the drugs scene. What European cover was the sleazy little trafficker using to get cannabis onto Britain's streets? Now that would be a story to nail!

BROADWAY DRAMA SCHOOL, LONDON E15

They were in Jenny Tongue's studio with a class waiting noisily outside. Paul looked at the schedule that she had given him – the first night was just over a month away.

WHITE ENSIGN PRODUCTIONS

SHE-PIRATE TOUR

London, England

Sun. 24/7	London Cambridge Theatre Get-in	
Mon. 25/7	London Cambridge Theatre Tech. and Dress rehearsals	**10:00 BST**
Tue. 26/7 – Sat. 30/7	London Cambridge Theatre (Mats. Wed. 27/7, Sat. 30/7)	**7 perfs**
Mon. 1/8 – Sat. 6/8	Free	
Sun. 7/8	Tour bus/ferry call London Victoria	**10:00 BST**

Holland

Tue. 9/8	Rotterdam Luxor Theatre Get-in	
Wed. 10/8	Rotterdam Luxor Theatre Tour Tech. and Dress	**10:00 BST**

Wed. 10/8 – Sat 13/8	Rotterdam Luxor Theatre	**5 perfs**
	(Mat. Sat. 13/8)	
Mon. 15/8	Coach call	**09:30 EST**
Mon. 15/8	Apeldoorn Orpheus Theatre	
	Get-in	
Tue. 16/8 – Sat. 20/8	Apeldoorn Orpheus Theatre	**7 perfs**
	(Mats. Thu. 18/8, Sat. 20/8)	
Sun. 21/8	Train/ferry call	**09.00 EST**
	Night at home – London (cast)	

England

Mon. 22/8	Coach call	**08:30 EST**
Mon. 22/8	Bolton Imperial Theatre	
	Get-in	
Tue. 23/8 – Sat. 27/8	Bolton Imperial Theatre	**7 perfs**
	Mats. Wed. 24/8, Sat. 27/8	
Sun. 28/8	Plane call – Manchester airport	**07:50 BST**

Germany

Mon. 29/8	Dresden Staatsschauspiel Theatre	
	Get-in	
Tue. 30/8 – Wed 31/8	Dresden Staatsschauspiel Theatre	
	3 perfs	
	(Mat. Wed. 31/8)	
Thu. 1/9	Coach call	**09:30 EST**
Thu. 1/9	Regensburg Theatre, Regensburg	
	Get-in	
Fri. 2/9 – Sat. 3/9	Regensburg Theatre, Regensburg	**3 perfs**
	(Mat. Sat. 3/9)	
Sun. 4/9	Coach call	**15:00 EST**
Sun. 4/9	Munchen Gärtnerplatz Theatre	
	Get-in	

Mon. 5/9 – Wed. 7/9	Munchen Gärtnerplatz Theatre	**4 perfs**
	(Mat. Wed. 7/9)	
Thu. 8/9	Coach call	**10:00 EST**
Thu. 8/9	Göttingen Concert Hall	
	Get-in	
Fri. 9/9 – Sat. 10/9	Göttingen Concert Hall	**4 perfs**
	(Mats. both days)	
Sun. 11/9	Coach/train/ferry call	**06:30**

England

Mon. 12/9	Bristol Dominion	
	Get-in	
Tue. 13/9 – Sat. 17/9	Bristol Dominion	**7 perfs**
	(Mats. Wed. 14/9, Sat. 17/9)	
Mon. 19/9	Cardiff New Empire	
	Get-in	
Tue. 20/9 – Thu. 22/9	Cardiff New Empire	**3 perfs**
Fri. 23/9	Coach/ferry call	**06:00 BST**

France

Fri. 23/9	Le Phénix de Paris	
	Get-in	
Sat. 24/9	Le Phénix de Paris	**1 perf**
	12 noon	
Sun. 25/9	Train/ferry call	**09:30**

End of tour

**(Call times above are mainly for cast. Tech. crew see
supplementary trucking sheet)**

'There's no script come through,' Jenny explained – 'but they're calling you for tomorrow, you'll get it then.'

Part of the time Paul still couldn't keep the smile off his face – although no script meant that he'd have to do the read-through at sight. Well, so be it, he was a pro, he'd manage. The rest of the time he was bugged by what his father had said on the phone, revealing the blueprint he'd been sitting on. The man was seeing this as the furthest Paul was to go in the theatre – one job! His mother had seen it differently, angrily, talking *divorce* and *High Court* – but whoever won, such a case would be covered in grunge like all nasty, messy, family feuds. Hundreds of plays thrived on that sort of thing. Blood on the boards.

'Mo's having the checks done,' Jenny was saying.

Mo Beckett was the firecracker of a co-founder of Broadway.

'Meanwhile you can travel to rehearsal from home. Don't go off to stay elsewhere till you've heard from us…'

Paul frowned. Was this PHSE or 'Health and Safety'? Was Jenny Tongue worried for his body?

'You're a Broadway student, under eighteen. It's our duty to check that this company's all above board, carries all the insurances, isn't going to leave you stranded in God-knows-where-istan. So don't let them take you off anywhere…'

'It doesn't go to—' He shut his mouth, his brain catching up with his ears.

'After the joy of the good news it's always bureaucracy and hassle.' Jenny pulled another sheet of e-mail from a thin folder marked *White Ensign*, and handed it to him.

PROPOSED TERMS AND CONDITIONS

<u>Payment</u>: Equity minimum for the run of the tour. Rehearsal daily rate for part week of 13th June, rehearsal weekly rate for period prior to opening.

Actual <u>travel costs</u> to and from rehearsals to be reimbursed weekly.

Daily <u>subsistence allowance</u> at London rates for rehearsal period, 20 Euros per day while touring.

All rehearsals to be held in London. London-based actors receive no <u>accommodation allowances</u>. Others receive £20 per day accommodation allowance.

All <u>accommodation on tour</u> to be provided by the company in registered hotels.

Actor to be <u>contracted</u> for the known length of the tour (see separate schedule).

Actor will <u>play as cast</u>, maximum of eight (8) performances per week.

'Anything you don't understand?'

'What's the Equity minimum?' Paul hardly liked to ask, it seemed so mercenary when he'd have done it for nothing.

'Your mother will have all the rates. I'm not sure–' said as Jenny went to the door and asked the people outside to keep the noise down; a moment to himself in which Paul realised for the first time that the job was going to make a bit of difference back at Kitchener Road. It might even mean that for a couple of months, instead of wearing herself out in some school, his mother could concentrate on her own career, sending out her details, chivvying her agent – unless his father had been serious about this money paying for his autumn term at Broadway.

He pointed to the last item. '*Play as cast?*' he queried: that was a more professional question to ask.

'That's a catch-all. It means they can take you off Ardal if they want.'

Paul nodded – although that was a scary thought, having Ardal taken away from him altogether if he didn't do well – and it led to the one question he'd promised himself he wouldn't ask, because in a way he'd rather not know. It was the question that had been bugging him all night; the one he hadn't broached even with his mother.

'Who's the other boy, the other Ardal – do they say?' He looked at the thin folder in Jenny's hand as his need to know ran off and away with him. The night before he'd actually had an unpleasant dream where the two people at his audition – Martin Kent and the singer Flame – were treating him as second best, only giving him the matinees and the early parts of the week – to a wake-up climax where he wasn't playing Ardal at the performance his mother came to see. And of course, the other Ardal was the super-confident boy he'd run across twice at the Old School.

'I've got no other cast details,' Jenny said. 'But cheer up, Paul – look on the bright side – they want you!' She waved the folder at him. 'Is your mother's agent going to act for you?'

Paul shrugged. He didn't know: they hadn't discussed it. Last night had been a dashed hopes sort of celebration.

'Anyhow, I'll ask Mo to fill you in on all that: she's the expert.'

'Cheers.' Paul knew that Mo had done everything from street theatre to circus to Palladium to the Royal Shakespeare. And outside the business she would still chain herself to a railing for a good, Trotskyish cause. She wouldn't let some third-rate, cut-throat outfit treat him like dirt, would she?

The class outside was noising-up to be let in, or dismissed – but the real business between Paul and Jenny was done, so she opened the door. And in they came – each and every one of them done up as a pirate: the Broadway wardrobe robbed for eye-patches, bandanas, headscarves, cutlasses, pistols, and a stuffed parrot. They entered heaving on an imaginary rope:

> *Fifteen men on the dead man's chest,*
> *Yo-ho-ho and a bottle of rum!*
> *Drink and the Devil had done for the rest,*
> *Yo-ho-ho and a bottle of rum!*

Jenny clapped her hands. 'Fantastic!'

Paul looked at his classmates' exuberant faces – and desperately fought off what his emotions threatened, crying at this generously shared success. He let them shoot him, slash him, clap him on the back, surround him like a marauding band – and it all ended up in a hugging, jigging dance of joy.

'Cheers!' was about all he could manage, and with a couple of kindly kisses from she-pirates and a few shipmates' hugs, he escaped from the studio to somewhere quiet where he could read the tour schedule and his contract conditions.

Good old Broadway! That had been a terrific thing to do. He went off singing *Fifteen men on the dead man's chest* – knowing from somewhere that the pirate song used in *Treasure Island* was never about a chest of dead man's treasure, but about the pirate punishment of leaving condemned men on a bare rock shaped like a torso, with nothing but a bottle of rum for company – to bring drunkenness before death. *Marooning*: a dreadful fate... Like a promising career left high and dry on the rocks.

THE OLD SCHOOL REHEARSAL ROOMS, LONDON WC1

From plays at Broadway, Paul knew there was a great coming together at a read-through. All the cast was there, with the director, producer, costume and scenic designers, the musical director and stage management; the biggest assemblage of a production there will be until the technical and dress rehearsals weeks further on. At the Old School that day there was also a great inequality, because finding enough seats for everyone was difficult – and chairs, thrones, bar stools and church pews had to be pulled in from every available source in the building. So, some sat high in the reading circle and some sat low; and Paul found himself perched on a bar seat half a metre above the leading lady, feeling very exposed.

He had spotted the alternate Ardal early on. Coming into the room he'd been on the look-out for matey and, failing him, for another person about his own age; which turned out to be a white boy with a shaven head, who looked as if he'd just come from playing a yobbo in *The Bill*. Further, unlike Paul, he seemed to know people there, laughing with a couple of men as they dragged seats into the reading circle.

Paul had reintroduced himself to the director, the man who had auditioned him.

'Paul.' The man had nodded, good on names, poor on warmth, and scrabbled in a briefcase for a clean-edged script. 'Sit down somewhere.' No introductions, no 'well-done', no welcome aboard. The only other name Paul knew was Flame's.

At home, Paul had been studying Flame. His mother knew who she was, and so did most of the Broadway staff.

Her fame was remembered in the corner shop and at the hairdresser's – and from the internet Paul called up more pictures of a fiery, aggressive, twisted-mouth microphone eater, rocking under purple lights. But she looked nothing like that today. Instead of the granny glasses of the audition, today she had slightly tinted glasses worn a bit crookedly, not the star shades the corner shop might expect, with a mid-brown linen suit, flat shoes – and altogether seemed to be one of the least impressive people in the room. The winner on the striking front was without doubt the tall, broad, round-headed bouncer who, it turned out, was playing the pirate Roarin' James. And there was Paul, sitting head and shoulders above even him.

Meanwhile, without actually looking at the other Ardal, Paul could have said where the kid was the whole time; his eye kept being drawn back to him – as he ducked out for a few moments, probably for a smoke, and came back to stick with his mates, and sit alongside one of them when they were all clapped to come to the table.

'Come on! Time! Time!' Paul would discover that this was the constant cry throughout the rehearsals: the room renters, the Bectu crew members, the rehearsal pianist – the cost of everyone's time was paramount. To go into overtime meant a haggle, and extra production money being spent; clearly why there was no time for warmth and humour from the bossy Martin Kent.

'Time!' The director clapped his hands again, sat next to a woman with a stopwatch and notebook. 'Introductions. I'm Martin Kent, co-writer and director. This is Maidie, who's on the book and likes ad libs even less than I do, and—' he pursed his lips and nodded at the *She-Pirate* herself, 'you all know Miss Baker.' Who didn't look up from her script. 'Beyond her—' Martin Kent raised his arm like a maestro and conducted the next person to speak, going anti-clockwise around the long table. Names were given, along with the parts people were playing, or their job in the production. But Paul was waiting for two names only: the other boy's, playing Ardal, and his own when his turn came, his stomach doing a first-night twist for fear that he'd fluff on his own details.

The first moment came. 'Bradley Turner, playing Ardal.' That was all. The boy had the front not to even look in Paul's direction, with no acknowledgment that the part was shared. Up there on his bar stool Paul felt light in the head, willing his knees not to tremble as the names came slowly around the circle. Everyone sounded so confident. They all probably knew each other from other things before, and he was the untried new boy... Until he thought of his mother, imagined her being the actress sitting across from him, and he remembered his Broadway class coming in as pirates, all proud of him.

Now!

'Paul Filey from "Broadway",' he told them. Yes, let them know he was a new boy, and let them know his pride in his drama school as well. 'Playing Ardal – when Bradley's "off".' Which got him a big laugh around the circle – *being "off"* the jargon for missing an entrance.

'Nice one!' Sadie Baker said, turning to him. Paul stared ahead, deliberately not looking at Bradley, but Bradley suddenly didn't bother him: with the laugh, and Flame's response, all at once Paul Filey felt at home in this company.

Martin Kent clapped his hands. 'So, we all know who everyone is – but what about this play? Some of you have had scripts, some haven't, until today. I should apologise for this, but I won't.' He took a sip of coffee from the cup Maidie had filled from his flask. 'We are keeping this piece confidential to those who need to know, when they need to know.' He put Paul in mind of a tetchy headteacher introducing the SATs. And across the room he saw an actress with the memorable name Tootie frowning hard. 'So, strictly five minutes' reading...' Martin Kent checked his watch and nodded at Maidie, who went into the middle of the circle to a small table where a pile of A4 paper lay. 'The "book". A quick run-down of scenes and calls...'

The stapled sheets were passed round, and those who weren't in the know bent over the 'book' like students in a supervised private study period. The others started busily marking up their scripts or talking technicalities. With another quick look at Bradley – whom he was pleased to see hadn't been given an early script and was reading the 'book' fiercely – Paul got into it himself.

Like every other person in the room his eyes skimmed and scanned for mentions of his own part in all this. He looked for Ardal, while other actors, singers and dancers sought out their own characters and chorus parts. And there was no big surprise for Paul, but he was pleased. He was on the stage a lot as Ardal, and he had two really big scenes – the one he'd read with Sadie Baker at the audition, and a fight with a pirate who had bad-mouthed his mother. His part tailed off a bit, and he ended up more or less in the chorus, although he'd be on for the final song, 'Supremacy', after Meg Macroo has flashed her breasts at the rival captain, Roarin' James. And what else should he expect for a first job? Wouldn't his mates at Broadway give their braced teeth to be sitting where he was right now?

'Time!' More clapping. Martin Kent rapped on the table

and said he wouldn't take questions, these could wait for the coffee break. It was time to read through.

Paul looked at Bradley, and for the first time Bradley looked across at Paul. Bradley looked away and called along to Martin. 'Martin—'

'I thought I said, no questions!' Martin Kent was definitely no luvvie.

'Who's reading Ardal?' Bradley persisted.

Martin Kent didn't look up from finding his place at the start of the script. He marked it with a long finger. 'You first act, the alternate Ardal second.'

A stomach plunge. On that word Paul's spirits sank. *Alternate.* The alternate was always the number two. And under pressure the director hadn't remembered his name. After all the 'up' of getting the part, now for the 'downs': the cold shoulder, the being ignored and forgotten, the getting mistaken for someone else, the having a director shout at you in front of the company and crew, all that stuff that went with the job. As his mum would say, because she always did, *'That's show-business, cockie!'*

But luck was at least going to have Paul Filey reading the big Ardal scene in Act Two...

At his desk in the newsroom Ben felt back at home. Perhaps – now that he was half re-instated – he had never really felt away. He and Meera had decided to shelve for a while any big decision about legal challenges, they definitely didn't want to do anything hasty. Meanwhile, what were Kath Lewis's real intentions? When she'd sent him to the picture library backwater, had she just been skidding her stones into the sea to see how well they bounced? Had her *Get-thee-from-hence!* been nothing more than a power plug-in? Because the crucial factor that Ben suddenly realised was that she had never had Ben locked out of his computer. Traditionally, when a journalist is dismissed it's done away from the room where they work; and while the sacking is happening the IT people are in the office and freezing their computer – so that an ex-employee leaves the building with no more than their car keys; and not even those if it's a company car.

But Kath Lewis had done none of that; and Ben had started wondering whether Jonny's intervention had been the catalyst it had seemed. Meanwhile, he had done his first stand-in showbiz assignments.

Dame Rebecca Fowler in her dressing room at the Garrick Theatre near Trafalgar Square had been just what older theatregoers might have imagined: a dressing-gowned but fully made-up Dame sitting before light-bulb mirrors that were framed with well-wisher cards. But 'Dame Trot' – as the business knew her because she went on political marches – was very much herself until the camera was switched on for the live interview: no glitz there. She was nervous, noisy, smoking heavily despite the regulations, and swearing like a cultured granny who's trodden in dogs' muck. But she seemed to like Ben, and she acted very pleased when he described her to the camera as 'up there among the greats to play Lady Bracknell'.

'You're too kind, Ben, too kind...'

For Ben, that interview had been his own 'first night' – he hadn't had the stomach-flutters of a live count-down for months. At the end, when the camera lights were off, she held both his arms captive, stared him in the face, and told him, 'That was lovely. So professional. Give my love to the South Bank' – and she propelled him and his camera operator out of the door.

Sunday at the Hen and Chickens had been a let-down, though. Robert Douglas had pulled out of the cast – no doubt his agent had painted-up the pub theatre somewhat – and he'd gone back to the States. The notices were up in the pub windows:

DUE TO CIRCUMSTANCES BEYOND OUR CONTROL MR ROBERT DOUGLAS WILL NOT BE APPEARING IN THE CURRENT PRODUCTION OF 'THE DUMB WAITER'.

'He's got a film!' was all the director would tell Ben. 'Came up suddenly when Richard O'Mara died – there's no story, truly.'

'Who's playing the part today?' Ben asked.

'Me, love, on the book. But we'll have someone Tuesday...'

So there was no story there – not without a Robert Douglas interview, and would Zephon fly Ben to Hollywood for that? The story had been the great actor on the London fringe: he *wasn't* on the fringe, so Ben had a drink in the bar and cycled home for the tennis from Queen's: showbiz had gone dead on him.

Now, back at work, he read what he'd just printed up from the internet.

COURT RECORDS SERVICE

● ●

EXTRACT – CROWN VERSUS FREDERICKS
SNARESBROOK CROWN COURT
BEFORE LADY BRYANT
27th MAY

<u>Prosecution summing up by Bertram Winters QC</u>

Members of the jury, you have before you two men whose principal aim in life is to make money out of the drug dependency in our culture, a dependency that they themselves have already helped to promote. They create the need, and then they fill it.

The Crown contends that Tony Dean Fredericks and Callum Neil Fredericks who stand before you have been proven beyond any

reasonable doubt to have been at the head of a drug supply operation that encompasses Britain, Europe, and the Americas.

We have shown that these two evil men – yes, I use that word with all the weight of disgust that it carries – jointly own the property at 131 Palmerston Road where the conversion of millions of pounds' worth of cannabis resin into the substance known as 'crack cocaine' was made between October and December of last year.

Interpol evidence – and you will remember, members of the jury, the scrupulous evidence of Inspector Rochette from Paris – has shown the bravery of agents in marking identifiable chemical traces within a consignment of cannabis resin imported into Rotterdam from the Americas. You will also remember that this same identifiable chemical trace was subsequently proven to be present in the cannabis resin found at 131 Palmerston Road.

Furthermore, these two men in the

dock – and, again, you will recall the police searches of their Essex country homes described in detail by Chief Superintendent Fellowes of the Drugs Squad – were found to possess banknotes at both their addresses that had previously been marked by the police and used by police personnel posing as addicts to purchase crack cocaine at Piccadilly Circus on December 15th of last year.

Members of the jury, I ask you to consider those facts most carefully. What innocent explanation can there be for the presence of identified cannabis resin in their Palmerston Road flat, and of marked money used for the purchase of drugs at their home addresses? Can they be anything other than drug traffickers...?

Ben flicked through to the closing statement of the Fredericks brothers' defence counsel, Rebecca Simmonds, QC.

Let's face it, shall we? What you have just heard from my learned friend is a cooked-up, corrupted fairy tale! One milligram of a trace element was found in a flat in East Ham rented out by the defendants to people they did not know, other than as tenants. Who are where, we ask? Have the police tracked *them* down? No. Doesn't this suggest that *they* might be those guilty of drug trafficking – typically gone to ground – and not my clients, who simply own the address and rent it out through an agent? 'A chemical trace element'. The element to trace is the missing tenant! And let's consider this damning forensic evidence. Has every kilo of cannabis resin in Europe been tested for this trace element? Might it not be found in cannabis resin in many other places? Yes, cannabis resin might have been there, but who is to say that those missing tenants simply didn't buy it in Britain – which would convict them of possession, but not of trafficking. What confident speculation is it that enables Inspector Rochette to say that it is only present in the sample entering Europe through Rotterdam, and subsequently taken to this rented-out flat in London? What confident speculation that it doesn't occur in nature! Don't forget that the witness for the defence, Dr Speigel, told the court that many trace elements from a myriad of sources can be found in easily obtainable powder anywhere.

Oh, and the marked money found in my clients' houses in Essex! In *both* houses! How likely is it that a couple of notes used for the police purchase of crack cocaine in Piccadilly Circus on 15th December came to be separated, and one was found in one house, and one in another, thirty miles away? Doesn't it all seem a trifle tidy, a file stamped 'CLOSED'?

And has the prosecution enlightened you as to the route the defendants allegedly used to bring their alleged substances into Britain? On this my learned friend is bewilderingly silent. To prove illegal importation, surely the route of that importation needs to be shown in evidence. Possession is one thing, although my clients deny possession, but trafficking is another – and the prosecution has produced nothing whatsoever in the way of evidence to support that charge.

This really is a dodgy case. My clients' names are Tony Dean Fredericks and Callum Neil Fredericks, although you might be excused for inserting 'Scapegoat' in both their names. I recommend you, as sane members of the community on whose shoulders rest British justice, on the evidence, or rather on the *lack* of evidence, to clear these legitimate businessmen of these charges.

Ben pursed his lips at the court records. The defence summing up had been good – he'd hire this QC himself when he was up in court for pouring a carafe of claret over Kath Lewis's head. But the prosecution had won with a majority verdict: and, with a leaning for his brother Pat's Scotland Yard point of view, probably rightly so. Absence of evidence was not evidence of its absence. But Rebecca Simmonds QC had also been right. There was a big hole in the case when it came to the drugs importation to Britain. And Ben reckoned that he knew who the toad in that hole might be: one Gary Fredericks, the still-free young brother. This sort of operation needed masterminding, and what was being brought in was more than a few grams here and there in toothpaste tubes and razor handles. Regular stuff in sizeable amounts was being shifted across the Channel. Ben thought back to Pat's text message. The clear implication there was that it was coming by some of the routes he'd mentioned, in chunky items carried by regular travellers. It just needed tracking and proving.

But if Scotland Yard and Interpol couldn't do it, how could Ben Maddox, working at the show-business desk of Zephon Television? Well, he told himself, perhaps that was where undercover reporters score – not so much by being unidentified as by not even being on the radar. *No one knew what you were up to till you hit them with an exclusive!* And, right now, that definitely included Kath Lewis!

```
┌─────────────────────────────────────────────┐
│                                             │
│     RASSEMBLEMENT CONTRE                     │
│     RACISME EUROPÉEN                         │
│     SAMEDI 24 SEPTEMBRE                      │
│     PLACE DE LA CONCORDE,                    │
│     PARIS                                    │
│                                             │
│     Se montrer la solidarité contre          │
│     les racists de droite qui souiller       │
│              la société                      │
│                                             │
│     S'affilier à le protestation contre      │
│     le racism le plus grand connue          │
│        en Union européenne                   │
│                                             │
│              ALLONS!                         │
│                                             │
└─────────────────────────────────────────────┘
```

The leaflet was pressed into Bloom's hand by a young Frenchman weaving his way through the world's press, camped in the Paris suburb of Levallois Perrett, outside the hospital where Princess Leanna lay.

They were all on stand-down. The medical bulletin, in English, had just been read to the battery of cameras by the hospital director, with copies handed out to journalists.

> ## Her Royal Highness
> ## Princess Leanna's condition
> ## is unchanged and remains critical.
> ## She has not recovered
> ## consciousness but is "comfortable".
> ## Her parents are at her bedside.
> ## Another bulletin will be issued at
> ## 18:00 hours.

Of the two pieces of paper in Bloom's hand, the anti-racist rally leaflet looked the more interesting. The princess's condition hadn't changed for two days, and the word on the street was that it wouldn't. An American neurologist who specialised in coma was flying in that evening, and it was the ten o'clock bulletin for which Europe was waiting – especially the French, whose interest in the British royal family took some beating. Meanwhile, cameramen were at the feet of their step-ladders, sound booms stood against railings like idle brooms, and 'runners' were heading their bikes and 'motos' for the nearest *créperies*.

'That anti-racist rally's going to be big!' the Asian royal correspondent for the BBC said to Bloom.

'First I've seen of it...'

'Biggest ever in Europe!'

Bloom folded the leaflet away. She'd often told Ben that such rallies made everyone feel good – the ethnic minorites, and the whites who wanted a world free of bigotry; but when racists struck, none of the marching class ever seemed to be at the bus stops on the estates, or under the bridges, or on the buses. And, however big the rally, who could legislate against the private, loaded look of a White Alliance shop girl serving Bloom?

'I'm off to find some lunch,' the BBC man said. 'Coming?'

Bloom smiled. 'Cheers – but I can't. You've got your back-up—'

The BBC News 24 Paris correspondent was there as well as this specialist royal reporter. If anything happened, the other BBC people would have this guy back from his *déjeuner* before he'd pulled his napkin out of his shirt front. But Bloom couldn't leave, and had to get by on fast food through the day and whatever sleep she could grab in her down-time from eleven pm to six am. Decent lunches were definitely off the menu.

Bored, she texted Ben.

**Hi, super-sub!
How's my desk?
Got a feeling
there's a story
with Flame &
She-Pirate. Not
much else in view.
B good for Kath.
Bloom.
PS Wish u were
here!**

And she settled down to a cold slice of pizza and a Diet Coke with her local *Canal Media* cameraman, and practised her French. And her patience.

'THE FILEY FILES'

Paul Filey's laptop notes on She-Pirate
(White Ensign Productions)
His first job – 'Ardal', the She-Pirate's son

Notes being made because I'll forget everything otherwise – and every actor who gets to the West End or Hollywood writes their autobiography at some time. And in spite of certain threats, that's where this bloke's heading. (Big-heading.) So, with my crap memory, I'd better start now. I'm not saddling myself with a daily diary – *'not much', 'same as yesterday'* – just important stuff and the things people say, so I don't have to make up conversations in sixty years' time.

Settled in OK this first week. Bradley Turner, the other Ardal, hates my guts, but that's OK because it's mutual. He's too neanderthal to even say 'kiss my backside', which suits me fine. I dropped my egg in the spoon race when Sadie Baker said something nice to me on the read-through introductions, and I'm having to live with it. Anyhow, there seems to be something binding him to a couple of the adult actors, so he's not going to bother with some kid like me.

Sadie seems OK, gives me the Aunt Dolly smile-that's-not-a-smile when she passes. That first day she read her first act a bit flat – all the love stuff, I somehow don't think she's greatly into all that – but my big scene with her in Act Two went well. I've been off-book with those couple of pages since the audition, so I turned and looked her in the eye – and a few people came out of their scripts to watch us do the scene. Turd-face Turner counted the knots in the wooden floor, but that'd be tough going for him if there were more than ten. Look and learn, son!

Day 2 we started blocking Act One (serious theatre talk for doing the moves), and by the end of the week we'd blocked the play. It's going to be a fair-sized stage in most places, especially the Phoenix in Paris, but we might have to shrink the moves in the smaller venues. Talking venues, being on the road they've got to keep scene changes simple: no electric lifts, revolves and trucks, all the scenes changed by hand, so there'll be a fair-sized crew.

Reading that back I sound luvvie already; but this company definitely isn't. It's more Band Tour than Royal Shakespeare Company; not surprising since Sadie Baker was once Flame.

The play's a real vehicle for Flame, it's all about her character, Meg Macroo, this eighteenth century pirate woman who became a rip-roaring captain. Looking at Macroo's biography on the net I think she goes down with Anne Bonny as a gay icon – but Flame doesn't play her that way, it's all very hetero. She falls out with her father and then with her lover Felix Lawes when he drinks wine from the same glass as a black slave. I'm her son, and I agree with her, got a song in Act One, Scene Three when I sing, 'A slave is a slave is a slave' – attitudes of those days, actors aren't the parts they play!

But when the slave kisses me on the lips, my mother Meg Macroo stabs her. And we all know it's not the being a slave, it's the being black. The play's a romp, but I suppose it's got a bit of modern meaning. Look at the bigoted racist filth that goes on today, where whites in some places think themselves superior. Come to Stratford East and see how inferior my black friends are! It's fear: racism is all about fear, which is the real inferiority.

Meg becomes a pirate under her new lover Ned Smart because she's helped by me (Ardal) on account of my maths, geography and navigation skills – and by the end of Act One we're heading for the African coast for gold, where slaves will do the dirty work. The Act One curtain comes in on a company song and dance of *Dirty Work*.

Then, like all second acts, it has to go wrong! Ned Smart gets killed by a native servant when he makes the King of Dahomey kiss his backside, and Meg Macroo becomes captain. And after the brutal flogging of a captured native, Ardal wants out, and that's when Sadie and I sing our big duet, *Seek the Life*, the one I did at audition. But it's the climax of the play that everyone will remember. A rival pirate captain – Roarin' James – challenges Meg Macroo to a duel (under the strict pirate rules for duels). He thinks she's a man, but just as he's about to cut and defeat her, she flashes her boobies at him, makes him stumble and kills him. And with her foot on his chest she sings *Supremacy* – and we all come on to join in the rousing chorus. End of play.

I've not made any real friends yet. Some of these people know each other from before. There are a nice couple of women, Tootie and Jo, who sometimes give me a smile – but they've got each other. The main dance boys are a tight foursome, and the singing chorus mostly know one another from other jobs. A couple of the older actors, like Judge Macroo (doubles the King of Dahomey) and Turd-face Turner's mate Roarin' James (doubles Ned Smart) – seem to be old friends from other jobs. If Turd-face had been a member of the human race – if he'd even been Snobby Boy from the auditions – the other Ardal and I could have hit it off, been a twosome of our own.

Sadie Baker smiles at me now and then, so I'm better off keeping a bit of distance – I've heard about these older actresses and juveniles who might want a leg up the show-business ladder. I'm all for a leg up, but you can count out a leg over…!

Now to get on top of some more lines.

Ben would have liked to text Bloom back for a few more of her thoughts on White Ensign, but pride wouldn't let him. They'd joined Zephon at the same time, and there would always be competition between them. Yes, they helped each other out – one would always back up the other – but when it came to digging the first shovels of dirt, that was solo stuff.

He started with the print-out he'd made of the White Ensign announcement of its first musical, *She-Pirate*.

Ben phoned the Bristol office first, and got a recorded message, which he recorded himself for transcript.

> You're through to White Ensign Productions. The company is currently touring but picks up messages from this number daily. Please speak clearly, identifying yourself, your telephone number, and the nature of your enquiry. For urgent enquiries during the tour please telephone Maidie Cobbley on 09736 615 2068; otherwise, please leave a message after the tone.

Definitely not West End! To Ben the accent on the answerphone was local Bristol talking posh – more like a shipyard than a theatre company – and he'd got no further than a small lead to Maidie Cobbley's number. But when he tried that, it was on voicemail, and he didn't leave a message. Reporters try not to leave any strings dangling that can be pulled from the other end; it's they who like to do the pulling.

He looked through Bloom's notes of her disastrous attempt at an interview with Flame on 9th June, and those of her lunch with Bunny Fortune from the Rusel Hudson agency on the 15th. There was nothing to glean from the first, but here was Bunny offering to take Bloom to a rehearsal! He was saying that he'd phone her; but, no, Ben would phone him – get in first: catching people cold gets the hottest response.

Ben Maddox (put through to Bunny Fortune at Rusel Hudson agency):
Bunny?

Bunny Fortune:
Bunny Fortune, yes. Who's this?

Ben Maddox:
Ben Maddox, Zephon Television. You met my colleague Bloom Ramsaran last week...

Bunny Fortune:
Yes, I did indeed. A very interesting lady.

Ben Maddox:
And sitting here's an equally interesting man, holding Bloom's desk together while she's off on another assignment...

Bunny Fortune:
'Another', or 'more important'? (Chuckle.)

Ben Maddox:
Princess Leanna. The royal granddaughter, in a coma in Paris...

Bunny Fortune:
Poor ducky. She's forgiven – your lady, that is.

Ben Maddox:
Bunny, I'm picking up on the White Ensign show – *She-Pirate*; do you know anything about this Martin Kent and Nick Cannon who wrote it? Newcomers, I believe... Are they your clients, too?

Bunny Fortune:
No, sir, we're theatrical, not literary. Never heard of them before I saw Sadie's press thing in *The Stage*. But she seems to have some back-story with them somewhere. The Bristol area they say, poor dear! Could be old school friends, I don't know. They've got their hands on some money, though, to mount a show like—

Ben Maddox:
(Cutting in.) Bunny, I believe you offered to take Bloom to one of the rehearsals...

Bunny Fortune:
I did – and I will if Sadie lets me. They're a bit touchy, these icons, you know, even with their agents...

Ben Maddox:
Well, it'd be me, not Bloom, but tell Sadie there's a chance we can do her and the show a power of good. It says on the information I've got that it's mainly touring Europe – well, let her know that Zephon ties in with all the European Union TV companies: we're known as the 'Eurovision' of the news and documentary networks. We can get the show air-time in all the countries the show's playing...

Bunny Fortune:
Well, she won't be averse to that! Euro-bums *are* for putting on seats, aren't they...?

Ben Maddox:
So you'll give me a ring? No cameras, just me sitting quietly at the back of a rehearsal? We can go from there, Bunny...

Bunny Fortune:
We can indeed.

Ben Maddox:
Thanks anyway for talking to me.

He gave the agent his details – mobile and work number – and hung up; he'd give it a day or two to see if Bunny Fortune kept his word. Meanwhile, he looked up Martin Kent and Nick Cannon on the internet. But there was nothing there for either of them, which somehow didn't surprise him, so, on a whim, he looked up 'Companies House' – every public company in the UK had to register with them. He entered a search under White Ensign Productions, and within seconds there it was:

Company Details
Name & Registered Office:
WHITE ENSIGN PRODUCTIONS LIMITED
WHITE ENSIGN PRODUCTIONS LIMITED
THE OLD SAILING LOFT
BRISTOL DOCKS
BRISTOL BS6 7QQ
Company No. 018660847

Status: Active
Date of Incorporation: 08/04

Nature of Business:
9231 – Artistic & literary creation

Previous Names:
No previous name information in this category of business

Members:
Martin Keith Kent (co-chairman)
Sadie Ruth Baker (co-chairman)
Leonard Clive Parker (secretary)
Margaret Binny (financial officer)

Changes since incorporation:
Nicholas Daniel Cannon (resigned)

Branch Details:
There are no branches associated with this company

Overseas Company Information:
There are no Overseas Details associated with this company

It was laid out before him. Freedom of information was a marvellous thing. *Because what was this?* Nick Cannon, with no telephone details on the White Ensign web page – had resigned from the company since its recent setting-up. So was there something a bit fishy about Nick Cannon? Either he didn't exist, had never existed, or he'd been a naughty boy since White Ensign had been set up. Bankrupted? Deported? Imprisoned?

Well, Ben thought, let's find out! And where did he usually start with potentially naughty boys? Brother Pat at Scotland Yard, of course.

Pat – what have u got on Nicholas Daniel Cannon? Bristol man. Suddenly off the radar of White Ensign Prods. Ben

Ben knew that Pat wouldn't tell him anything not available somewhere else if Ben had known where to look. Pat was a professional policeman who had risen to being a DI in the Flying Squad, and he knew where his duties lay: *compromise* and *corruption* weren't words in his thesaurus. All the same, he could point Ben in the right direction sometimes – and, of course, he had access to stuff like the car registration computer, the up-to-date list of British bankrupts, and criminal records from all over the UK. What Pat would never do was pass on anything connected with a current case, or discuss things with Official Secrets embargos stamped on them. In exchange, Ben would sometimes feed a news item to the editors for Pat; something to make a criminal think the Yard was off the scent. It worked between the two of them, each one aware of the tender areas. As brothers in the bath they'd always washed each other's backs.

Ben left it at that – reporters never wait for a phone to ring, there's always another story to chase – and Ben had his personal search for Gary Fredericks to pick up on. And – just handed to him by a messenger – here was an invitation for Bloom from an *EastEnders* actor celebrating his 'Fifty Golden Years in the Business' bash at the Theatre Royal, East London on Sunday night. George Bailey. Ben pulled a face. *Never heard of him!* But Meera watched *EastEnders*, didn't she? Maybe she would like to go? Plus, thinking more about it, Ben reckoned there were bound to be a lot of showbiz people there – and it wouldn't hurt for him to get to meet a few 'faces'. Who knew, if young Princess Leanna hung on, Ben Maddox might be Bloom Ramsaran for a little while yet...

ZEPHON TELEVISION TRANSCRIPT SERVICE

**Programme 07682
Zephon News 18:00**

Monday 20th June

Newsreader: Gerald Black

Reporter: Bloom Ramsaran

GERALD BLACK (STUDIO):
News is coming from Paris on the condition of Princess Leanna, the royal granddaughter. Bloom Ramsaran, our royal correspondent, is at the British Hospital in Paris. Bloom, there's been a new development?

BLOOM RAMSARAN IN PARIS – EXTERIOR HOSPITAL:
Correct, Gerald, and it's a worrying one. The consultant treating the teenage princess here at the Hatfield British Hospital is Sir Philip Granville-Palmer – and he's just come out and read us a statement...

Cut to PACKAGE 1: Granville-Palmer reading statement:
The princess remains in a critical condition. She is still comatose, and has been examined by Professor Peter

de Vere, a United States neurologist called in by our team. In the light of his findings, the decision has been taken, together with the princess's parents, to transfer Her Royal Highness to the Brain and Neural Clinic in New York as soon as an ambulance flight can be arranged. This is expected to happen in the next three hours, and this statement ends the series of bulletins issued by the Hatfield British Hospital for the time being.

(Off-camera, sounds of clamorous question, but Granville-Palmer withdraws into the hospital without response).

PACKAGE 1 ENDS

BLOOM RAMSARAN:
That was fifteen minutes ago...

GERALD BLACK (VOICE OVER, CAMERA STILL ON BLOOM):
Do you have any details of flights and timings?

BLOOM RAMSARAN:
No – we're expecting the royal press officer to come out with information when he's got it...

GERALD BLACK:
There's been no more medical information – what's the US clinic hoping to do?

BLOOM RAMSARAN:
We've only got guesswork to go on – there's no word from in there. It could be a viral attack on the brain, that's what the American professor specialises in, so we're told. But to be honest, information is very hard to come by.

GERALD BLACK (VOICE OVER, CAMERA STILL ON BLOOM):
What about the royal parents? Are they—

BLOOM RAMSARAN:
For what it's worth, the French press are running stories about late night parties at the princess's school's hotel, and—

CUT TO GERALD BLACK:
Bloom, I think we'd better leave the French press to their own inventions. (To camera.) That was Bloom Ramsaran at the Hatfield British Hospital in Paris where teenage Princess Leanna remains in a coma. To other news...

EXTRACT ENDS

Swearing and twisting her mouth at her *Canal Media* cameraman, Bloom pulled out her earpiece and unhitched herself from her microphone feed. 'I'll murder that smart-arse Gerald Black! Is he on the take from Buckingham Palace? We all know what *E* stands for in HRH's alphabet. Why can't the British bear to hear what the rest of the world knows...? That kid's in a pin-eyed collapse.'

'So why is she going in America?' the cameraman asked, lighting a cigarette.

'My guess?' Bloom took the cigarette from the cameraman, puffed at it, and handed it back. 'Justification. To justify investigating this viral brain thing. As if, would they be spending that amount of dosh if they know what's up, right here? They do know what's up but they're going to come out with a cover story.' Bloom looked across at the shuttered windows of the room where the princess lay in her coma, the royal parents at her Intensive Care bedside. 'Justification, distance – and time,' she went on. 'News moves off to other things, people get used to thinking she might die. Plus, if she dies over there and not in a British hospital, it can't be a British failure, can it?'

The cameraman laughed. 'And everyone says paparazzi are the cynical ones...'

Bloom wound the wire of her earpiece round and round her hand. 'Cynical? I'll say cynical! You guys with long lenses don't get close to us hard-boiled hacks for calling a dead dog a sympathy-seeker!'

Her mobile shrilled, just once. She opened her Message Inbox – and three words said it.

Follow that plane!
Kath

'Us cynics keep all our visas up-to-date for a start!' Bloom told the Frenchman. 'Because we always need to be ready to chase the ambulance...'

Over the weekend, Paul got on with learning his lines. For student productions at Broadway people had different techniques. Some recorded their scenes in the different voices and played them back through earphones, walking around talking to themselves like Blue Tooth idiots. Others read the script over and over, with their parts underlined or highlighted – 'seeing' the scenes and mentally turning over pages as they stood on stage. Paul, though, was lucky in having a mother in the business, who helped him. With a photocopy of his scenes, she read them with him – her doing all the other parts – until gradually Paul could come off-book.

Which backfired when she started getting critical. 'Who wrote this nonsense?' she asked as they circled each other in the front room, scripts in hand.

'Martin Kent – the man at rehearsals – and some Nick Cannon...' Paul was frowning at this, he wasn't into dramatic criticism, he was into getting these lines secure.

'It's crap!' his mother said. 'Full of clichés – and half the sentences are arse about face...'

'What sentences?' He had to give her the courtesy of telling him what she meant – she was giving up her school preparation time to help him.

'Well, here. Meg says, "I'm going to flay his skin when I meet up with him."'

'Yes?' What was wrong with that? How could 'flay' and 'skin' be in any other order?

'Basic rule – keep the audience waiting for the climax of what you're going to say. "When I meet up with him I'm going to" – slight pause – "flay his skin", as opposed to "cook him a fish supper". Much stronger. Keep the important bit to the end of the sentence.' She waved the script as if she was in front of her class. 'Sloppy writing!'

Paul kept his finger on his place in the script. 'Anyhow, this sloppy writing – I've got to *learn*.'

'And, "flay his skin" – that's such a hackneyed saying. Why not "lay him open to the bone"?'

'I'll tell Martin Kent on Monday and suddenly become Mr Popular!'

'Yeah, I'm sorry – you can't do anything about this. Except breathe some life into the lines – and you're doing fine.'

'Cheers. Shall we get on?'

'Sure. Sorry. *Scusa grosso!*'

'THE FILEY FILES'

File 2

For a whole day we didn't mention Dad. I phoned to let him know I couldn't go over on Sunday so I could learn my lines – but he said he was going out anyway, had meant to ring me. But there was no repeat of his threat to have to tell Mum about.

On the other front, she's right. The script is crap, and some of the attitudes to black slaves disgust me, although that's the way it was, historically. Anyhow, I can't do anything about it, and being critical means I'm going in there tomorrow with doubts. Actors do have to have views on what the material's like – and on the director, and the design, and the rest of the cast – but it's easier when you feel 100% behind the show.

To be fair to Mum – I'm not 100%, but not for her reasons. It's great having the job, and I'm the envy of Broadway, but there's something about White Ensign I don't feel at home with. Only Tootie and Jo seem as if they could be kindred spirits, but I couldn't imagine any of the men becoming a mate.

The show is definitely a vehicle for Sadie Baker aka Flame – but somehow it seems about something else, too. Are there double meanings to the concept of pirates that I don't get, is there some hidden agenda in *She-Pirate*? Were gay men part of Flame's following, like Shirley Bassey's and Judy Garland's? I'm not against that being the case – but I'd like to identify what's swimming under the surface. If anything. I could be totally wrong – and I'll be deleting this later. Or should *any* thoughts of the moment be deleted from autobiography notes?

For now, back to learning lines. Then Monday rehearsals move to a bigger, cheaper space – a church hall in Romford. Number 86 bus. Touch the Oyster!

126 Jimmy Seed Close
London SE7 8ER

Ben –

See attached trace on your Nick
Cannon – don't know what you're
chasing with him, but tread with care.
He looks tasty.
Looked up his case: too time-
consuming to copy, but basically he
was with others in a town centre
affray prior to local elections.
Attacked local councillor with bottle
('glassing') – claimed extreme
provocation and self-defence when
surrounded by councillor and
aggressive party workers. Denied
racial element in attack.

Pat

METROPOLITAN POLICE

SCOTLAND YARD

CRIMINAL RECORD TRACE

Name: Nicholas Daniel Cannon

D.O.B.: 03.08.84

Last known address: 27 Draybury Crescent Bristol BS6 7QQ

Conviction court: Bristol Assizes

Charge(s) brought: Grievous Bodily harm / wounding

Plea: Not guilty

Finding: Guilty

Sentence: 3 years custodial

Ben read it through twice. So what was that all about? What crowd of local politicos had surrounded the writer, according to his defence? Was he black – and the target of a BNP councillor and his heavies? Surprisingly, the trace didn't give his ethnicity. And, given the court's finding – guilty and three years down the Swanee – where had he been lying in his defence? This show-business brief got meatier, Ben thought: already *She-Pirate* was starting to look a million miles away from Shakespeare at Stratford-upon-Avon.

Just as far away, too, was the other Stratford theatre, the Theatre Royal in east London. Put on the world map forty years before by Joan Littlewood, it had survived theatre closures all around and was still 'the people's theatre', in the culturally diverse Newham. If Stratford-upon-Avon was a temple of theatre then Stratford East was a vibrant mission hall. George Bailey, the *EastEnders* 'soap' actor could well have started there. Ben looked again at the invitation to the man's *Fifty Golden Years* celebration – on Sunday night when most actors would be free to attend: and definitely Ben and Meera would be there; already Meera was listing the favourites she might meet. It would be a good night out for the pair of them – one of very few recently.

Ben knew the century-and-a-quarter-old theatre as a treasure in the midst of modern development and Olympic

Games venues. East London's Stratford was a metaphor for renewal, change and development – hardly a day went by without a Zephon Outside Broadcast van raising its dish in Stratford. He and Meera loved the Theatre Royal: its sloping corridor from entrance to long, busy bar with food and bands, and its gilt auditorium where challenging plays sometimes scorched the stage. Real, true theatre – and would a musical like *She-Pirate* ever be allowed to play a venue like this? Somehow, Ben couldn't see it happening.

After a wary word with Kath Lewis – sort of civilised, but eyes like cats at next-door's dog – Ben didn't take a camera crew. Zephon wasn't into marking the career of someone best known for earning a pension on a BBC soap. But if anything newsworthy happened on the night, Zephon could get a news camera to the theatre inside fifteen minutes. If a top TV executive or a big name politician arrived drunk, or half out of a dress, Ben was to call up the stand-by camera crew and summon a taxi to get him and the pictures pronto to the South Bank studios.

But what Ben and Meera saw that Sunday night was neither a drunkard nor a bared bosom, nor anything the theatre management would have endorsed – and certainly nothing Ben wanted on the news, not yet. Instead, he received a journalist's dream reward for just being at the right place at the right time.

For Meera the evening started like *Holi* all over again. As she and Ben were ushered in she took one look at the faces in the stalls.

'It's "Spotlight", in person! You could cast a film just looking along the rows.' She shone her eyes at Bob Twist, who played a heart-throb on Saturday nights in *Loving London*. If this had been the BAFTAs he'd have been shrieked at and mobbed on a West End red carpet. As it was, he was quietly sitting among rows of familiar faces, those with real names and those just known as 'the one off *Casualty.*'

But what electrified Ben was a not-so-familiar face, one that would have hidden from any first-night flashes. There, up in the front row of the circle, sat a still man among a group of others with equally frozen expressions – six seats of men who demanded no attention, quietly reading their George Bailey Tribute programmes. And the little-known features that transfixed Ben belonged to the man both he and brother Pat were dead keen to locate. Up there was Gary Fredericks, the still-free third member of the Essex drug-running gang. And he was sitting here among friends.

The sad stage show was a series of 'turns' – speeches, scenes, reminiscences and filmed thanks for a gutsy career – tributes to George Bailey, all aimed at the actor and his wife sitting up in a box. These were pros doing their party pieces, a string of London telly faces – predominantly white with a couple of black actors obligingly playing stooge – whose material was what Ben's mother called 'off-colour': sleazy, sexist, and subtly racist, the stuff of strip clubs and stag nights. This was a private hiring the theatre was unlikely to repeat.

Finally, with a spotlight trained on his box, George Bailey thanked everyone for coming – this elderly, white, cockney actor, who put the deepest freeze into Meera by telling an out-and-out racist joke: *It's all right, all my coloured friends laugh at this* – and as the lights went up for the audience to find its way to the bar, Ben noted how predominantly white the audience was.

This wasn't a sociological assignment, though, and it

wasn't part of Ben's showbiz brief any more, either. This was turning into a crime story. He told Meera they couldn't go straight out, and left her to queue for the lavatory while he headed for the foyer – where he could keep his head in his programme but his eyes on the stairs from the circle to see where Gary Fredericks went. If his target went out to a car, Ben would follow him and get its number – which might lead both him and Pat to an address.

And here he came! As Gary Fredericks appeared at the foot of the stairs, Ben's heart started thumping and his stomach tensed. Fredericks didn't know him from a hopeless addict, so it was no problem to follow him in the general drift towards the bubbly reunions in the bar. Immediately, Fredericks found George Bailey, who was fawningly pleased: old East End actor and young Essex villain.

'George—'

'Gaz – thanks for coming, mate...'

'Wouldn't miss, George, would I?'

'Sorry about...you know. Everything...like...all right?' After years of screen camera work the actor's face could say a lot with the cast of an eye.

'Cheers. Yeah, we're sorted.'

'Anything—?'

'I'll let you know. You know Allen Green? He's in your line.' Gary Fredericks – angular, sandy-haired, blue pins of eyes – pushed back against the thronging George Bailey friends who wanted to say a word, opening space for a well-built middle-aged man to give a small nod, hands in his corduroy jacket pockets.

'Well done, George, nice speech,' Allen Green said, large eyes hooding.

George Bailey just nodded, his attention now on others beyond this unknown actor who was going through the necessities.

'I like the day job you're doing,' Green went on. 'You're not coming out of it, are you?'

'The soap? It's crap,' said George Bailey – 'but ta, anyway...' And he leant to kiss his TV wife, who really was a famous face.

'Georgie...!' she squeaked in her household voice.

'Cut it an' get us a glass o' something. Me stomach thinks me throat's cut.'

Which was all Ben could hear before the throng in the bar pushed him too near to the piano and drums – and by the time Meera came into the bar and saw him, Gary Fredericks had disappeared. Nor, when Ben could get there, was he outside.

'How was that for naff?' he asked Meera.

'Appalling! It's the implicit racism that gets me: never mind out-and-out abuse, it's the we're *us* and they're *them*.'

Ben pushed his way into Angel Lane. 'Still,' he said, 'as work it was useful; very useful...' And he led the way through to more civilised life in the real Stratford.

'THE FILEY FILES'

File 3

It's only a bus ride out of the East End before the bungalows start lining up like little Monopoly houses, with spaces for garages in between – tons different from Kitchener Road. St Barnabus's church hall is on the corner of one of these streets, planets away from anything to do with theatre. The caretaker who opened up was totally confused by us walking in on Monday morning – actors! He was a meaty man who seemed years too young to be jangling keys twice a day, but he shot Martin Kent a really peculiar look – like, *rehearsin' a play?* – as if that was the last thing on God's earth he'd ever heard of sane people doing. Then, having cottoned on to that, he couldn't get his head round the fact that we weren't some local amateur group all taking sickies off work – till Martin Kent told him that someone called Steve Lord had arranged it, and then the man went all 'secret service' with us – winks, and nods, and even a clenched fist as he went out through the door. Yo Steve Lord!

It wasn't long before I had my first bust-up with Turd-face Turner, the other Ardal. I say 'first' because I'm definitely not likely to go three months with that pillock and not deck him – even though he looks harder than me.

We were rehearsing a fight, with a proper fight arranger brought in from Pinewood Studios: a stunt man, short and fit who does most of his days dressed up as a lead actor, doing the dangerous bits, definitely not at the 'luvvie' end of the job. In Act Two Ardal sorts out a pirate called Frenchie Roche who's bad-mouthed his mother, and awkwardly for the two of us, this other pirate's being played by whichever one of us isn't on as Ardal at the time – so we have to learn the fight moves for both characters, attack, defend; defend, attack.

This fight arranger really knows his job, he rehearsed us like ballet, and wouldn't tolerate a foot out of place, or a missed cutlass slash. He worked us hard and swore at us, but I enjoyed it, it was a professional step up from the fencing at Broadway. He reminded us of the golden rule of stage fighting: *acts of violence do not occur on stage, they only seem to happen*…and told us we had to live or die by it.

So, Turner was Ardal and I was this other pirate, Frenchie Roche. Ardal has to win, of course, but Roche, being made to pay for his garlic tongue (as Martin Kent puts it) gives him a good fight. In a rare explanation of what he's written – what dictators ever explain themselves? – he told us it's in there to show that Ardal's a strong son in the pure blood-line of Meg Macroo and Felix Lawes.

We worked through the moves without weapons at first, doing it like a dance, feet choreographed and us counting beats the whole time – thrust and parry, high level, mid-level, low level; parry and thrust, high level, mid-level, low level; with me as Roche advancing then retreating, counting up to twelve with four beats to the bar. That's when Roche leaps up onto the capstan, and Ardal tries to ankle chop him on the count of sixteen; but Roche jumps over Ardal's slashing blade and leaps back down to deck level. That's the end of the first sequence, what the stuntman calls 'phase one', before Ardal draws blood in phase two.

We did the first sequence for timing, then the stunt man threw us these bamboo canes standing in for cutlasses, and we did it again, very slowly, then again a beat quicker, then up to fight speed, the stunt man clapping his hands and shouting out the timing. I was breathless at the end but phase one went OK, then we had to swap parts and I was Ardal and Turner was Roche. Which was no problem for me, but Turner started acting instead of counting – didn't seem able to do both – and keeping time was hard for him. His 'beef' was natural, but the moves twisted him up, he tried to do it more like a playground fight – all over and around the place, with one of us somehow winning at the end.

And it all went disastrous when we got to 'weapons' again, him still being Frenchie Roche. He just about managed the forward and back counts, did the leap up onto the stage block 'capstan', but then he lost the count between twelve and sixteen – and when I slashed in with the bamboo cane as if to slice his feet off, he didn't jump fast enough. He was still standing there, when whack! – I caught him a stinger on the ankle!

'Ow! You bastard!' (But worse than that!)

160

I shouted sorry as quickly as I could, but he wasn't having it. He leapt and hopped about on the stage block like a monkey on a hotplate, shouting out that I'd done it on effing purpose.

'He did not!' The stunt man shouted at Turner – who was calling for first aid – asked him whether or not they'd ever taught him to count up to twenty at drama school. Which put me in the frame as the goody favourite when the class bully gets bawled out. Mr Ever-so-Popular! Being the one in the right put me well in the wrong.

So now Turner's got a purple welt on his left ankle and a blood red grudge against me. I haven't told Mum – I can fight my own battles, thanks, and why worry her with my stuff? She's seething enough already over Dad and what he said about pulling my plug – on top of which the school don't need her next week, there's no acting work going, and the only talk she really wants is someone down the phone with a supply job or an audition call.

Life upon the wicked stage
Ain't ever what a girl supposes...

Roll on, the tour!

Hi Ben! Howz my
chair? Hot? Cold?
U'r luckier thn me –
no news on the
princess, no change.
Boring!
Mistake 2 cum 2 USA –
story's back at the posh
school. Wot wer
those kids taking at
their late-nite
dorm party? Any1
talking – girl with
a loos tung or
irate dad?
But will Kath
send some1 2
leafy Surrey to dig
around? No!
She must b after
a dame-ship!
Luv Bloom XX

Ben thought about the teenage princess and the likelihood that she was in a drug-induced coma. And part of him could see the story that might be lurking there – but the *Sun* and the *News of the World* were already making sure the royal shame wasn't so much lurking as exploding out of the bad girls' closet. Besides, Ben Maddox, disobedient TV reporter, was skiing off-piste enough already, taking a sneaky interest in Gary Fredericks and his drug trafficking routes. One scoop at a time was enough to dollop on Kath Lewis's head. Although, how off-piste was he, with Fredericks suddenly showing up at George Bailey's showbiz tribute? Showbiz and criminals sometimes tended to be mixed up in a very small world!

Ben snapped his mobile shut as the desk telephone rang. It was Bunny Fortune with Flame and *She-Pirate* promotion on his agenda.

'The point is,' he told Ben, 'White Ensign's got bums to put on seats for their British dates as well as foreign bums on the European tour – you were talking European television networks, weren't you?'

'I was, Bunny, I was.'

'For whatever reason Sadie, you know, Flame – the lady just didn't take to that Zephon...girl – but I thought she might do something for you.'

'Thought? You mean she might not?'

'Well, she wants the publicity but not the press, awkward lady – doesn't want interviews and media people around. But I'm her agent, and she does need a PR push. Flame was a hundred years ago, people need reminding about her, and if I'm going to get my fifteen per cent I want it to be fifteen per cent of something with a few noughts on the end... She's on a slice of the box office,' he added, confidentially.

Ben sighed, but inwardly, kept a light bantering tone for the mouthpiece. 'Bunny, you sound as if you're pinned to the ground by the prongs of a forked stick!'

Bunny snorted. 'I've got a plan, dear boy.'

'Go on.'

'I'll get you in to a rehearsal, but you're just with me, sort of thing…'

'Just with you?'

'Personal, a friend…'

'Aaaah!' Ben didn't want to snuffle around that concept for too long.

'You're meeting up with me, we're going on somewhere.' There was a long pause that Ben didn't cut into. 'Can you be at St Barnabus Church hall in Romford on Wednesday afternoon, three-ish?'

'This Wednesday?'

'This Wednesday.'

'Have you got the postcode? I'll print a map.'

Bunny Fortune gave it to him.

'And I'll see you there?'

'Remember, we just happen to be meeting up. As far as the company's concerned we're going on to a late matinee…'

'What late matinee? Let's get our story straight.' Ben had been in the news business long enough to know that undercover meant over-prepared, if need be.

Bunny Fortune riffled a paper. 'There's a five o'clock show at the Criterion – *The Duel*, political drama.' He riffled again. 'Check – five o'clock and eight o'clock, Wednesdays…'

'OK, we're meeting up to go on there. And what am I?'

'I said, you're a personal friend.'

'But I've got to have a job, haven't I? What do I do? Am I in the business?' Ben hated not to be 'solid': reporters should never take a chance when it was easy to be cast-iron.

Bunny went quiet for a few moments. 'Be something boring, so actors won't want to talk to you. Personal financial adviser – you're mine, that's how we got to know each other. And you just sit at the back and look through your portfolios till we go to the Criterion.'

'OK...' Ben could slip into a bank and pick up some life insurance schemes. 'That's good, financial adviser – they work their own hours, get about seeing clients.' Ben would remember that job for other undercover times...

'You fancy the Criterion?' Bunny Fortune suddenly sounded hopeful.

'I fancy nothing, Bunny – I'm washing my hair...'

And on that note of banter Ben replaced the phone and sent his smile back into hibernation. A Wednesday afternoon in Romford! But if he had to do this showbiz job he'd better do it properly. Although, why should Flame have taken against Bloom Ramsaran the way she had – could it be something she'd got against women? And why didn't she want to go full strength for some press coverage? At any rate, he decided, Flame and White Ensign were going to be very interesting people to meet...

ST BARNABUS CHURCH HALL, ROMFORD, ESSEX

It was a hot day, a record-breaker, and Ben took Meera's air-conditioned Astra. In his shirt pocket was an Olympus voice recorder that looked like a mobile phone. He could switch it on discreetly if someone started sounding quotable – or he could talk his first impression notes into it later, back in the car.

Bunny Fortune was already there. He seemed to know his priorities, to hold the client's hand and ensure that life was smooth. But as Ben came in, he patted Sadie Baker on the arm, shut his Filofax and went to meet his Financial Adviser friend...

BEN MADDOX MEMO – DICTATED NOTES – WED. 22/6 16:00

I was met by Bunny with a smile from Minehead to Margate. But his greetings were a bit too noisy and effusive, men rehearsing a scene at the far end of the hall looked round as if to say, 'Do you mind – we are ac-tors at work', although nothing like a Kath Lewis scowl when a visitor gets shown into the news directing suite!

I sat at the back of the church hall, where Bunny put me, just about avoided a kiss on the cheek as he over-did the 'friends' bit.

I recognised Sadie Baker straight off. I've now seen most of her Flame pictures on the web, and listened to a couple of her top ten hits. She looks nothing like that these days, but I can see how a wig and some slap would transform her: it's all in the driven eyes.

Bunny sat her down near an open window on the shady side – so I could hear their conversation while I did what he'd told me to do – bury my nose in a financial portfolio. God, what boring stuff those things are. But I certainly wasn't bored by the chat to my left. For my benefit, said so falsely that I thought he'd give the game away, he asked her some stuff about the show – topped it by looking along to see if I was receiving loud and clear!

He asked her what the *She-Pirate* USP was, but had to explain 'Unique Selling Point' to her. She thought long and hard. 'Human rights.' Said very defiantly. Bunny asked, 'Whose human rights would those be?'

'*Our* human rights.' Then she waved her arm round the room to include all the company in the sweep. 'The human rights of the people in this room are – to be allowed to like what we like when we like, to admire what we admire, to hate what we hate, and to live the way we want to live…' It was quite a little speech: she sounded like a candidate in a local government election.

Now Bunny started to sound genuine – he wanted to know what a former rock star was doing with stuff like this? (Doing his own hand flutter around the room.) 'Sadie, love, I'm a bit befuddled – how does what you want come out of *She-Pirate*?'

She gives it to him, as if, how could she be represented by an agent so far off her beam? 'Meg Macroo's a woman with rights, she asserts those rights against the odds. It doesn't matter what she's told she's got to believe,

or what her attitudes should be, she knows the life she wants, and she leads it! At the risk of hanging at Execution Dock. That's the theme of *She-Pirate*.'

Fair enough, says Bunny, with a barely disguised nod at me. He wants to look as if he agrees with her, so that I'll be positive for the show. Then she got called to rehearse and I went back to my portfolio. Bunny slid along next to me – 'Did you hear that, Ben? That's good stuff! Plenty of meat for a musical! You should get some mileage out of that.'

I told him straight – 'I'll need an interview. Listen, Bunny – she can't have it and not have it!'

Then this little Adolf Hitler of a director told us to shut up or get out of his rehearsal!

As a younger newspaper reporter, Ben had realised that watching a play rehearse is preferable to watching a film being shot. There's a more solid core to what's going on – no constant checking for sound and lighting; no hold-ups through 'hair' in the camera-gate. There's no make-up, props, or shooting the reverse angle to wait for. With a play 'on its feet' you get to see a scene run through, picking up a bit of momentum, and mostly the only people involved are the director and the actors. The rest are out of the way drinking tea, mouthing lines, knitting, doing crosswords and texting their agents.

Now Sadie Baker had been called and Ben watched her run through a scene with two younger actors playing the same part, one after the other. It followed a flogging in the story, and the character – her son, as far as Ben could tell – dislikes the life and threatens to throw himself into the sea. She forcefully persuades him not to. The first boy remembered his lines perfectly – better than Sadie did – and he acted well. When the second boy's turn came, he kept clicking his fingers at the woman on the book and calling 'Line!' He was much less secure than the first – but his acting had an edgy power to it that gave off a real sense of danger. Ben thought this character really might lose his head and leap into the sea. Both times the scene stopped short of a song that ended it – but with just a few director's notes for each of them, and none for Sadie Baker, the man in charge clapped his hands and went on to something else.

'Martin Kent,' Bunny whispered.

He almost naively enquired, *Not Nick Cannon?* but he was intrigued with something else right now. What struck him was how strong the script was on eighteenth century attitudes. Powerful, even. Sadie Baker had a line about 'the best place for a black skin is floating in its own blood on the quarter deck'. So *She-Pirate the musical* certainly wasn't intended as a Christmas show for the Hackney Empire! Bunny was right, there was meat on this bone. And thoughts of Nick Cannon evaporated completely when something else suddenly pricked Ben's ears. A couple of bored stage-hands were called from having a smoke outside to shift some rostra for another scene. One was early twenties, the other older in a black leather jacket; both white, complexions that said they saw more artificial light than sunshine, and as they sauntered back outside again, Ben just caught something one of them murmured to the other.

'Shall wi lay some white around the clubs later on?' Said in the quietest voice a Geordie could manage.

Ben's ears strained, flat to his head. *What was that he'd said?* He strained even harder for the reply, eyes focused on a page of financial growth, seeing nothing.

'Don' call for me – they're sitting on my place. I'll do a jiggle an' meet you,' this younger one a Cockney lad. Then the pair were outside again, and Ben found himself rigid in his seat. He quickly slumped before Bunny looked at him, but the agent didn't seem to have heard what they'd said.

That had been drugs talk just now! It wouldn't be white sugar they were going to lay around the clubs later. Their 'white' had to be cocaine. And why would anyone watching the Bow Bells boy be anything but police? *Sitting on his place.* Ben frowned as he pretended to make a couple of notes against a profit forecast. What to make of that little exchange? Probably no more than two stage crew being into supplying on the side...

Except for what happened next.

With Ben's backside losing all life on that church-hall chair, Martin Kent dictated a tea break.

'Bunny, come and meet a *real* man!' Sadie Baker called to Bunny Fortune, as a burly actor looked up from talking to a woman with a tape measure around her neck. 'This is "Roarin' James", the pirate captain who sees my titties and dies a dramatic death at the end of my cutlass!'

Roarin' James left the costumes woman and went to Sadie's beckon. He was one of those actors often seen playing tough guys on TV without anyone knowing their real name.

'Hi! Allen Green.' Roarin' James gave Bunny a meaty handshake.

'It's a strong script,' Bunny said. 'Powerful stuff for boys like me who just like being entertained.'

'Needs to be,' the actor said. 'This isn't kiddies' theatre. I'm enjoying it. You represent Sadie…?'

'Till she sacks me.' Bunny sounded as if he meant that – and Sadie kept her mouth shut. 'You specialise in musicals?' he filled in quickly.

'Anything going!' Allen Green said.

'Never out of work! European tour after European tour for someone or other,' Sadie Baker put in.

'Very nice.'

'…Gets through three passports while I get through one, all that coming and going.'

'Which must be a touch strenuous,' Bunny sympathised.

'No way!' Allen Green corrected. 'If there's a purpose behind it.' But he didn't explain himself, just nodded at the agent and went for a cup of tea, other cast and crew making way for him – a big man in jeans and a striped suit jacket. Which *no way* fitted him. No way did he seem like an actor to Ben, whose brain – still bent over his financial forecasts – was ringing inside his skull with a muffled bell. His voice when he spoke seemed to be coming at him from outside himself, sifted through sand. 'I'll see you outside, Bunny,' he muttered. 'I've got a cold flask in the car…' He hurried out of the church hall, went to Meera's car and ran the engine to cool the interior.

Roarin' James! *Roarin' James?* And OK, some actors' names get forgotten – but not their faces: sight is the number one sense. There he was, right now, big-framed, round-headed, balding, with hair cropped short at the ears, and no mistaking those hooded but staring eyes, nor the deep actor's voice that belied a man who looked more like a minder. That man in there was Allen Green! The man Ben had just seen introduced to Bunny was the man who'd been introduced to George Bailey at his benefit gala. *Allen Green, the brought-along friend of Gary Fredericks!* Ben *knew* he'd seen him before. He'd been one of the guys tightly tucked into Gary Fredericks' party: sitting in the same front row of the dress circle and later introduced in the bar as one of Fredericks' mates.

Two stage-hands talking about 'laying some white'. And the cast of *She-Pirate* including a close friend of a suspected drug smuggler – an actor who wore out his passports with European travel, but didn't mind if there was a purpose behind it.

Was that what the *She-Pirate* tour was all about? Ben shivered in the sixteen Celsius of the air conditioning, but not from the cold. What had hit him was an intense shiver of excitement. And thinking Pat and *modus operandi*, the first thing he was going to do when Bunny Fortune came out would be to ask the agent for a copy of White Ensign's tour dates.

Had following Bloom's brief helped him to hit upon a neat little drug smuggling scam?

In deciding what action to take, Ben rooted deeply into his conscience. His brother at Scotland Yard had been very good to him in his professional life. Now Ben was thinking of deceiving him: or, at least, not sharing some useful information with him. It was a tough decision – he should have tipped off his brother – but then, Ben reasoned, what solid facts did he know that Pat and the Squad could act upon? All it came down to was Gary Fredericks knowing an actor who was in a touring company that had a couple of crew members who might be into drug dealing, an actor whose travel purpose could simply be seeing more of a French girlfriend. Now what did that stack up to?

How long could the police hold anyone on suspicion of dealing or trafficking with that sort of flimsy evidence? No, the more he ran it through his mind, Ben persuaded himself, the sketchier it seemed. Pat would need more than a hunch to go on. Which perhaps Ben Maddox could provide... Yes! He could sit on it for a bit – for his own purposes – and *then* do his duty by Pat.

And for these purposes of his own, what he needed to know was where this *She-Pirate* tour was going, and whether it went backwards and forwards to Europe, giving opportunities to bring drugs in.

Back in the office he telephoned Bunny Fortune to double-check; he hadn't hung around out at Romford for long. It was just a casual enquiry for future reference, as if it was something to help him gauge likely interest in the show's star from European television networks. But the finger on the pulse of Ben's conscience – necessary to separate him from being a 'red top' hack – told him that he wasn't being fair to Pat. Because when Bunny Fortune read over the tour itinerary to him, he was pretty certain that he *was* onto something. And, by all the piratical thunders, it could be something big...

'THE FILEY FILES'

File 4

'You're going *where*?'

For some reason Dad had my passport in an old briefcase over at his place, probably from that last unhappy holiday in Corfu, and after rehearsals I had to shoot across to Wandsworth to get it. From the tour list I read out the towns to him, just to let him know what a proper, major, professional tour this was going to be. It was pretty impressive, I've got to say, and if I'd been one of his probation service clients who'd been offered a job like this he'd have been Delighted Dick.

London, then Rotterdam and Apeldoorn in Holland; back to Bolton; then over to Germany – Dresden, Regensburg, Munich, Göttingen. Back to Bristol and Cardiff – and finishing up in Paris. Yes! Pretty impressive for a first professional job!

But when I looked up from reading out the list, Dad had got me fixed with his formal father stare, that look that goes with the twisted mouth, as if he's just bitten into anchovy in the middle of his strawberry gateau.

'What are the sleeping arrangements?' he wanted to know. 'Are you booked into a single room in all these places? Or who are you sharing with?' He was clearly dead worried for my body.

'I'll be all right,' I told him, 'I can look after myself...'

But he was making a sort of growling sound in his throat – I swear he doesn't know he does it, please God he doesn't do it in court – then suddenly Turd-face Turner came to my rescue.

'No prob, there's another lad in the cast – we alternate the part. It'll be him and me sharing, bound to be, both of an age.'

'Oh? What sort of a lad is he?' *Like, GAY?*

'He's dead straight, I know. Looks a right thug...' Which seemed to satisfy.

'You let me know if it's not him,' he growled, Captain Cautious. And I just about got out of the house with my passport – and the ugly, repulsive, likely reality in my head of twelve weeks of nights in a room with that poxy kid!

ZEPHON TELEVISION
TRANSCRIPT SERVICE

Programme 08001
Zephon Rolling News 13:23

Thursday 23rd June

Newsreaders: Gerald Black / Val Geeler

GERALD BLACK (STUDIO):
Now with more of the tragic breaking news from
Manhattan, we go over to our royal correspondent,
Bloom Ramsaran. Bloom, is the news as grave as we
feared...?

**Bloom Ramsaran to camera (live OB from the street
outside the Manhattan Brain and Neural Clinic):**

Certainly, Gerald. The official bulletin was read to us
five minutes ago. (**Looks down and to side.**)

Cut to PACKAGE 1:

AARON GREY — SMOOTH, SUITED — READING FROM A STIFF SHEET
OF PAPER:
The Manhattan Brain and Neural Clinic sadly proclaims
the death at six am today of Her Royal Highness
Princess Leanna of Great Britain. Her royal parents were
at her bedside. The death certificate was signed at
07:30 hours by Consultant Surgeon Raymond Fletcher.

The immediate cause of death was organ failure caused by ultra-hypothermia, the underlying cause of which is to be investigated in an autopsy examination to be conducted at the Manhattan District Morgue later today. No further announcements will be made from this clinic, nor questions answered at this time, and I refer you to the British Embassy in Washington, DC.
(Against a background of thrown questions the spokesman retreats into the clinic).

PACKAGE 1 ENDS

BLOOM RAMSARAN (TO CAMERA, SUBDUED):
The official word there, from Aaron Grey, the hospital spokesman. As you can imagine there's a heap of speculation surrounding the viral or other cause of the hypothermic coma and organ failure that has killed the young princess. Gerald, we'll have to wait on the result of the post mortem – meanwhile, I spoke earlier to Dr Louise Weatherby, the *Washington Post* medical correspondent, who knows this clinic and its work well. Recorded before the royal death, the opinions she gives are hers and hers alone. **(Looks down and to the side.)**

GERALD BLACK (VOICE OVER):
Reported without comment by Zephon Television…

Cut to PACKAGE 2: interior
Dr Weatherby at her desk. Establishing two-shot with Bloom nodding, before cutting to a close-up on the doctor.

Dr Weatherby:
The Manhattan Brain and Neural Clinic specialises – among other areas – on aspects of drug abuse, focusing on effects on under-age kids. We've seen the vulnerable teens of Hollywood names and political heavies come through those doors. George Randall was transparent about his son, who was treated at MBNC for a cocaine spasm two years ago in the President's first term. Now your young princess has been admitted from France in a deep coma.

Bloom Ramsaran (off camera):
Which we mustn't read too much into – but do you have any hunches?

Dr Weatherby:
I'm not prepared to go to the racetrack on this, but she presents to me with all the streamers in the wind of some sort of Ecstacy substance reaction. That's where my money goes.

PACKAGE 2 ENDS

Bloom Ramsaran (live to camera):
Dr Louise Weatherby. Of course, everything is guesswork at present. But whatever the cause or causes of Princess Leanna's illness and her sad, premature death, the post mortem will surely shed some light on a personal and constitutional crisis for the British royal family – with whom many hearts and minds will be joined in the coming weeks. This is Bloom Ramsaran for Zephon News in Manhattan, New York.

(Transcript ends)

KITCHENER ROAD, LONDON, E7

Paul waited until he got home to open the envelope on the first Friday of his professional life. He knew what was in it, because he'd been given it by Martin Kent's assistant, Maidie Cobbley, as if it were an OBE for Services to British Theatre. His first pay cheque! In the theatre, only money came like this. Directors' notes were spoken; and contract terminations and show closures were traditionally 'put up' on theatre notice boards.

Like most mothers, Sylvie Filey said she'd frame the cheque; while Paul's father would have snorted, *Don't spend it all at once!* But Paul scanned the slip that went with it into his autobiography file, a sugar lump to sweeten a bitter entry.

'THE FILEY FILES'

File 5

WHITE ENSIGN PRODUCTIONS
24th June
Paid to: Paul Filey
The sum of 250 pounds only
Being rehearsal rate for She-Pirate
Signed: Martin Kent

There it is. Who knows – it could be historic in a small way, like that prime minister photographed as a boy standing outside the door of Number

Ten Downing Street. My start! Or it might be part of a big regret that I'll look back on from some boring, nine-to-five life. *There you are, kids, I might have been famous!*

But if I am ever famous, I swear it'll be over Bradley Turd-face Turner's dead body. He hates me because we always have to rehearse our scenes together, and I stand and wait while he gets put straight over moves and business. Keeps looking to see my face. He's come from an NVQ course linked with the Bristol Old Vic, knows Allen Green, which could be one reason why he's been given the part. But to be fair, there's another. There's this sort of threat in his acting, people stop talking, stop blinking as they watch him. His stage presence makes me feel ordinary, safe, boring– because I've had longer training. But then he goes and gets his feet tangled up, doesn't do anything the same way twice, and Martin Kent *will* bloody say, 'Watch Paul do it! God, learn from Paul...' He's *always* being told to learn from me, but I want to learn from him. I really want to get that threat into what I do. Meanwhile, daggers aren't in it, the looks he gives me. Radioactive lasers, more like.

What brought the 'iron' in between us was something he said during the flogging scene. He's doing it with our 'mother', Meg Macroo, when after a look across the rehearsal room at Allen Green, he suddenly turns to Martin Kent and says, 'Am I supposed to feel sorry for some black idiot?' Only, he didn't say 'idiot'.

It came like a slap in the face: me from the multi-ethnic Broadway at Stratford East. Straight off, challenge words out, I jump in with, 'What the hell's his colour got to do with it?' You don't come from an East End background where it's proved to you every minute of the day that skin colour has nothing to do with intelligence or character – and then let a crap remark like that go past your ears.

He swung round on me. 'Everything, Filey! Everything!' He had a snarl on him like a rottweiller. So he saw the guy being black as cancelling any reason for being sick at the sight of him being flayed to the bone. I stared at him, and shook my head: that stare that goes with an obscene hand gesture, up and down.

I forget what Martin Kent said – something about everyone digging for their own motivation – because my red mist was filled with Turd-face and his attitude; and the gut-dropping thought that I might have to share a room with him on the tour. But that's going to be over my dead body, I tell you. Never mind my dad, I'm going to get this accommodation thing sorted my way a.s.a.p. I'm not spending twelve weeks sharing with a mini-minded racist.

TOP FLAT, 130 LEYTON HIGH STREET, LONDON E10

Ben pressed the 'mute' button on the small drop-down TV in the kitchen, where he was baking a trout. He called through the dining hatch to Meera, who was half-watching the news while she worked on the costings for a new book. Bloom's sombre piece from Manhattan had just finished.

'You see that?'

Meera looked up from her mathematics. 'Now it's going to be all Elgar and mounds of flowers outside Clarence House. All the suck of a Nation in Royal Mourning for weeks...'

'I'm talking about Bloom...'

'She'll have to stay out there for the autopsy. So you're still Mr Showbiz for a bit longer...'

Ben sighed. The post mortem was only the start of it: there'd be the heart-rending royal funeral to be covered, the white coffin, the sobbing crowds – with a half-hearted press observance of the royal family's privacy while they did each other down to get the best shots of the grief. Meera was right: it was going to suck for weeks. Tragedies like this were slippery gifts to Zephon and the British media. The printing presses would run short of purple ink, and the archives would be worked skinny for the tributes. Box and Cox in Cardigan Bay would themselves be kings.

He selfishly cursed his luck. Since speaking to Bunny Fortune and reading the agent's e-mail attachment of the *She-Pirate* tour, he had been ready to go to Kath Lewis with a bold plan. But that would be on the back of Bloom being called home from America while the world waited on Princess Leanna's luck. Now her luck had run out, and so had his. The royal family wouldn't be off the screens and front pages for weeks.

He stood up, restless, and laid the kitchen table, forgetting the fish knives. He was bugged with an idea, and the irony of it was, it could just tie-in with the likely mood at Zephon. If the royal granddaughter's death was from stupidly pill-popping Ecstacy at some dormitory party, then the whole drug supply issue would be a red-hot topic – until the next war, or terror attack, or tsunami. And what was hotter than the harder stuff that was being smuggled into the country by the likes of Gary Fredericks?

But would Kath Lewis see it that way? And would Ms Lewis even see *him*, to discuss it? Was he still in the doghouse? Or, again, even if he was, might she allow him a little wag of his tail?

'Ben Maddox, are you ever coming back to me?' Meera was at the hatch, sniffing at over-baked trout.

'Eh?'

'You're never here! You're always off somewhere else in your head! Do all journalists' wives have to share their husbands with a breaking story?'

Which brought Ben back like the clatter of a dropped knife. What had she said? Two simple words: *wives* and *husbands*? Meera had turned down his proposal of marriage in Paris last spring, then promised to marry him if he came straight back from Lansana. But Ben hadn't returned when Jonny Aaranovitch was kidnapped – which was Meera's big beef as well as Kath Lewis's. So, what was this? A proposal of marriage?

He rescued the fish, then stood and stared her in the face. She didn't smile. But could that be because she could see that he was still elsewhere? And he was, too. What he was really thinking was, if Meera is in such a forgiving mood, might Kath Lewis be, also? Might she be prepared to shuffle her Zephon pack once more and put real life over show-business...?

'I've got three minutes, Maddox. What's your pitch?' Hard-bitten language from Kath Lewis, but her eyes were foreign to the words, signalling, by the size of her irises, that she was over the worst of her anger with him.

Ben didn't sit. He stood across from her desk and pitched, as invited.

'Drugs,' he said, 'at the top of everyone's agenda. Corruption of the young. Two out of three Fredericks' brothers banged-up for trafficking, but Gary, the youngest, still uncharged. And Scotland Yard as certain as they can be that he's still bringing in the white stuff – but no proof to hit him with...'

'While Ben Maddox has that proof, of course...' After her first glance Kath Lewis had looked down and started shuffling papers on her desk. He hadn't grabbed her yet.

'...A friend of Fredericks' is an actor, one of a company about to go backwards and forwards to Europe, touring a new musical. Two of the musical's stage crew are dealing, I've heard them talking about it. They probably go backwards and forwards, too, with all sorts of bands and shows. Roadies. Regular travellers – a typical pattern, according to the Yard. Stop and search the familiar faces a number of times, always clean: known travellers, cheerful waves, walking through the green channel as clean as Clearex. Then in starts coming the goodies with the touring gear...'

Kath Lewis looked up with an obvious question. 'And Ben Maddox is on to that but HM Customs aren't?'

Ben shrugged. It was a good question. 'Customs are – that's how two of the Fredericks' are doing time. And bands, groups, they're always going to be top of the hit list for being searched. But plays, shows, orchestras, they're more respectable, less suspicious…'

'OK. So?' Shuffle, shuffle. Ben was running low on time.

'So – I go undercover as crew on this show. My theatrical agent contact is looking for publicity in Europe for his client who's starring in the show…'

'Being whom?'

'Sadie Baker. "Flame".'

'Flame! I remember her.' Kath Lewis looked up. 'Quite a specialised following, she had…'

'Well, this Bunny fellow – her agent – he wants publicity, and Flame sort of wants it but doesn't want microphones and cameras around. But Bunny can get me into the company as crew, pushing out "puffs" to the Dutch and Germans, while *I'm* there for my own purposes…'

'*Zephon's* purposes!'

But she wasn't shaking her head! 'Of course, Zephon's!'

She was still giving him the shrewd stare. 'Is Flame in on this trafficking?'

'I don't know. I don't think so. I think Bunny Fortune's idea is to please her with the publicity – welcome foreign interest: the first of many come-backs.' Ben was ready to turn and go – back to Bloom's desk. 'What do you think?'

'I think it stinks!' Kath said. Now she started really shuffling the papers on her desk. 'But Bloom's better on show-business than you are, and I'll need a senior presenter with gravitas for all the royal funeral stuff, that's not her scene…' She held up one of the shuffled papers, a CV with a photograph of Royston McCall, a grey face in a suit. 'And you're right: drugs stories are going to sell news – and adverts – for a good few weeks to come.' She flipped at a desk calendar. 'How long's this theatre tour?'

'About twelve weeks.'

'And you can fix it to go?'

'I reckon I've got a fair chance. And I know the lingo, know a border from a cheater, did my share of show-biz lugging and humping with the circus.'

'Tell me you were a clown.'

'I was a clown – Maddo – a holiday job in the long vacation.' But he knew that she knew what was on his CV. She just wanted to say it, which was a good sign: the catty Kath Lewis of old.

'And when I say "come back!" you bloody-well come back?'

'Faster than a bullet train.'

She went on staring at him, through him, at the monitors that were always playing on her office wall – Zephon's output, Sky's, the BBC's. 'All right, have a go.' And without another blink or a wave of her hand, she went back to something more important than Ben Maddox.

While he tried not to skip out of her office. He was out of the dog-house, even if it was on one of those retractable leads.

WHITE ENSIGN PRODUCTIONS
SHE-PIRATE TOUR
PERSONNEL (non-cast)

Director	Martin Kent
Assistant to the director	Maidie Cobbley
Musical Director	David Rainham
Company Stage Manager	Ronnie Hammond
Deputy Stage Manager	Lisa Flynn
A.S.M.s	Fliss Combe
	Lee Philips
	Connor Proudland
Chief Technician	Neil Strong
Asst. Technical	Liam Wolfe
Production Master Carpenter	Mike Samuels
Production Electrician	Simon Shanks
Lighting X 2	Roy Martin
	Sheila Green
Production Wardrobe Mistress	Shelley Tame
Sound X 2	Marvin Steel
	Scott Donaldson
Driver X 2	Fred Lynton
	Jonny Ransome
Painter (and crew)	Jess Good
Crew	Rod Mountjoy
	Lee Conyers
	Ben Maddox

Ben sat in the stalls bar of the Grand Theatre, Southend, and read through the list. The theatre was closed for a week due to the cancellation of *Seaside Fun* whose comic Billy Froth had suddenly died. So White Ensign had got what it needed, a couple of days to set up the *She-Pirate* scenery and the lighting and sound plots prior to the premiere at the Cambridge Theatre in London.

Ben was using his own name, which he wouldn't have done had the tour not been going abroad; but where passports and health insurance were concerned he couldn't sail under a pirate flag. With the rest of the crew he'd been called for eight-thirty am, to await the scenery lorry and the equipment van. Up a side street in the older part of the town off Queensway, the Grand was a Victorian theatre with a large stage. White Ensign carried its own false proscenium – the traditional stage 'picture frame' – for those venues on the tour that didn't have one; but Southend's Grand boasted its own, done over for the summer in yellow ochre, understudying gold. Otherwise – as Ben would learn – the significant bits of the White Ensign scenery were the black flats that would cover the gaps on the different sized tour stages. *She-Pirate* was a flexible fit-up.

Bunny Fortune had done the business. Without compromising Flame he had telephoned Ronnie Hammond and told him how a 'very dear' chum of his – a stage technician – needed a few months' work; and since Sadie Baker was Bunny's client, the Company Stage Manager had given Ben Maddox the nod. First he had required a few details – for an EU work permit, he'd said – of age, sex and ethnicity; and when those answers seemed to satisfy, he needed to know Ben's experience; and on the strength of Bunny Fortune's assurances Ben had been slotted in as one of the stage crew. 'As it happens,' Bunny had told Ben, 'he's lost a man to Her Majesty, last weekend.'

'Called-up?' Ben had asked. 'Army reservist?'

'Not in Belmarsh prison he's not!'

A bell rang for Ben. 'Like Nick Cannon, the co-writer?' And straight off he regretted letting on that he'd done his research. That was slipshod, and he'd better be more careful in the next few weeks.

He told the caretaker his name at the door – going in through the front; nothing romantic like strolling past a stage-door keeper sitting in his little cubby-hole. On the magic words 'White Ensign' he was admitted to the foyer where the crew was assembling, smoking under the No Smoking signs. And the first people he looked out for were either of the pair he'd set this up to watch: the two hands who'd been talking drugs, and no doubt friends of the actor Allen Green who came and went in Europe for a 'purpose'. None of the cast was there today, so no Allen Green, but one of the hands was – called Lee Conyers, about thirty, in a black leather jacket. Ben nodded at him, and the man stared back – like, *What's this?*

Ben knew he mustn't be over-eager, like some new kid at school who was desperate to make a friend. He pulled out a packet of chewing gum and unwrapped three sticks, shoving them in like someone giving up smoking. He looked around to find the main man – and there he was, walkie-talkie in his hand and a radio pack at his belt. Without doubt everything was under the control of this guy, Ronnie Hammond, the Company Stage Manager, a young, fat man who moved as lightly as a dancer. Suddenly stepping over to Ben – black T-shirt with a Betty Boop logo – he stood, chubby hands on a huge waist.

'Maddox?'

'Ben.' Ben held out his hand, which was taken very briefly.

'An't worked with you before.' The voice was light, and West Country.

Ben shook his head.

'What've you done?' No casual enquiry. Ronnie Hammond was staring, a big, impassive face.

Ben was ready, but not for such focused attention – this man's authority was magnified by him being so young. After Bunny Fortune's leg-work he had thought his fictitious experience would just seep out among these people as he worked.

'Writ it out for you,' he said, taking his accent into the street; the same way that he'd not shaved, just trimmed the edges into some sort of designer stubble.

BEN MADDOX - PRO EXPERIENCE

THIS YEAR:
Jan. to April. Spring season cover for assistant technician at Greenwich Theatre (8 shows, 1 in-house, 7 received med-sized tours). Involved all aspects – inc. working with tour CSMs and techs.

May: 2 one-off jobs for Southwark

Playhouse & London Boro. of Lewisham.

LAST YEAR:
Early part, non-theatre stuff.
Summer: Monthly music concerts at
Charlton Athletic FC (the 'Valley') with
'Stage-Force'.
Nov./Dec. Pantomime at East Grinstead –
DSM.

PREVIOUS:
Various – mostly south or south-east
England. Long Theatre-in-Education tours
with 'See-Hear!' and 3 Far East tours for
Cameron Mackintosh shows – 'Saigon',
'Phantom', 'Cats'.

WAY BACK:
Circus work, etc.

He had thought hard about his stage-crew CV – put his mind into Pat's south London world for recent work, which would be less well-known than the West End scene. Now Ronnie Hammond was looking hard at the paper, as if he were checking the spellings. 'What happened with the Jock, then?' he asked. 'Number one stuff, that is.' Meaning, why ever work for someone other than Cameron Mackintosh, at the top of the theatre tree?

Ben sniffed, took the paper back. 'You won't like the answer.'

'Try me.' The big face settled lower on the neck, pushing out jowls.

'I can't stand bloody musicals!' Ben said. 'That's the honest truth, but I need this job, an' I'll love *She-Pirate* for sure...' He had read his spy books, picked up a bit about what they called 'tradecraft'. *Everyone's life story is complicated and messy – filled with regrets and missed chances – and we all tell lies about them. So give the people you're deceiving something on you, be vulnerable where you can afford to be vulnerable. Let the people you're fooling have a safe lie to nag at because it could divert them from your big pretence. But never believe in the first place that you're fooling them...*

Ronnie Hammond stared at him, didn't smile. 'All right.' He shrugged. 'We got a week to suss you out, 'fore it gets serious...'

'Cheers.'

And the CSM went round the foyer checking boots. No one worked on one of his stages without the steel-capped boots that protect from dropped stage weights. Which Ben knew about, and had brought a pair in his rucksack, borrowed from a studio hand at Zephon. He also had that other essential, a leather safety lanyard which attached to tools, for hitching to the belt or the wrist when working at height. Health and Safety was no less stringent in touring theatre than it was in film and television, and wasn't he supposed to be a pro?

After a quick coffee everyone filtered through into the

auditorium and up onto the stage. Off stage right, the tall scenery doors were open, and within three minutes of getting his boots on, Ben was shifting stuff off the truck outside and onto the stage. The 'get-in' had begun.

Most scenery flats are two-person carries. These were soft flats made of wood and painted canvas, a metre and three-quarters wide and four metres high and, without too much manoeuvring, Ben managed to get himself partnering his target, Lee Conyers – without his druggie mate of the other day. A bit later Ben would find out whether he'd been the one put inside. For now, he let Conyers pull the first scenery flat off the truck, and stepped in himself to take the other end.

'Looks like panto at Sunderland Empire!' Conyers sneered, looking at the tropical beach painted on it. 'Reckon they got mermaids?'

'Bags top 'alf if they 'ave!' Ben came back – and into the theatre they went, to stand the flat against the back wall – and then outside for their next one.

Meanwhile, the front line lighting bar was being raised, followed by the black border that would mask it: from both the circus and the studio, Ben knew that everything worked from the top down. Lights and borders first, then the Master Carpenter would take over to supervise the getting up of the set. Ben had a feel for professionalism. He could always watch a skilled plumber at work, or a potter, or a bricklayer, admire the tricks of the trade. Now he was part of a pro team of theatre people setting up a musical on a provincial stage. And Ben had thought that he was part of it all until Lee Conyers suddenly stopped him by the back wall as they rested a flat against it.

'Wor you bin before?' Conyers frowned. He had

stopped and taken off his leather jacket now he was hot, hung it on a cleat. He ran both gloved hands down it, a check of the pockets, and turned his thin face at Ben, an arm across him, resting on the brickwork. This wasn't casual chat.

'Just before this? Greenwich.'

'Left your mittens there, then?'

Ben spat on his hands and shrugged, a vital couple of seconds to think. His mind frantically thought what he'd seen that morning, and he realised that all these others were wearing leather-backed gloves, this Geordie with the yachting type, giving protection to the palm but leaving feeling at the fingers.

'Yeah! Stupid! Gotta get some…' Ben spat again on his sore palms – because he certainly needed a pair. 'Nicked!' he said. ''Alf-inched by some git on *Porgy and Bess*…'

'Huh! Actor?' Lee Conyers wanted to know, pushing off the back wall to go out to the truck again. 'Never leave nothin' about an actor c'n eat. Leather? Tha's sirloin steak to soom…' He rubbed his nose with the back of his glove.

Ben laughed. 'Make you right!' He followed.

'Might 'ave a pair of old 'uns—' Conyers tossed over his shoulder.

'Cheers.'

'Nah bleedin' mittens!' he sneered, as Ben Maddox followed him out for the next flat. With quite a bit to think about, one way and another…

The light in Sylvie Filey's eyes would have lit up London. She brandished her Thursday's copy of *The Stage*, open at the 'what's-on-and-who's-in-it' professional listing on page twenty-six. The print was small but the pride was huge as she read it out to Paul, ducking under her arm to see his first theatrical credit in national print.

LISTINGS

LONDON
Cambridge Theatre (020 7850 8710)
She-Pirate (from July 26th)
Flame/Allen Green/ Robert Tremaine
Paul Filey/Bradley Turner/Judy Gold/
Jo Beckford/Tootie Sylvester/Ron Quick
Lee Fletcher/Bailey Trust/Little Johnson
Fay Carter/Den de Sousa

'Wow!' he said, and his smile almost needed stitches at the sides.

'So!' she said.

'So!' he said.

'How about that?'

'Not bad, eh?' And he filled his lungs with bursting pride, one of a special band of people that even included William Shakespeare. He was an actor, a proper actor. It said so here.

'Snip it out!' his mother offered. 'Start a scrap-book.'

'I'll scan it,' he said. 'Let's keep the whole paper intact.'

He didn't want to explain why. When it was yellow and old, it might fetch a few bob at a charity auction.

'Nah! I'm going up the newsagents to buy two more – and one's for your dad.'

But Paul shook his head. 'Just get one,' he said. 'Dad won't be impressed with *The Stage*, but he might respect a *Guardian* review, if we get one...'

'Yeah, if you get one,' Sylvie cautioned. 'Don't count any chickens, dear boy.' And her serious face suddenly showed the lines of bitter experience.

'THE FILEY FILES'

File 6

I can't describe the take-your-breath-away moment when you suddenly see the show you've been rehearsing up there on the stage. Except, it takes your breath away.

Our call was for ten o'clock at the Grand Theatre, Southend, and some of us had been on the same Liverpool Street train to Southend Victoria. I got on at Stratford, and found a carriage where Jo Beckford and Tootie Sylvester were waving through the window at me.

Of all the people to do with the show, these two are the nearest to being mates – nothing special, but if a seat is free at their table, I go for it. They know each other from before, they like a laugh, have both done a fair bit, give stick where stick's due, and always clap on a good exit. My luck is, since the second week of rehearsals they've sort of adopted me like a stray dog that's walked in. But I don't lick their hands, and they don't throw balls for me to chase. It's liking, and respect, both ways.

They were quiet, talking about getting through a difficult day. Today was going to be the 'tech', where we make-up and wear costumes and run the play through for the sake of the lights and the sound and the scenery changes. Even at Broadway a tech's a pain, a long old slog for the crew. It would be the next day, the Thursday, when we'd run it twice as 'dress' – which are full 'performance' rehearsals, with everything coming together. Please God.

Jo and Tootie were carrying their own make-up cases, but they'd have liquid black provided by White Ensign for their slave scene and as 'nubiles' at the court of the King of Dahomey. So why haven't black actors been cast? Only Tootie has anything 'white' to do – but I'm glad these two are in it, they're a sparky pair and great to be with. It was definitely a plus not to be stuck in with Turd-face Turner on my first company transport call.

And my good news is that Turner does the tech and I do the first dress as Ardal. So, what's Martin Kent up to, who's the 'alternate'? Search me!

I've got three costumes: my Ardal's, first as the young grandson in Judge Macroo's household, then the pirate son of Meg – and my pirate crew gear for when I'm Frenchie Roche, which is hardly a costume at all, me being bare-chested most of the time. And, thanks very much, one make-up does me for the show.

Being a tour in all sorts of different-sized venues, the show's design is nothing like *Les Miserables* or *Phantom*, but it's cracking enough to see for the first time. The designer's created a good sense of depth by the way she uses perspective, and the cloths at the back are painted as if they're further away than the flats at the front. And on the different ships, the curved cyclorama sheet gives the sky and the horizon a deep sense of distance.

On Wednesday morning at the Grand the scene we walked in on was what the tabs would go up on – Scene One, Act One, the fancy grand saloon in Judge Macroo's house in Barbados. It's got flush 'mahogany' doors set between two wall flats on each side of the stage, which say posh, very posh, to the audience, and a cross-stage balustrade in front of the cyc – with a couple of hanging palm trees in between – which really gives the feel of cool money looking out over the Caribbean.

The scene was fully lit – and a few people clapped at the sight of it – which none of the crew seemed to appreciate. They all think actors are big girls' blouses.

No surprise – the tech was every bit as hard as any tech I've done for end-of-term shows at Broadway. Lighting couldn't get the focus groups of lamps co-ordinated, and sound had the usual battery problems with the head mics; but the recorded overture, and the backing for the vocals was real heady stuff. There was a rock rhythm we thought we knew about from the piano at rehearsals – till we heard it at a hundred and fifteen decibels with the bass twanging our spines inside our bodies. Fantastic!

And that was the moment I discovered what Flame was about, and the show, and the attraction for the Europeans who'd been her fans before. She was electric. With the beat of the backing, the breath was sucked out of my lungs. And the thought that I was a part of all that was mega. *Mega mega!* I was so knocked out by it, I nearly cried.

Till Bradley Turner came and sat behind me, after he'd come off in Scene One. 'Load of old toss!' he told anyone and no one. 'A right trawl this is... Should've done it as a pod-cast!' Which wouldn't have been theatre at all. What sort of attitude's that for an actor?

So why's he here at all, I ask myself...

LEYTON, LONDON E10

Ben snatched up his mobile and checked who was calling him. *Call from Bloom.* He answered it.

Ben:

Hi!

Bloom:

Ben!

Ben:

Bloom – how're you doing?

Bloom:

Good! I'm good!

Ben:

What did you think of New York?

Bloom:

Hated it! Except Broadway. Loved Paris. God, the Americans know how to eat – but the French know how to dine.

Ben:

Are you back at Zephon?

Bloom:

Yesterday. An' you left my desk really neat, Maddox. So you're following up a showbiz story, you dog…

Ben:

No competition, girl – it's a drugs story with a showbiz background... The rest is all back to you, the Dames and the premieres. But I followed up on Bunny Fortune—

Bloom:

Dear Bunny!

Ben:

—And I've seen your Sadie Baker, from a distance...

Bloom:

La vache ancienne! Is she part of—?

Ben:

No, I don't think so. But have you ever heard of an actor called Allen Green...?

Bloom:

Allen Green? *(Not sure)* No. *(Certain)* No! Is he in on whatever's going on?

Ben:

He's in the show, and ten gives me fifty he's in on something for sure. Constantly touring Europe with different companies – says he does it for a purpose...

Bloom:

I'll look him up. If I see anything significant I'll be in touch.

Ben:

Different from what he'll have printed in the programme?

Bloom:

Could be, but I doubt it. You seen the programme yet?

Ben:

Nope.

Bloom:

I was goin' to say. They're usually very last minute – yours'll be just before opening next week. They'll print a whole-tour programme, the same one for all the venues.

Ben:

In English?

Bloom:

If they're playing the show in English.

Ben:

Glad you rang—

Bloom:

You just wanted to hear my voice...?

Ben:

Are there different make-ups for the West End, or for a big theatre like the Cambridge...?

Bloom:

Different? You mean, for the same character...?

Ben:

Yeah. Before the dress rehearsal today, this Allen Green asked the director whether he wanted the 'tour' make-up for this character, or the 'London' one. Martin Kent – the director – said, 'We're "dressing" for London...' Which Green seemed to understand, went off and got made-up...

Bloom:

As what?

Ben:

Roarin' James – a pirate captain.

Bloom:

Looking like what?

Ben:

A pirate captain. 'Blackbeard', or 'Captain Kidd'. What you'd expect...

Bloom:

Heavy make-up?

Ben:

Not all that. Good wig.

Bloom:

Because the Cambridge is a big barn of a place. He'd need more make-up there than somewhere tiddly like the Royal Court.

Ben:

Just struck me as weird...

Bloom:

There's a hellova lot that's weird in the the-atre, luvvie. You'll get used to it.

Ben:

Yeah...

Bloom:

Is that it, or did you miss me while I was gone?

Ben:

Goes without saying. Missed you like hell, Ramsaran.

Bloom:

Well, look out for me in Paris...

Ben:

In Paris?

Bloom:

If they haven't 'outed' you by then, your tour winds up in

Paris, doesn't it?

Ben:

That's right...

Bloom:

Well I'm in Paris that weekend. 24th September...

Ben:

Has Kath got you following up on the Princess Leanna story?

Bloom:

I've got me following up on a nice French *Canal Media*
cameraman. And an anti-racist rally.

Ben:

Good for you, Ramsaran, on both counts... Might see you
there, then.

Bloom:

If you haven't already uncovered what you're uncovering –
and if Kath Lewis gives me the leave I'm due.

Ben:

Look forward to it. OK, gotta go – or my rice is going to weld
itself to the saucepan.

Bloom:

Ciao, then, Ben!

Ben:

Ciao, Bloom! Luv ya!

Bloom:

Oh, yeah?

Ben flipped his mobile shut and concentrated on his late supper. After the second dress rehearsal down at the Grand there had been notes for everyone in the auditorium, and then a drive home up the A12. Meera was still out at a publishers' 'Book Circle' meeting, and he was grateful for that, because she wasn't a theatre person; and with his head full of what was going on it was hard to talk politics and literature in the evenings, and then go down to Southend to be a *Sun*-reading 'roadie'. On tour it would be different; but right now what he didn't want was a double life.

He poured his stroganoff onto the rice and sat to eat it one-handed, elbows on the table and scooping like a kid at school dinners. He'd caught himself in the theatre bar eating an Indian take-away, holding his cutlery the way his mother had taught him. 'For God's sake, don't hold your knife and fork sticking up like a couple of pens...' Which was exactly what Ben had suddenly remembered to do in the bar – in the hope that his table manners hadn't given him away.

Already, he'd made a gaffe over the gloves, which had surprised Lee Conyers, who'd lent him a pair, but who was keeping a bit closer an eye than was comfortable. Yes, there was definitely more to being undercover than a false CV, Ben thought, shovelling the food into his mouth.

THAMESIDE ROUTE

Paul read his notes from the director on the train home. A crewman called Ben who lived in Leyton had offered him a lift to Stratford Town Hall in his car, but after the dress rehearsals Paul wanted time on his own; so he dodged off quickly to the station for the nine-o-five, standing well behind the Coca-Cola machine. As it happened, most of the others were going for the nine-thirty-five or the ten o'clock, after a drink in the King's Arms. But that wasn't for him. He was still shaking after the rehearsals and from the tension of sitting in the auditorium for the great dictator's notes. But Kent had said nothing to him in public, written his notes instead and thrust the folded paper at him like a court summons. He'd said nothing public to Sadie or to Bradley Turner, either, but concentrated on re-blocking the bigger scenes, where getting on and off was different now that the set was up. But, by and large, he'd been satisfied – he was never pleased.

Meanwhile, Paul had his own opinion of Bradley Turner. Turner had done the second dress as Ardal, and he'd hardly moved on from day one. Nearly three weeks of rehearsal and he'd hardly changed. Paul had thought the dress would bring something out of him that they hadn't seen up to now, but, no way! Then what had worried him was that Paul Filey hadn't moved on, either.

But reading his notes put his mind at rest. Now he had to keep on improving, not slip back and disappoint. Already, he'd tried to put some of Turner's threat into the part – you can always learn stuff – and it was up to him to do the business at performances. But the first big question

Paul Filey — Ardal

Your training with a TV/Film bias means you're not giving enough facial expression for the stage and some of our bigger venues.

Don't over-do it, no mugging, but notch it up a gear.

Pace! Remember what I tell you — jump on others' lines a bit quicker — even Sadie's. It's a long show.

Singing's good and true, keep practising the breathing for the main duet.

Stagecraft — I'm happy with this. You seem aware of sight lines and where others are. You're less predictable in your movement and dialogue — which is good: remember, always be prepared to be surprised.

Specific — the Bradley fight — at Ardal's victory, come down left a touch more, find the lighting spot we've plotted. We did it for a purpose! Today you were out of it.

Overall - creditable. On track for a good performance.

M.K.

was, who would play Ardal on opening night? Which of the two of them would the critics see next Tuesday?

And how would three months of such Martin Kent decisions play with him and Turd-Face?

We've got in at the Cambridge and done the 'tech' and
the 'dress'. The Cambridge permanent staff have seen
everything, done everything, and they've got a big
American musical coming in next week with a waterfall
and an erupting volcano, so with our squirts of dry ice
and a few 'stage fright' cannon noises, we must seem
pretty small-time stuff. Hear that? I sound like I'm
getting under the skin of this part.

It went OK. I'm busy, busy, busy during the show. The
way the crew has to move about with the scene changes
are as choreographed as anything in the action. There
aren't fly-towers everywhere we go, so instead of scenery
whizzing up and down on counterbalanced weights, it's
pulled on and off from the sides on 'trucks'. By hand. By
muscle. We make the ships different from one another by
swapping pieces stage left for stage right. The painted
scene 'drops' that go across the stage at the back – like
'tropical' and 'cabin' – aren't dropped at all, but pulled
in from left to right like curtains. All of which is hard, on-
your-toes work.

Lee Conyers is still keeping an eye on me. He can be snide
with some funny Geordie remarks about actors, but
whenever I look round, he's just looked away. Whether
that's all down to me not bringing gloves on the first day,
or me coming in out of the blue, I can't say. If he'd
remembered my face from TV almost a year ago I think
he'd have challenged me before now. All the same, I'm

holding-off talking to him too much. Except, on the Cambridge get-in I made sure he overheard me say something to one of the scenery truck drivers as we off-loaded against the scenery dock.

'Bet there's plenty of "serving" goes on round here,' I said. 'Wouldn't know,' Jonny Ransome said. But Conyers made some sound in his throat behind me; the trouble was, I daren't turn round to see the look on his face that went with it. Still, it's early days yet.

And the big day's to come. Tomorrow. The first night. We'll all have to be on our toes for that – and I'm getting so much into this, I'm starting to feel a bit twitchy.

'THE FILEY FILES'

File 7

It's going to be me! It's going to be me! Martin Kent told me today – it's me doing Ardal, opening night! I knew he'd told Turd-face already because the clown wouldn't look at me – but if I'm 'up' like this, he's bound to be 'down', so I mustn't be triumphant.

I've organised first night tickets for Mum and Jenny Tongue from Broadway, but I've not involved Dad. They'll sort of understand if it's a disaster, but he'd treat it as making him right all along; like, what a waste of space actors are in the real world. They'll also be there on business – at least Jenny will. She'll look up the cast in her Broadway copy of Spotlight and see who their agents are, because it's on the London dates that they'll drop in to see their clients – and Jenny can send my CV to the decent ones. They'll have seen me in action, won't they – and none of us can work without an agent.

There aren't any previews. Most London shows that hope to run have a week or more of cheaper tickets while the play beds-in before the critics see it. But White Ensign are treating this just like any week in the tour schedule. We're called for eleven am for a 'line run' in the bar, then a 'music run' in the theatre – voice, not movement, then a lunch break, and a 'tech/dress' at three o'clock. After which we're free until 'the half' at six twenty-five.

The calls for a show are 'beginners' – five minutes before curtain up, and 'the half' – half an hour before that, by which time you're supposed to be in the building to be allowed to go on. So I'm not going to take any chances. With make-up to do, and an Ardal costume with buttoned breeches to get into, there won't be any chance of me missing the 'half' on first night. I won't leave the building. I'll get ready, and then take myself off under the stage to do the voice warm-up routine they teach us at Broadway before we do the company warm-up, which for Turner and me involves running through the fight. This business is all about discipline, and focus.

So, fingers are crossed. If it goes well, I've worked out that having done the first night as Ardal, I should also do the Wednesday matinee, Thursday night, and Saturday matinee. Turner will probably do Wednesday night, Friday, and Saturday night – if we alternate equally, which could be the plan. But I can't be sure. I might wait for a good moment when his impatience is out to lunch and ask Martin Kent if there's a schedule for the part yet, because Mum's on the top line to buy up a row of seats for the staff at Hartley. What she won't want is a Bradley Turner performance by mistake. The other part we play when we're not Ardal are OK with a couple of nice moments as Frenchie Roche – but it's not like being Flame's 'son' and singing a duet with her. Will it be Thursday for me after tonight, then – or has Martin Kent got other plans? Who knows? Does *he*?

Although the thought has just crossed my mind – I bet
Sadie Baker will have something to say in all this...

Ooer! So – putting everything together, with Mum,
Jenny Tongue, Martin Kent, Sadie Baker all in the frame,
I've got a fair bit to get nervous about...

Bloom had briefed Ben on theatrical first nights.

'Never say "good luck" – that's bad luck.'

'I know that one.'

'And send the leading lady a lovely card wishing her well.'

'Telling her how brilliant she's going to be...'

'You're there, Maddox, you're there! Me too. I shall be there—'

'What?'

'At the Cambridge. I'm coming to the first night, going to do a short news piece for *London Late-nite*.'

'Excellent! That'll please Bunny Fortune. And come backstage afterwards...'

'I might. See how I go. See if I feel like looking that cat in the eye when I bump into her.'

Ben frowned. 'You can't. *London Late-nite* goes out at eleven. You'll have to scoot.'

'Best, then.' Bloom laughed. 'I don't bear a lot of grudges, but that woman really treated me like something scraped off the bottom of her shoe.'

'So it'll be an unbiased piece...'

'Natch. I'm a pro, Ben Maddox – don't you ever forget that!'

Ben said he wouldn't, and finished the call. There was work to do. The first scene of Act One had been re-set after the dress rehearsal but there were still flats and props to be lined up in position for the rest of the show. And wearing his blacks like everyone else, Lee Conyers was leaning against the back wall of the building, waiting for Ben to give a hand with a balustrade for the Act One mansion.

'C'mon, man – set this fence for tha' ponce to rip his tights on...'

Ben took his own end. It was better to be busy right now. Meanwhile, his real assignment would have to be on hold till they were over in Europe – although he ought to chase off an e-mail to Bunny Fortune to keep his back covered.

From: Ben Maddox [benm@talktalk.net]
Sent: 26 July 11:45
To: b.fortune@ruselhudson.co.uk
Subject: She-Pirate

Hi Bunny

Everything's going nicely leading up to the first night. Perhaps I'll see you at the drinks afterwards?

I've got my list of Zephon TV associate TV companies in Holland, Germany and France. You can tell your people that I'll be feeding publicity to the following outlets:

France: CANAL+ TF1

Germany: ARD + its regionals – BR, HR, MDR

Holland: NPO + NOS TeleTekst

Europe-wide: ASTRA + EuroTV

My colleague Bloom Ramsaran is coming to the Cambridge tonight and is hoping to get a news spot on Zephon's *London Late-Nite*. Although this is local TV and London-based, the item gets syndicated to Zephon North West, Midlands Zephon, Zephon West and Zephon Tyne if the story warrants it. And if Flame gets mobbed by her old 'rock' fans it will doubtless make national Zephon news.

Hopefully see you tonight!

Ben

For Paul it was eerie backstage. It was quiet, and nervous, and the laughs were high and forced. The temperature was in the high twenties and humid, but when he met anyone it wasn't all sweat but shivers. He shared a dressing room with Ron Quick and Robert Tremaine, and talk was cut to the murmuring of lines and the odd phrase of a *She-Pirate* song. Ardal would be onstage a lot of the time, and both Quick and Tremaine had quick changes for their doubled parts, so the dressing room was on stage level, and handy. Bradley Turner was in with Allen Green and Bailey Trust, while Sadie Baker had a dressing room to herself – the number one, with 'FLAME' pinned to the door. The theatre billing and the programme credited her as 'Flame', answering the query in Paul's head. Was this a fresh start or a comeback?

Meanwhile, the first thing Paul did when he saw the counted-out stack of tour programmes in the Green Room was to grab one and look for his name on the cast list – one of those times when fingers can never be quick enough.

WHITE ENSIGN PRODUCTIONS

present

SHE-PIRATE

A new musical by Nick Cannon and Martin Kent

Directed by Martin Kent

CAST

(in order of appearance)

Judge Macroo	Allen Green
Meg Macroo	Flame
Felix Lawes	Robert Tremaine
Ardal Macroo	Paul Filey
	Bradley Turner
Carmenita Savilla	Judy Gold
Nelly Laidlaw	Jo Beckford
Alice	Tootie Sylvester
Ned Smart	Ron Quick
King of Dahomey	Robert Tremaine
Frenchie Roche	Bradley Turner
	Paul Filey
Captain Bright	Lee Fletcher
Roarin' James	Allen Green
Quartermaster	Ron Quick

Seamen, pirates, slaves, passengers: The company, with Bailey Trust, Little Johnson, Fay Carter, Den de Sousa

The action takes place in the Caribbean and the west coast of Africa in the early seventeen-hundreds

And there it was, with a blood-red pirate skull on the cover. The centre pages opened out onto an advertisement for a Lancashire travel company on the left and, facing, the cast list; prominent on which – no, jumping off which – was the name 'Paul Filey'. OK, it was a pity that the credit wasn't his alone, but never mind, there it was, in bold black print on glossy programme paper: and on the back page were the tour dates. It all looked so professional that a light-headed surge of excitement suddenly puckered Paul's skin into goosebumps.

He flicked through the pages. Next was his biography, beneath a small black and white version of his photograph.

PAUL FILEY – ARDAL
This is Paul's first professional engagement. He is a student at the Broadway Theatre School in east London. His mother is the actress Sylvie Filey, known for her performances as 'Trish' in

EastEnders a year or so ago. Paul says he is proud to be following in his mother's stage footsteps, and is looking forward to the tour.

Paul sighed. Would his mum be pleased with that? Maidie Cobbley had caught him off-guard one afternoon at the church hall rehearsals, and he hadn't realised quite what she'd been after. When he read some of the other biogs – Flame just listing her hits, and Allen Green with a string of touring credits – Paul reckoned his looked pretty amateur. Worse, Bradley Turner had unfairly linked himself with the Bristol Old Vic and listed a string of student productions as if they were for the main company. The crud – he looked one step down from Sir Ian McKellan, while Paul Filey was going on about his mum...

But, stop it! Paul had enough to think about right now without vanity rearing up in the dressing room mirror.

'Plenty of slap!' said Bob Tremaine, larding it onto his face. 'Like playing the Emirates Stadium, this is. Else, from the back of the Upper Circle you'll look like Morph.'

Paul got on with his own make-up, and all too soon, the dreaded voice came over the backstage tannoy.

'Beginners, please, ladies and gentlemen – Miss Flame, Mr Green, Mr Tremaine, Mr Filey, Miss Beckford, Mr Trust, Miss Sylvester – this is your Act One beginners' call. And this is your ten minute call, Miss Gold.' Somewhere in the distance from front-of-house, Paul could hear the audience play-in music, and he pictured his mother with Jenny Tongue down in the fourth row of the stalls – the 'company' seats.

And he wondered who might be sitting at the centre aisle ends of rows two, three, four and five – where the critics sat – scouring his brain for some reason why anyone ever took up this torture for a living...

'THE FILEY FILES'

File 8

He's a sod. There's no other word I can use right now. No, there are tons, but this is meant for my autobiography one day, so I'll keep it professional and try to put a lid on my volcano-hot anger.

It was in the fight scene – the one where Ardal duels with Frenchie Roche, punishing him for bad-mouthing his mother – the sequence after Ardal slashes and Frenchie jumps the cutlass, choreographed to the count of sixteen. It's where I caught him in rehearsal when he didn't jump on the count, and he cursed me. After this, Ardal goes on to win – the moves rehearsed like a dance till I run him through with the sword-under-the-arm trick.

Everything was perfect at the dress rehearsal – but on the first night the bastard doesn't let me win! My solo in Act One had gone well and we'd got a round for it after Tootie had joined in for the duet finish. My duet with Flame had gone even better in Act Two, with whoops and whistles in the applause – and now Frenchie Roche has got to be put down for bad-mouthing my mother. As Paul Filey I'm on top of the world. I'm over my nerves. The first night shakes have gone, I've hit my high notes, I'm on a West End stage and going great on the most important night of my life. I've just stood staring into Flame's eyes, holding a pose to audience acclaim. She exits, in comes Bradley Turner as Frenchie Roche, and

I've got a showy fight scene that'll cap everything, and make my night. *And bloody Turner won't let me kill him.* As Frenchie Roche he's one of the captured crew of a merchantman, most of them played as disabled and useless; but Frenchie's got some spirit, so it's got to be a good fight, not a walk-over.

Even so! When we got to the end of the choreographed, practised, rehearsed and step-perfect scene, right up to the kill, he suddenly slides out of the way on my final thrust and gets round behind me. I turn and fight on – go into a sequence we both know from the first part of the duel, me staring into his eyes trying to reach some sort of understanding with the dog – when I slash at him and miss (deliberately, rehearsed) but he pretends I've struck him and drops down like a boxer taking a dive in the second round. He makes it look as if *I've* gone wrong, and he's had to do something drastic to end the scene with me winning.

Big anti-climax. A couple of murmurs in the audience. When the stage blacks out for the ship scenery to be reversed, the *Smiling Rover* turning into *HMS Chatham*, he gets up, says, 'Sorry, Filey – went wrong!' And disappears stage-left.

It took the shine off everything for me. I forgot the applause and the whoops and my professional joy at staring eye-to-eye with a rock legend in a big duet on a London stage. All at once I looked like a theatre school kid who couldn't remember his moves!

Mum and Jenny said they didn't notice anything wrong – but they must have done. I wanted to kill Turner. I ducked out of the first-night drinks party as soon as I could and went home.

And I'm sitting here, gutted, with no chance of sleep and two shows to do tomorrow.

Dad's right. He's bloody right!

Ben wasn't a bit surprised to see him. There in the bar at the first-night drinks was Gary Fredericks, smoothing it like a show backer – which, of course, he might have been, talking to his friend Allen Green. Trays of red and white wine and orange juice went round, while requests for beer were politely smiled off. Ben, deliberately still wearing his black KREW sweatshirt, sidled up to Allen Green and Gary Fredericks.

'Went a treat, Allen!' he said.

A residual smear of Roarin' James eyebrow make-up extended into the gap above Green's nose. It wrinkled into a *who-are-you?* frown. But the actor must have known Ben was on the show, they'd side-stepped and dodged throughout the performance in the scene changes.

'Be better next week,' Green said. 'Do it properly then!'

'I thought it went OK,' Ben repeated. 'Didn't you?' he asked Gary Fredericks.

Fredericks' eyes shrewed back at him, slate-grey, impassive. 'Yeah,' he said. And that was all. Silence. Without being told to leave the two of them alone, Ben was being told to leave the two of them alone. There's something about a hardened criminal that gives commands without word or gesture.

Ben went. As expected, Bloom hadn't shown, but she'd have stood out in that room, and so would Meera. It was solidly white. Meanwhile, Bunny Fortune was one of a cluster syruping round Sadie Baker; so Ben found Lee Conyers, drinking from a bottle of Budweiser.

'*Beer!* Where'd you get that?'

'I c'n get stuff,' Conyers said. 'When I wan' it.'

At which Ben was so tempted – *so* tempted to dig for his Zephon mission; but something held him back. Every journalist has the instinct that someone might be testing them.

'Won't ask you who to see. Hop an' vine don't combine.' Ben looked down into his glass of red wine: and thought *what a stupid, middle-class thing to say!*

'Poncy stuff!' Conyers swigged again. 'Wine. Gi' me sup cats' piss, sooner.' And he drifted off for another beer.

Ben looked around the room, in particular at the Sadie Baker cluster. The few outsiders allowed into the first night party were of a type: mostly male, youngish, short haircuts, white shirts – a no-nonsense band of 'rockers'. And Ben recalled the shouts of 'more' at the ends of Flame's songs, and the cheers at her curtain calls: throaty, almost threatening. With a welcome-back like that, Flame was definitely about to kick-start a new career.

Ben refocused on Gary Fredericks to see Lee Conyers walking over to where Allen Green and the crook were still talking quietly. Using the bar mirror he watched the three of them, heads close like Guy Fawkes, Catesby and Percy, no brush-off for Conyers but instant inclusion in a serious conversation. A bit more confirmation, then: the way they were standing, Conyers and Fredericks had to know each other already.

Could Ben really be on to something? This had all been a hunch up to now – his fancy, an indulgence that Kath Lewis had allowed. Now it seemed quite likely that he was on the right track.

Another glass of wine as the party broke up and he went home to catch Meera's recording of *London Late-*

nite, walking from the Tube with a jaunt that said how chipper he felt to be an active reporter on the road again. Doing the show-business job would have bored him out of his mind.

ZEPHON TELEVISION
TRANSCRIPT SERVICE

Programme 10332
London Late-nite
Tuesday 26 July

Package 11
Bloom Ramsaran

BLOOM RAMSARAN (SOLO, TO CAMERA):
Her real name is Sadie Baker, and twelve years ago she
was known internationally as a rock star – under
another name. Tonight she reinhabited that 'rock' name
on the West End stage. Who is she? 'Flame'! – who's
rockin' again, at the Cambridge Theatre.

*Cut to publicity footage of 'Flame' fronting her rock
band.*

BLOOM (VOICE OVER):
Yes, Flame is rocking again in a new musical, and her
fan base seems never to have gone away, judging by
the reception she got from a full house.

*Cut to shots of (mostly) young and middle-aged men
walking purposefully to join a queue around the
Cambridge Theatre.*

Cut to Bloom:
The fans were reluctant to be interviewed, as was

Flame herself when I caught her at rehearsals. I presume she preferred the show to speak for itself. Well...

Cut to front of theatre with She-Pirate *signage and posters.*

Bloom (voice over):
She-Pirate, by Nick Cannon and Martin Kent, who also directed. And how well does it speak for itself?

Close-up of 'swashbuckling' Meg Macroo, poster detail.

Bloom (voice over):
She's in good voice. And you can see her appeal as a rock star. Her flaming hair flames and her voice goes to places no voice has a right to go: throaty one moment, high and ringing the next. Her timing is superb, her acting is good, and somehow you know that you're seeing someone very special up there on stage. It's a rock concert around a play, and maybe she has found a new outlet...

Cut to Bloom, close-up:
... but what is this musical all about? It's a strident, power-seeking re-write of pirate history, relying for shock value on the legend of the real female pirate who, posing as a man, won a crucial duel by suddenly baring her breasts and slaughtering her gawping opponent. 'Supremacy!' she sings. Well, if that's all it takes, watch out fellows...!

Bloom puts both hands to the neck of her blouse as if about to pull it open.

Black-out.

Package Ends

TOP FLAT, 130 LEYTON HIGH STREET, LONDON E10

Ben was still in bed when his mobile rang. He'd got a matinee that afternoon, but with everything rigged and set at the Cambridge he wasn't called before two. So this was a first chance after the early starts of the past couple of weeks to catch up on some shut-eye.

'It's Bunny Fortune...'

'Bunny!' Ben tried to sound up and about.

'Drear! What *were* your people playing at last night? That *London nighty-night* wasn't what our plan was all about...'

Meera murmured something beside Ben in her sleep so he turned the other way, leant on an elbow, and spoke quietly into the phone. 'You wouldn't be meaning Zephon, Bunny?'

'I decidedly would! Who else? Your black reporter. The lady I lunched. Sniffy, Ben, she was very sniffy about *She-Pirate*, dear.'

'Yes, I'm sorry. But she was complimentary about Sadie, and it's Flame I'm trying to promote. I can't write all the reviews, now can I – all through Holland, Germany and France? Bloom plugged the show's strength – Flame and the rock music – and rock's going to be the audience base, don't you reckon?' He was awake now; very awake. He mustn't fall out with Bunny Fortune or he'd get pulled from the tour; and he'd need to keep his job with White Ensign if he was going to get a good long jail sentence for Gary Fredericks. And his own scoop to go with it! 'Tell you what, read the newspaper reviews, and if – no, when – you get a good one, I'll get Zephon to invite the writer onto one of our shows later this week...I do think Flame's very good, myself.'

'It's more than a tad disappointing, Ben.'

'Wait for the papers, Bunny. Someone's bound to like it. Look at what's running in London right now...'

Bunny Fortune sighed into the phone, the sound of a wave on shingle. 'Hey-ho, my hearty! I'll be in touch.'

'Look forward to it.' And Ben clicked himself off. But that was it for sleep. Now that he was alert there was a lot to think about. And most of it wasn't about Flame, nor the merits of the show, but about what was going on behind the scenes.

Because thinking back on the first night party, he had a strong sense that he was getting nearer to the real action now...

THE CLARION

★☆☆☆☆☆

She-Pirate
Cambridge Theatre

Why? If former 'rock' tourer Flame is intent on a come-back, why do it in this travesty of a musical by Nick Cannon and Martin Kent?

The red-haired singer might have to dye those curls these days but she's still in good voice – less screech, more boom – but the vehicle she's chosen runs on wonky wheels and goes nowhere.

The story would embarrass a primary school end-of-year production, written by the leavers. Meg Macroo (Flame) with her son Ardal (nicely acted and sung by Paul Filey) take on the pirate world seeking supremacy in all they do. In the final scene (yes, I stayed that long) Macroo bares her 'breast' (modestly in a body stocking upstage) and thereby tricks and wins the day over her pirate rival Roarin' James (Allen Green playing pantomime).

The canned music thumps without effect and the lyrics are banal. *She rules the waves who waives the rules* being about as clever as it gets.

This production is at the Cambridge for a week only, before touring – a good decision by the Cambridge, which would be better dark than so poorly lit.

James Kershaw

KITCHENER ROAD, LONDON E7

Question: How to get hated by your colleagues?

Answer: Receive the only decent mention in a clutch of dire reviews.

While Paul slept in, Sylvie Filey ran to the newsagent's and bought up the likely morning papers. With experienced accuracy she found the show-business page in each and skimmed through the *She-Pirate* reviews. Not everyone covered it, but of the four who did, each was damning; all of them welcoming to Flame but panning the show. Only the *Clarion* was different, for a very special reason. As soon as its review page was opened, the name 'Paul Filey' leapt at Sylvie like a loved face grinning out of a class photo. Her insides flared as she took in the whole piece in one gulp. A name check! In the *Clarion*! '...nicely acted and sung by Paul Filey'! The show was panned, but Sylie's grab was her son.

'*Excrement!*' Paul said when he saw it. '*Blocked lavs!* Green will hate me! Turner will hate me! Martin Kent will hate me! I'm the only one to get a half-decent mention!' Paul knew the feeling well from Broadway – when someone was singled out for praise and the rest flayed, the big reaction was a stab in the back, not a slap on it.

'Flame did all right. She'll be OK with you,' Sylvie smoothed.

'No, she won't. It's her show, her vehicle, and it's heading for a crash...' Paul huffed into his toast, and dropped marmalade onto his first national review, an altered state for ever.

'I'll get you another one,' his mother said. 'Does Dad see the *Clarion*?'

'He's a *Guardian* man.'

But the *Guardian* review was one of the worst, went on about 'a pointless plot' and 'lyrics to die from'. Paul didn't know how he felt. Normally he was up, down, or – mostly – in between. Today he'd got a great mention and Jenny Tongue would be pleased with it. Between them they could quote it on his CV for jobs and agents, so, OK, he was 'up' over that. But working for weeks on a project does demand loyalty. *She-Pirate* was what he was about right now – and he definitely felt 'down' about it. And then there was the outright fear that he was going to be the target of some very sharp tongue.

Were all jobs like this? he wondered. He looked at his mother and pulled a face. She was out of work as an actor and temporarily unwanted as a teacher. And as she folded the papers, her face said, *Nice problem to have, luv!*

Which was true; so Paul told himself he would just have to get on with it, wouldn't he?

Martin Kent called a short company meeting in the stalls. Before the matinee. It was a bit like Kath Lewis after a Zephon programme has taken a panning. On the back of the poor reviews everyone was pretty subdued – to start with, anyhow.

I've got to say I'm not sure about Kent. He's the dictator, what he says goes, and he must have cast Allen Green, and taken on Lee Conyers and the crewman who's in prison – so is he part of what's going on? Is his company White Ensign funded by drugs money? To be fair, I didn't see Kent talking to Fredericks at the party last night, but what does that mean, one way or the other?

Anyway, Kent gave out a few notes – criticised a late entrance here, and asked what happened there (where one of the fights went wrong and a pirate didn't get killed fast enough) – neither of which would make or break a show.

Then, suddenly, to whoops and cheers, Kent grabbed up the morning papers and tore each and every one into shreds. Passionate. Powerful. Small men getting angry can be cold-sweat sinister. (I cheered loyally with the rest – while Conyers muttered, 'It's uz gunna hae to pick up that lot!') Then Kent stood up on a front seat and really rallied the troops.

SANYO RECORDING TRANSCRIPT:
MARTIN KENT:

*'Critics are vermin. They sip up our dropped sweat
and they sup on our scaled skin. They scuttle into
their corners and work in the dark, striving to blacken
the talent they haven't got themselves. Or they suck up
to those who throw scraps to them, and fawn as
they puff themselves up.*
*They're a sub-race, unable to function at our level
of creativity.*
*In every way we are superior. Like Roarin' James
in our final scene – we can place our feet on the
chests of such people, and say, "We are the
superior breed, and you are where you deserve to
be – toiling on the droppings of our artistry."*
You can't close us – and you won't put us down—'

His voice rose to a hoarse screech.

'We have the ultimate supremacy!'

And as he screeched the words 'ultimate supremacy' the
piano down in the orchestra pit started to play the
introduction to the Supremacy song that ends the show.
No one knew there was anyone down there. But Flame
had gone to the front and now she started to sing her
verse, and straight off the entire company stood up in the
stalls to join in the finale chorus.

Supreme we stand above all other,
No one fit
To call us sister, call us brother –

We are the world's superior crew
The rest inadequate
To touch the hem or kiss the shoe
Of such as us!
Supreme in mind,
Supreme in spirit,
Supreme in strength,
Supreme and designate
To rule these seas.
To rule these seas,
To rule these seas,
Supreme, God-given designates
To rule…these…seas.

It was like a marching song, like a rally – and Martin Kent and Flame had rallied the company big time into making the same, scary threat as the All-Blacks with their *haka*. My skin prickled with goosebumps, and even Lee Conyers was up and at attention to sing the chorus as if it were a national anthem, his head lifted and proud, his fist clenched in the air.

Yeah, it was really scary stuff – and the matinee audience was going to be at the receiving end of this defiant trumpeting!

'THE FILEY FILES'

File 9

Martin Kent and *Supremacy* did more than a regular warm-up could ever do. Everyone was really up for the matinee – where it turned out I was to be Ardal again – and Turner could play him at the evening show. Then it was going to be me for Ardal on Thursday night, Turner on Friday and the Saturday matinee, and me for Saturday night. So, one way and another, I was getting the better of it here in London.

But no one apart from Tootie and Jo said 'nice mention' to me, or 'well done', which I could understand; except that they said it to Sadie Baker, when she wasn't keeping herself to herself.

She's a funny customer. All through the rehearsals she's stayed distant from all of us, done her stuff on stage, said something to people if she couldn't avoid it, but all the time making it clear she isn't ever up for a chat. And now that we're in the theatre, she's got her star dressing room for keeping herself more private than ever. Martin Kent goes in, and Allen Green, and Shelley Tame (wardrobe), who's also more or less her dresser, but otherwise that 'No 1' on the door definitely says 'KEEP OUT' to the rest of us.

Turd-face Turner ignored me like I was creeping leprosy, and when our casting for the rest of the week went up on the company notice-board he stood behind

But I lost my sword. Did I mean to? Can't say – but in his last thrust at me, which I dodge, I was a bit slow and his weapon caught mine, just a nick. And straight off, I dropped it. Did I have to drop it? Who knows – but I did, and I 'accidentally' kicked it out of the action, downstage and into the orchestra pit – where there was no getting it back. And now I knew what I was going to do…

He stared at me. I stared at him. He had to die. I knew he had to die, Turner knew he had to die, or the scene was nonsense. So, how – me with no weapon?

With a great growl I kicked at his cutlass, leapt at him, and got him in a neck lock. He let go of his cutlass to have his neck broken, another quick stare into each others' eyes saying this is what we're going to have to do. But I didn't make it easy, or painless. I let go of the neck lock and grabbed a handful of his hair, started to shake his head from side to side. Which is supposed to be a stage trick. It shouldn't hurt.

But this time it hurt like hell! I knocked Turner's right hand down and grabbed it with my left, and because of where my body was, he couldn't get his left hand up to hold my wrist, for him as victim to be the one in charge of the shaking. So, my grip on his hair was for real, he had no say in it. I shook him left, I shook him right. I hurt him, really hurt him.

He yelled out, he screamed – and coming round behind him after a good, final tug, I changed grip, got both hands round his throat, and he had to let me pretend to throttle him – when I say Ardal's final line in that scene:

<u>Ardal:</u> No one goes against Captain Meg Macroo.

To which I added, in the same quiet voice he'd used on me: *Nor against Paul Filey, Turd-face!*

We got a clap and a cheer for the realism of the degradation: but backstage, Martin Kent went ballistic. He marched up and down and threatened to fire both of us, got us in the Green Room and nearly took the plaster off the wall with his fury. He threatened to go on himself as Ardal for the rest of the London week till he could rehearse a replacement for Rotterdam. Or we could bloody-well get the scene right that night.

Which we did. Roles reversed, Turner as Ardal, me as Frenchie Roche, we played it to perfection. Because neither of us wanted to leave the show under a cloud.

But now Turner understands me. He knows he started it, and he knows I finished it. And whatever else happens between us, we both know it isn't going to happen on stage.

Probably.

A29, HOLLAND

Ben was in the back of the crew bus, heading for the first foreign date on the tour, the Luxor Theatre, Rotterdam. The cast mini-bus was somewhere behind; the crew would be the advance guard, as always. They'd been travelling long enough that Sunday for talk to have drifted off into heads nodding against windows, and paperbacks and magazines coming out.

And Ben was ready for all this. He had researched the business side of the operation: learned how the European legs of the tour had been organised by a specialist Dutch company – Podium Amsterdam – who'd fixed the theatres and done the deals, and taken their fees off the top. They'd also arranged all the accommodation – mostly in cheap motorway hotels outside the cities and towns.

Meanwhile, Ben was like a ghost crab in a sand hole, his eyes out on antennae. He wanted drugs trafficking evidence but he had to keep his story straight – who he was, and what he'd done before. Over a few weeks a lot gets said on long journeys, people soon find out they know others you've worked with. Show-business is a small, inbred, nepotistic world, and no one knows whose friend or offspring they might be talking to. So as well as generally keeping himself alert, Ben's 'back story' had to be rock solid, or he'd have to sleep a lot on journeys like this. There was always the danger of tripping over some discrepancy.

On his nights at home during the rehearsal period, and thanks to Meera and her lunchtime research at the publisher's, he'd learned a string of names from the theatres at which he'd said he'd worked: real names. But what he relied on – mainly through growing designer stubble, not quite a beard – was no one remembering a year back to his Zephon front-of-camera days. That would finish him, especially since he was having to use his own name.

But that Sunday evening in the crew bus on their first long journey together, he started to feel more secure. They'd all talked, they'd all laughed, and he told himself that if he'd been going to be spotted, it would have been in the rehearsal weeks, or at Southend or the Cambridge. Surely he was 'in' by now. Although he also told himself that there was no such word as 'surely' in his business. So, if he ended up sharing a room, he had to be very careful not to talk in his sleep. Because if he was going to have to share with anyone, it would be Lee Conyers, and there was something about that man with the snide wit that made him deeply suspicious.

With some consultation between the driver and Neil Strong and a *Big Road Atlas Europe*, the bus turned off the A29 and onto the A15, and within fifteen minutes, there, with its international sign spluttering on the far side of a roundabout, was the Tourist Europe, an ugly concrete box of windows, sitting at the roadside like a large, washed-up houseboat. And within a quarter of an hour the *She-Pirate* crew had unpacked the roof-rack and done their own personal get-in.

To find, to Ben's relief at the reception desk, that everyone had their own room.

It was that cheap.

'TOURIST EUROPE' HOTEL, ROTTERDAM, HOLLAND

Paul hefted his travel bag onto the bed in his single room. There was a television on a bracket for cracking his head on, and an ensuite bathroom with missing tiles, but it was great – because he didn't have to share. Touring theatre companies live out of one another's pockets; there's no 'down time' for the whole of the travelling and performing day, so turning the key in that door is like reclaiming your name. He stood in the narrow space by the bed and said it.

Paul Filey.

But he hadn't finished drying his hands after the longest pee in hotel history when there was a rap on the door.

Room service? A call girl? Paul's solo experience of hotels was in the thrillers he read. He unlocked the door.

'What you up to, locking your door? Naughty boy!' It was Tootie Sylvester. 'We're going into town to get a meal. Want to come?' She couldn't have had time to do more than sling her bag on her bed, and there was Jo Beckford along the corridor, waiting by the stairs, combing her fingers through her hair.

They were a great pair. Tootie, blonde with her bright, sparky London attitude, who would make a marvellous solo stand-up in any club in Britain; and Jo, a bit older and not so pretty but more the quiet actor.

Nice of them to invite him, Paul thought: including him in their jaunt. But, 'No, ta, I've got some grub,' he said. His mother had packed him up with a school-journey-supply of bits and pieces to see him through the day – and he'd have felt bad, wasting any of it.

'OK, love. See ya.'

Tootie went – and Paul really did dig out the plastic box marked *Supper*. He sat on the bed and thought about his mother, on her own tonight. He looked at his watch; England was an hour behind, so what would she be doing right now? Watching *The Royal* for sure, picking out her mates who were in work while she wasn't – which was what most UK TV drama amounted to in Kitchener Road these days.

He'd take a quick look to see what she'd packed before he rang her; like a good review, he'd give it a mention. But his phone needed charging, so he'd eat his supper first.

But he'd hardly got the cling-film off a tuna baguette when the door was rapped again. Now who? Who else was going into town and wanted his company? One thing was for sure, it wouldn't be Bradley Turner.

It was the Geordie crewman, Lee, his leather jacket creaking, and hovering behind him was Roy Martin, a lighting guy. 'Aah, sorry, mate. Wrong door.' Lee looked genuinely mistaken.

'That's OK.' So he wasn't so popular among the lads, then.

'No, ask him, he's a big boy...' Roy Martin had stepped forward.

Lee checked up and down the corridor. 'Just sayin', we're off inta the city if ye want to come...'

'Cheers. But I've got some grub, thanks.'

Lee snorted, and Roy Martin laughed. 'Weren't food we had in mind!'

Paul looked from one to the other. Now he understood. He'd heard about Holland. In the relaxed Dutch atmosphere, they were off into town after booze or girls or something to sniff, or to smoke. 'No thanks,' he said. 'Cheers, anyhow.' And gently he closed the door on them.

He could definitely use a DO NOT DISTURB sign to put outside, he thought. What next? According to his dad it would be a sexual proposition from Robert Tremaine or Bailey Trust, who trod the boards lightly. He locked the door again and made up his mind not to answer it next time. He'd be asleep. He'd be in the bathroom. He'd be watching TV. He'd be talking to his mum.

But as he lay full-length on the bed, not really hungry yet, he somehow felt as if he'd grown a few centimetres, this side of the Channel. Adventure! The coming weeks were going to be a real adventure into the show-business world; and – it seemed – into his own integrity.

THE LUXOR THEATRE, ROTTERDAM

After the Cambridge opening Ben was used to the get-in routine. When they arrived at the theatre with the truck for a nine am start, the scenery doors were open and the stage bared and ready for the show to arrive. The five or six lines of lighting bars were 'in', or down, hanging about a metre and a half above the stage. When the lights were 'rigged', in from outside came the stage cloth, which had to be laid and smoothed, then the scenery; and finally the furniture and props – which would be that for the first day.

Day Two in the morning had the lights focused into groups for the different areas of the stage, the sound was sorted – important in *She-Pirate* with its digitalised music – and there'd be an afternoon cue-to-cue rehearsal involving crew and cast. And at around seven-thirty in England and nine o'clock in Europe, the show would 'go up'.

When Ben arrived from the hotel the White Ensign truck looked sad outside the splendid, modern theatre. Ben could imagine the line of trucks that would be needed to bring *Phantom of the Opera* or *Les Miserables* into the Luxor. By contrast, *She-Pirate* was going to be like theatre-in-education.

But with the more relaxed day-and-a-half time scale for what they had to do – nothing like the stopwatch turn-around of a Zephon studio – they got *She-Pirate* in under Neil Strong's technical management.

Strong was just that – a tall, bony, shiny-faced man who could haul himself up a rope by his hands, and hold stage weights above his head while a flat was set – on top of every job in theatre. A Lancashire man, he'd worked in most theatres in the north of England, with dour criticisms of all of them. While actors remembered shows and venues with nostalgia, he remembered the rats in the 'flies' – 'Running across like tightrope turns!'

He always had his eye on Ben. Ben was being watched all round, he knew that. From day one when he'd come without his gloves Lee Conyers had been all eyes for the next ricket; and Strong, who'd had Ben wished upon him, was never as intent on a job as he pretended. Which wasn't helped today when Ben picked up the wrong lamp – a 'profile' when 'fre-nell' was shouted across at him – Strong swore.

'Get yeer act together, Maddox!'

'Sorry!' Ben was cross with himself, because errors like that were basic. Profiles and fresnels served different purposes. He'd lost his concentration.

'Didn't sleep too great,' he said lamely.

'Long as it was greet for some lass!' Lee Conyers shouted. 'Ye need an "upper"?' he asked, rigging a light on bar four.

And suddenly Ben's mistake seemed to have been a godsend. What if he said 'yes'? Was the time right to take a more active line with Conyers? But he didn't. Something still made him cautious. Might Conyers be trying him out? The man had stared a second too long when he'd asked the question. And there was time enough, wasn't there? This was a long tour, and he wasn't in a rush. He thought of what Pat would have done under-cover: and he decided to hang back. Patience, patience, patience, that was the essence of detective work; and it was crucial to the secret journalist, too. Ben shook his head.

'Please yorsel, laddie.'

'Cheers, anyhow.'

And Ben got on with the job. Both jobs now, it seemed. Because another little sign had hinted that he really was on to something.

Paul had the day off. But the first thing a touring actor does in a new town is to find the theatre, to time the travelling for the first day's call. So he walked there from the hotel with Tootie and Jo. The Luxor was modern, and large, and took in the best shows the world had to offer. After its week with *She-Pirate* it was staging *The Sound of Music*. And so impressed were they with the look of the place that Tootie did a little dance, and instead of going for a coffee in the city centre the three of them went in to look at the auditorium. They walked in through the scenery door behind a 'flat', hidden from Neil Strong, who would have bawled them out for being where they shouldn't, and scuttled to the back of the stage. Paul took a quick look out at the red plush 'house', humming with the sounds of vacuum cleaners. It was awesome – wide and deep, row upon row upon row! And he told himself it was just as well strong lights were trained onto the stage – or the sight of a house this size would petrify him.

Quickly, he followed the girls up the stairs to the dressing-room corridors. And there, outside the Green Room, was a set of pigeon-holes for company post. And somehow, before he really looked, Paul knew that there was going to be something there for him, in the 'F' slot. He knew it, and it was a weird, prescient feeling. There it was, bearing a European stamp with the Queen's head, the handwriting saying who'd sent it. His father; the letter was addressed to him in Alex Filey's crabby fist, care of the Luxor Theatre, Posthumalaan 1, 3072 AG Rotterdam, Holland.

Leaving Tootie and Jo to roam, Paul found a corner, leant against the wall, and tore open the envelope. What could this be? It couldn't be bad news about his mother, he'd spoken to her the night before and she'd sounded fine. So, what?

338 Balham road
Wandsworth
London SW6 3QQ
020 7674 3210

31st July

Dear Paul
I'm deliberately sending this to you in Rotterdam, so you can read it alone, away from anyone else's 'voice in your ear'. I very much hope it has found you. Also that you're well, and taking care of yourself, and being cautious of the Dutch attitude of 'laissez-faire'!
I saw your performance at the Cambridge Theatre. I didn't make a big fuss with your mother about coming, but I was there on Thursday night.

I won't comment about the play, except to say that I agree with the general newspaper verdict that it doesn't amount to much. (Although I suspect that makes one of my points in this letter.) But within the artistic constraints of a poor piece of writing - not your fault, of course - I thought you were very good. You've come on a long way since the first end-of-term offerings I saw at Broadway. Your voice is good, you look comfortable on stage with a certain presence, you bear yourself professionally, and you've gained an edge in performance - a danger - that I hadn't seen before: we know to expect something unpredictable.

However, and this is getting to the point of my writing to you , none of this is enough for you to fulfil yourself in life for a further three score years. You are a special person, Paul, and you have so much more to offer your fellow man than cavorting on a stage. You're bright, talented, and if I were religious I'd say that God has given you something privileged - that could be so much better used for the benefit of others who are less gifted.

You could make a difference. As a teacher or a doctor or a lawyer you could make real changes to people's lives. There are necessary things to do in society and you're one of those people who can do them. But you're wasted, doing what you do, and I am letting you know that I am reinforced in my decision to no longer fund your journey in the direction of player - observer on the stage of life. You must be a participant.

I feel it only fair to say this at a time when - thrust prematurely into that professional world, and distanced in time from what I said previously - you might feel that the die is cast, that you're destined to be a professional actor. I must reiterate that your place at Broadway will have to finish this year, after which time I shall do my utmost to point you surely - and happily, I swear - in the right direction for your promising life.

Please don't get sucked in further, do watch the real world's news, keep your sense of perspective, and prepare to join that real *world when your tour ends. Go back to your sport as a recreation, shout your head off at Upton Park, not on some stage - release your tensions there: it will help you to study and then to make a proper career for yourself.*

All this is meant in your best interests.

With my paternal love, as always,

Dad x

Paul's stomach took a gallows drop, his eyes filled with tears, and he screwed the letter into his pocket.

'What's up, Paulie? Your mum?' Tootie and Jo had come back too soon.

Paul shook his head.

'Come on!' Tootie put an arm around him and gave him a squeeze: and, God, that did it! He hadn't had such a hug for a long time; he'd had battles with Turner, he'd fought his nerves at every performance, and he'd just been told that what he did was worthless. Now Tootie's warmth and softness broke him up. He stood there and started to blub like a baby. He had to tell Tootie and Jo something about what had made him crack. So why not the truth? He blew his nose, pulled himself together, and said, 'My dad. He's pulling the plug on my training at Broadway.'

'Nice time to tell you!' Jo said.

'*Training*! What training?' Tootie asked. She was the direct, more maverick of the two of them, who played that sort of rebel part. 'You're in a professional show, you'll get your Equity card, automatic – so you're a professional already. You don't need *training* to do this rubbish!'

Which sort of made his father's point, Paul thought.

'Yeah, we could all be dead by the end of this tour!' Jo joined in – not helping either. 'Tons can happen by the middle of September. Cross that bridge when you come to it, love. Meanwhile, enjoy bein' a strolling player!'

And she was soon proved right in saying that. Significant things *could* happen before the middle of September.

For instance, they could happen the following evening, on the first night of *She-Pirate* in Rotterdam...

THE LUXOR THEATRE, ROTTERDAM

She-Pirate

Act Two

Scene Five

Theatre box

As if on his bridge, Roarin' James is standing alone in the box or on the theatre balcony with a telescope to his eye. Behind him hangs a 'Jolly Roger' – the skull and crossbones flag of piracy.

He searches the horizon with the telescope and sees something.

Roarin' James: (Roars) By the lights of Jamaica Jim – what's this? Helmsman! There's that damned Cap'n Macroo's bucket of gold. See it? Moored offshore to windward! Steer a course, man, take me to that upstart buccaneer!

He shuts his telescope with a crack and pushes the 'Jolly Roger' aside to exit the box.

Scene Six

A clearing near the beach at Cape Lopez

Through a gap in the trees we can see Captain Meg Macroo's ship 'The Smiling Rover'.

On the stage, the clearing is set up with barrels, boxes and benches as an impromptu court, with a black slave tied to a tree where a prisoner's dock would be.

Meg Macroo, the female captain, is sitting in judgement. On either side of her are her 'lords' and her son Ardal.

All around the clearing Meg Macroo's pirates are drinking rum and the sounds of more carousing is heard (off stage). The mood is relaxed – and the slave's fate is going to provide some amusement for the bored pirates.

There are sudden ad lib shouts of 'Enemy coming!' 'Attack from seaward!' Etc.

Macroo's pirates forget the slave and prepare for battle, loading carbines,
slashing cutlasses in anticipation.

Meg Macroo, helped by Ardal, swiftly yanks off her skirt to reveal pantaloons and buckled boots.

Meg Macroo: Johnson, Tiber – to the port!

Conceal yourselves! Weston,
Povey – to the starboard!
Ardal stand by me!

With drums and whistles, screeching and shouting,
Roarin'James and his crew come charging into the
clearing.

Roarin' James: Put 'em to the sword!
                       (Roars)

The two pirate bands fight, Meg as brave as any
man.

In the wings, downstage left, Ben Maddox banged at a
drum with one hand and blew a trumpet with the other.
'Pirates' raced past him onto the stage to fight. Across on
the prompt side he could see Allen Green as Roarin' James
standing where a profile spot would pick him up as soon
as he entered. And Ben couldn't believe his eyes. He stared
across at Green, standing ready for his entrance; Ben closed
and opened his eyes and stared again – to make sure that it
was Allen Green over there, waiting to go on as Roarin'
James.

'Good on yer, Greeny!' said Lee Conyers behind him.
'He said 'e'd do it prop'ly over heer!'

But Ben didn't reply. He was busy blowing his trumpet
– and if he hadn't been, his mouth would have dropped

wide open, gaping. This was something totally unexpected...

Onstage, Paul wouldn't see Roarin' James till he came on. He'd made the usual quick moves to help Sadie Baker get into her captain's floor-length coat, and he'd put her tricorn hat upon her head. Now he was standing prepared to fight the invading men – led by Roarin' James.

And as Allen Green came on, stepping boldly into the glare of the profile and picked up by the follow spot, Paul did a double take. He looked, he looked away, and back shot his stare. What the hell was this? *Who* the hell was this?

But when big Allen Green said his first line as Roarin' James there was no doubt in the world that this was the same man who had played the part in London.

Roarin' James: A curse on you, Captain!
                       Your pirate days are over!

Which was the cue for the fight between the pirate crews; with Roarin' James winning tonight as much through cast surprise as by choreography.

Sadie Baker ground out an ad lib to Allen Green, something the audience wouldn't hear but Paul would never forget.

'*Yes! This* is what *She-Pirate's* all about!'

And even a novice like Paul Filey knew that something significant was happening on the Luxor stage that evening.

CAFÉ MARS, ROTTERDAM

Tootie, Jo and Paul avoided the theatre bar after the show. Some of the others might have stayed in the Luxor where they could get drinks cheaper, but the three of them took themselves well out of the *She-Pirate* world. None of them said much, they just headed off along by the river and slid into the first place that sold drinks and pizzas.

The Café Mars wasn't very busy. The actors sat in a booth, gave their orders to the waiter, and looked into each others' faces with the stares they'd been saving for this moment.

'So *what the hell* was Allen Green playing at?'

'Why no warning?'

'That was *so* unprofessional, hitting us with that!'

'Green and Kent, both!'

Because what had happened was that Allen Green as Roarin' James had appeared that night not as the usual grisly, swarthy, captain of a pirate ship. Instead, he'd come on 'blacked-up' as a native Caribbean: same costume, same lines, same moves – but totally different. After curtain up, while the rest of the cast were busy on stage, Allen Green had covered the exposed parts of his skin with Leichner Negro Black and come on talking 'Uncle Tom' – a change of character that made everything different; more different, even, than another actor taking over the part. Other members of the cast wore black make-up like Jo herself in Act One as Nelly Laidlaw, and Tootie as a nubile wife to the King of Dahomey, and Robert Tremaine, who after he played Felix Lawes, became the African king. But this had all been in the play from the start – whereas Roarin' James had never been black, not at the read-through, not in rehearsals, and not at the Cambridge. And suddenly his being black put a completely different slant on the play.

'"Supremacy"!' said Paul. 'Think of those words!'

Tootie was nodding her head off. 'Yeah, they're different, love – they're *so* different when he's black...'

Jo could hardly get her pent-up anger out. 'It's just racist when he's black! When he was beaten before he was a defeated man – now he's black an' being beaten by supreme whites!'

Paul ran the words over in his head.

> *'Supreme we stand above all other,*
> *No one fit*
> *To call us sister, call us brother –*
> *We are the world's superior crew*
> *The rest inadequate*
> *To touch the hem or kiss the shoe*
> *Of such as us!'*

At which moment the café door barged open and in came one of the backstage crew – Ben Maddox. He looked around the tables and saw the three in their booth. He stared at them, they stared at him. Deliberately he stood in the doorway and dropped his mouth open, like *what about that?* – and they dropped theirs, calling him over.

'Are we touring *racism*?'

'Can you read it any other way?' Tootie asked him. '"*Supremacy*"!?'

Ben quickly ordered his pizza, while they all got stuck into the first of several lagers. 'If it's not about race, why didn't he do it in London?' he wanted to know. 'Plus the weapon – did you see the weapon?'

If they had, it hadn't made the impact that the blackness had.

'It wasn't his regular sword – it was a scimitar! Middle-eastern. Islamic. He's covering all bases! And did you see and hear the audience?'

The actors hadn't seen them. By the time they'd got their make-up off the audience had filtered into Rotterdam; but they'd heard them throughout the show. From Flame's first appearance as Meg Macroo they had stamped and shouted, greeted her with roars – this was her great European following that Britain knew little about. And when she'd killed Roarin' James they'd shouted slogans in Dutch that sounded as sinister as storm troops.

'Well, I saw them,' Ben went on. 'There were a hell of a lot of the sort you see at right-wing meetings...'

'The European Ku Klux Klan!' Tootie slammed down her glass. 'Does this mean we're part of something else, then?' she demanded. 'You an' me. Are we peddling what I'm not prepared to peddle?'

'I'm out of this show tomorrow!' Jo said. 'I'm not singing *Supremacy* if it's saying whites are better than every other race on God's earth. We're not, no race is superior to any other. Individuals, yes, tribal stereotypes, no! No way am I going on to make some spotty fascist feel good!'

Paul looked from one to the other; and his stomach did its lurch again. This show had been his break. Despite his dad, this had been his professional chance. But like the girls there was no way he was going to stay in *She-Pirate* to promote racism; that was against every decent instinct he'd ever had. You didn't grow up in East London and not know the brilliance of a wide mix of people. There were blacks, Jews, Arabs and Asians whose brains and wit were second to none.

'Shouldn't we talk to Kent, have it out with him?' Ben asked.

Tootie wasn't very keen on that. 'That little martinet! Criticise his play or his direction? He doesn't need a talk, he needs a kick in the front-of-house!'

Ben looked around the café as if in search of a menu, or the condiments, or a waiter. Buying time? Because he looked at the three of them, and suddenly seemed to come to a big decision. 'Right,' he said. 'Can you lot keep your mouths shut on a secret...?'

The three stared back.

At which moment the pizzas came. Food – or a waiter asking if you're enjoying your meal – always comes when you're far more interested in what someone at the table is saying than the food upon it. But the service and the re-ordering of drinks seemed to give Ben time for further thought: and as everyone started cutting into their bases, he told them.

'I'm not theatre, I'm television. I'm on a story – about peddling, as it goes. But what I thought was being peddled was drugs. Now I'm not so sure. Now I'm thinking it could be something else, just as insidious. And I want to know more. If *She-Pirate's* the sort of gutter stuff we now think *Supremacy's* all about, I want to nail it, blast it, expose it for what it is.'

'So...?' Tootie wanted to know.

'So we stick with it. Don't let on to Kent that we think anything's wrong – and if others talk to any of us about Roarin' James being black all of a sudden, we play it down. Say it's probably a change because he got bad reviews in London. If anyone wants to leave, we tell them we're going on, we've heard it's going to get sorted. Meanwhile keep an eye on those who might be part of what's happening...'

The thrill of conspiracy ran through Paul. 'What can you do, then?' he asked. 'How can you nail it?'

Ben looked at him intently. 'Paul, mate, I don't know where I'll get the proof. But nail it I will: or Zephon will. It'll be blasted out of the water on television – exposed for what it is. So we can eventually do much more good by hanging in there than by walking out of the door...'

There was some nodding as they started eating. Until Paul, the hungriest, finished first and wiped his mouth. 'What's your name?' he asked Ben.

'Ben Maddox. Like it says on the tin.'

'You said Zephon TV?'

'Zephon, yes.'

'Funny,' Paul said, 'I thought I knew your face. Didn't you do a job with the daughter of a politician...?'

Ben laughed. 'Sort of – if you put it like that.' Pride fading to prudence. 'But let's hope you're the only one who remembers me. Because there's more to this than we've seen so far. A lot more!' He looked at each of the eating or drinking heads. 'So we're hanging in there?'

And the four of them agreed to hang in there, and raised a glass to secrecy and conspiracy – like a handshake on a solemn promise.

'A TRAGIC ERROR OF YOUTH'

The royal chaplain the Very Reverend Charles Quentin spoke of the grief resulting from 'a tragic error of youth' at the funeral of Her Royal Highness Princess Leanna yesterday.

The teenage princess was laid to rest in a simple private ceremony in St George's Chapel, Windsor. Members of the royal family, the Prime Minister, close friends, and a small group of class mates from Heathfield School attended the service.

Speaking later at his monthly Downing Street press conference, the Prime Minister, Ian Prentice, said he respected the royal family's wish to grieve in private – while wishing to very publicly condemn those who profit from the sale of dangerous drugs to young people. 'Far from enhancing pleasure, these "recreational drugs" can bring death and family despair.'

He said that the government would be leading a campaign to rout out the abject criminals who feed off impressionable youth.

Read the papers?
Seen the news?
Respect for royal
grief is over now.
Media starts anti-
dealers campaign!
We want in on it –
so what news?
Any leads? You
haven't filed – heard
nothing from you.
Stay a team player
Maddox – or else!
Kath

Ben sat on his bed and threw his phone on top of the *European Guardian*. Yes, he'd file something for Kath Lewis – but something for *her,* not for transmission; a few words asking for patience. He mustn't let on to anyone at Zephon that the trafficking he'd half-suspected in the first place might not be in drugs but in racism. The mood Kath was in these days meant that she'd pull him back to London, pronto, if she thought he was on his own agenda. And besides, right now Ben had only a vague suspicion on which to base anything. Perhaps he and the three actors had been over-reacting last night; he'd felt sure there was some bigger agenda than making racist theatregoers feel good; but he'd need more evidence of some major racist mission before he started accusing White Ensign of being in contravention of British and European Union race laws.

Meanwhile, there was one thing he could do – as well as constantly keeping his eyes and ears open and his mouth shut. He could ask Pat to dig a bit deeper into Nick Cannon's court conviction and imprisonment; specifically, try to find out the reason for the original police charge. Cannon had co-written *She-Pirate*, his name was on the programme and his biography was printed at the back. So he was very much part of what was going on, whether in or out of jail.

Now Ben rooted around for a programme, to read what the co-writers Martin Kent's and Nick Cannon's biographies said. As he remembered them, they'd been pretty 'nothing' notes – but in the light of last night and Lee Conyers' 'Yes!' at what Green was doing, might there be a clue to link these two men with racism?

MARTIN KENT – *DIRECTOR & CO-WRITER*
Martin is a co-founder of White Ensign Productions, following his career as both actor and director. His aim in writing *She-Pirate* and in setting up a company to produce it, is 'to explore a period in history when people were not ashamed to be proud of what they were...'

NICK CANNON – *CO-WRITER*
Nick has written for specialist publishers of books and magazines, underlining his interest in the history of cultures and the growth of beliefs. He is active in local politics in Bristol, which is his base for travelling widely in the UK.

So – what did those biogs tell him? Anything more than they'd told him before? And the answer was, yes! Put together, they revealed that these two had deliberately chosen to reveal nothing of themselves! Martin Kent listed none of the plays he'd acted in or been proud to direct; and Nick Cannon neglected to mention a single book title of his that he might like people to buy. So, yes, Ben decided, in a negative way these biogs provided a very telling clue.

But a clue doesn't amount to evidence, and Ben would have to watch and wait for that before the job was done – perhaps even take action himself to reveal it.

If he was right.

File 10

The trouble with being a touring actor is that hotel staff always need to clean. Staying in your room after about ten o'clock just isn't on, they want you out. Ron and Robert – who share the dressing room – say it's good for geography – actors learn a lot about the towns they play because they're out on the streets during the day.

After that first night I walked around Rotterdam like a spy. I was undercover now, working with TV's Ben Maddox. It's funny how the place where you see someone makes a difference to who you think they are. OK, his face was a bit familiar to me – but no way in the world would I have connected stage crew with the kidnap rescue of the Home Secretary's daughter till Ben told us who he was.

I'd taken a bit of special interest in that story because Mum and I went to the opening production in the new drama block at Kensington Girls' High where Kenny Richards is head of drama. Kenny worked with Mum at Watford on a couple of shows before he went into teaching, so she got an invitation. But Princess Anne was going to be there so I went with Mum on the second night – neither of us are into doffing and curtseying – and afterwards it turned out that that's where the girl had been lifted. But not in a million years would I have seen Ben Maddox standing in the wings on the O.P. side of *She-Pirate* and tied him in with TV news. And now I've been trusted with his big secret – and it'll be interesting to see how he treats me next time we meet up.

Turner's doing Ardal tonight – and I'm Frenchie Roche. I'm doing Ardal Friday night, Turner on Saturday matinee, and me on Saturday night. If I were 'watching points', as Mum would say, I'd reckon I'm getting the better of the shows. But Martin Kent only puts up the shows a week at a time: Apeldoorn next week could be different. Then it's a night at home before we go up to Bolton, then back to Germany the week after.

On the theatre level I'd be really enjoying this if two crunch things weren't running through my life. Dad – and his threats (and Mum definitely not able to take over his Broadway payments); and of course this racism thing the show could be all about. But now I'm looking at people in new ways. Like, who's in on it, who isn't – because not everyone is: me, Tootie, Jo and Ben Maddox for a start. At breakfast in the hotel, Allen Green came in while I was still eating. He gave me a bit of a nod, nothing special; but, being in it himself, he'll know I'm not in the plot – if there is one! But when Lee Conyers came creaking in, he got invited over to sit and eat with Green.

I deliberately didn't wait for Tootie or Jo to come down: I don't want to seem part of a trio, a clique. Not because it wouldn't be good – they're great to be with – but because it wouldn't *look* good. From now on I've got to try to be friends with everyone – even Turd-face. Or is that stretching a good cause too far?

'TOURIST EUROPE' HOTEL, ROTTERDAM,
HOLLAND

From: Pat Maddox [pmaddox@tiscali.com]
Sent: 11 August 19:07
To: benmaddox@talktalk.net
Subject: request

Long time, no hear. Hope you're well.
Love to Meera. Here's the info you want –
but you didn't get it from me!

Pat

Attachments:

Bristol West Magistrates Court

Summary of proceedings on Metropolitan Police request (Scotland Yard)

Regina versus Nicholas Daniel Cannon

Cannon (29), of 27 Draybury Crescent, Bristol BS6 7QQ, was brought to court accused of grievous bodily harm and wounding in an incident outside Chipping Sodbury Town Hall on 13th September last.

He was found guilty of assaulting Marcus James Kingston (38), a local councillor, and sent for trial at

Bristol County Court where he was again found guilty and given a three year custodial sentence.

The GBH occurred at Chipping Sodbury at 21:45, shortly before the count for the local council by-election. Cannon, a registered member of the Bristol White Alliance, attacked Kingston for allegedly ripping a Union Jack from his (Cannon's) hands. Witnesses neither connected with the election, nor recorded members of any local political party, gave evidence in support of Kingston who, they affirmed, was attacked first by Cannon with a broken bottle, coming at him with strong verbal abuse.

The accused had been drinking, and denied a racist motive in 'responding to the aggression of this guy: black or white, I never knew he was a councillor, he could have been any bxxxxd out for trouble'.

A subsidiary charge of racial hatred under the Race Relations Act was not proven.

Ben folded the e-mail and hid it deep in his hold-all. It had told him what he wanted to know, which was not so much that Cannon's assault was racially motivated – although he bet it was, not everything unproven is untrue – but that Cannon was a member of the White Alliance, a right wing political party that fed on racial tension in towns with mixed ethnic populations.

White Alliance/White Ensign! It didn't need a genius to

see how Kent's and Cannon's thinking went. England was for the English, the white English whose jobs were being taken by inferior foreigners, whose wives and sweethearts were being violated, and whose taxes were being raised by immigrant benefit claimants and health service users. Never mind that statistics showed the overall tax gain from such people working here, nor the cultural advantages and the skills and sweat they contributed. That White Alliance sort of nationalism was simple, bigoted stuff, nothing intelligent or truthful. It was just saddening that White Ensign – the name of the proud flag of the Royal Navy – should become tainted the way the flag of St George always looked tawdry in the wrong hands.

Ben called Tootie Sylvester on her mobile. He liked Tootie – she was like Bloom Ramsaran with lots of 'go' and sparkle, and a strong sense of justice and right. 'Tootie – how're you doing? It's Ben.'

'No different, Mr Mole! Up for it! Just tell me what you want me to do: anything short of selling my body – my agent's on fifteen per cent!'

Ben laughed while he thought quickly. He hadn't expected to be leading a team of spooks! This was getting to be like Lansana when he'd led that crack squad to the rescue of Jonny Aaranovitch.

'Information, I'm after. I just wondered if you've had any reactions from the others: like, who might be in and who might be out of Martin Kent's scam.'

'Well—'

'Hang on, where are you right now? Can you speak?'

'I'm in my room painting my nails. And this is a secure line, Mr Bond...'

'Go on, then – what reactions?'

Tootie cleared her throat. 'Well, the girls in the cast I've spoken to seem definitely outside the bucket to me. I don't know about the Baker woman, our shining star – she's one on her own – but look at her following over here! There's only two others, apart from Jo. Fay Carter was dead surprised at what Green did – seemed to see it our way – but Judy Gold didn't sound as if she cared one way or the other; not part of anything, or I'm Madonna.'

'What about the men?' Ben reckoned that was more where the foot soldiers would be. 'Anyone been talking about last night's show?'

'Haven't seen anyone to talk to; shan't know till warm-up time. I saw Fay on our landing and Judy at breakfast, no men about. It'll be in the theatre when we need the bugs and key-hole cameras…'

Ben pulled a face, and began regretting his need to share his secret. But he laughed. 'Anyhow, thanks for that, I'll see you later.'

'Awaiting instructions, 007!'

And again Ben wondered how wise he'd been to come out into the open. Undercover reporters do that at their own peril.

LUXOR THEATRE, ROTTERDAM

The company did the Thursday warm-up on the stage –
where, for whatever reason, nothing was said about Allen
Green's appearance the night before. In a more relaxed
company there might have been wisecracks about a 'Dutch
sun-tan', but Ronnie Hammond, the Company Stage
Manager, took the session as usual – and no patch of his
time was ever sewn with idle banter.

Ben watched from the side. Hammond really knew this
business inside out, didn't seem like an upstart politico
who was dipping his toe into showbiz waters. He was
young and overweight but there was a strict command
about him that marked him as special; and he was so
focused on theatre that it seemed real-life issues like racism
could have no place in his world. But, you never knew! As
far as Ben was concerned, everyone was in on some secret
White Ensign business until they proved themselves not to
be.

He watched Paul warming up with Bradley Turner. It
was common theatre practice for everyone doing fights to
run them in warm-ups, and from the cocky body language
of the boy who shared a dressing room with Allen Green,
Ben had to put him in on the plot until proven wrong.

Otherwise, it was hard to tell which side anyone was on.
But based on his delight the night before at the sight of the
black Roarin' James, one person whose colours could be
clearly seen was the guy whom Ben had suspected weeks
back of drug-selling: his snaky friend Lee Conyers…

BEN MADDOX MEMO – DICTATED NOTES –
THURS. 11/8 23:00

Just played back some of my notes. Can't believe I was lucky enough to get Martin Kent's little speech after the Cambridge first night. Hitting back at theatre critics, he ended it:

'In every way we are superior. Like Roarin' James in our final scene – we can place our feet on the chests of such people, and say, "We are the superior breed, and you are where you deserve to be – toiling on the droppings of our artistry".'

Well, forget the artistry bit – look at the final scene the way it's being played in Rotterdam, with the vanquished Roarin' James now a black pirate. The White Ensign message is simple. Black is inferior to the likes of the white Meg Macroo.

Tonight Allen Green played Roarin' James the same black way again, and once he'd been beaten at the end, begging for his life, he upped the servile accent to sound like a white man's 'boy' in an old Hollywood film – and what a reaction that got from the audience – and from Lee Conyers.

We're both on the prompt side of the stage at the end of the show, ready to push on a rostrum in the final black-out. The spotlight suddenly picked up Allen Green in the box, and as he stood for his 'steer for the island'

speech, Lee Conyers grunts, 'Can't wait!' loud enough to be heard in the stalls. He thumps me on the back. 'They've go' it comin'!'

Quickly, in the dark of the wings I turn to him and stare him in the face. 'Bloody great!' I say, give a victory punch in the air – and he hugs me like a blood brother.

'Aah, this is gonna do the business!'

I held off asking, *What business?* because from the comradely way he's treating me I'm supposed to know. So I turn my back and concentrate on shifting the rostrum a millimetre this way and a millimetre that – fiddling till we're into the island scene where I've got a banging and a trumpeting to do for the Roarin' James raid.

With plenty to think about.

OK, now I'm cast-iron sure that Lee Conyers is one of them. But how many others are there? And what is this *business* that they're hoping to do? Racism is an attitude, not a business.

Whatever it is, some of us are resolved to send its stink down the nearest sewer...!

APELDOORN ORPHEUS THEATRE, HOLLAND

Moving on to Apeldoorn, Paul kept his profile low. The first thing he looked for on the Tuesday morning was the Ardal/Frenchie Roche performance rota. Bradley Turner had been strangely quiet during the Luxor run, their scenes together had all gone well both ways round, sticking to script and choreography.

Now that morning the company notice-board told Paul that Martin Kent was saying something without coming out and saying it. 'Filey' was listed as playing Ardal on the Tuesday night, the Wednesday night, the Friday night and the Saturday night. Turner was playing Ardal on the Wednesday matinee, the Thursday night, and the Saturday matinee. Which meant that Paul Filey was now the principal Ardal and Bradley Turner was the alternate. But for some reason Turner didn't seem to mind. Paul might have expected a sly trick onstage, or a trip in a corridor, something to say *Watch your back, son!* – but nothing like that happened at the end of the Luxor week, nor that Tuesday evening on Apeldoorn's first night. Surprise, surprise! Perhaps Turner was just overawed by the size of the theatres and good houses.

The Orpheus main house was a twelve-hundred-seater in a state-of-the-art building less than ten years old. The orchestra pit alone looked as if it might have lodged the Royal Philharmonic, en-suite! And even on a Tuesday night, the house was well over half-full – which for an unknown company touring a new musical couldn't be bad.

So was it Flame who brought the business? Or was it the same audience-type as in Rotterdam? Was it rock, or racism? She had been very big once upon a time – huge over here by the looks of things – and the sound was as big as her reputation. The company worked off digital sound that played through huge quadraphonic speakers out front. And was that something! When Flame as Meg Macroo went from the quieter intros to the chorus of her songs, the beat thumped louder and the accompaniment blared and boomed, starting Paul's heart racing whether he was onstage or off. And onstage as Ardal, duetting one of the songs, his spine went, too: the rock backing and Flame's seared-steak voice hit him like rubber bullets to the heart.

Which had to be what it was all about! Paul reckoned. Both! Rock and racism! When the words of the songs were looked at, the message read clearer every time: and when the black Roarin' James was destroyed, the words of *Supremacy!* saluted out like a fascist anthem. And the terrible thing was, as a performer, that song excited Paul – every performance he spiralled up in the elation of singing to a thousand people. Which has got a name. Power – theatrical power – and it lifts as high as any Ecstacy. And, likewise, it kills; except that in *She-Pirate's* case, *Supremacy* would kill the human soul, the way all fanaticism destroys humanity.

After a show like that, coming down always took a while; and even with the costume and the make-up off, the person who was Paul Filey within the actor still took a while to emerge. It's a 'stage door' that every actor goes through, back to the dirty streets of real life…

REUTERS NEWS AGENCY

Tuesday 16ᵗʰ August   23:03

Angry scenes occurred in Churchillplein, in Apeldoorn, Holland
tonight. At the end of a performance at the Orpheus Theatre,
fighting broke out between different sections of audience
members emerging from the building. It was quickly quelled by
local police.

Professor Bram Korthals said, 'With my wife I saw a disturbing
play which upset us both badly. At the end, as we emerged, a
group of right-wing youth shouted victory slogans, calling,
"Immigrants out!" My wife remonstrated with one of them and
she was punched in the face.' Asked the nature of the play Dr
Korthals replied, 'It was a stupid pirate story but the content
was of white superiority. It was banal if it was not dangerous. I
came because I remember the singer Flame from TV shows. Her
name should be "Enflame" I think.'

The theatre management and the production company White
Ensign, however, claimed that the confrontation outside the
theatre was between genuine fans of Flame and members of
the European Musicians' Union who were staging a protest.
Show director Martin Kent said, 'The EMU disapproves of our
use of recorded sound instead of a live band or pit orchestra.
But we couldn't afford to mount the show with live music – and
we have paid agreed fees to the British Musicians' Union. Our
actions have been whiter than white.'

No charges were brought by police.

MCDONALD'S, APELDOORN, HOLLAND

After the show Ben thought he'd escaped without being spotted. As soon as they'd reset the stage for the next day he slipped Lee Conyers by taking the backstage lift instead of climbing the stairs to the crew room. Few theatricals use backstage lifts: missing a performance in a stuck lift does no good to the heart. Ben was down again and away before Conyers had unhooked his leather jacket and run upstairs.

But within minutes of coming from the McDonald's counter with his Big Mac, Paul, Tootie and Jo walked in. Same-thinking minds acted alike! There was no company socialising for any of them till they knew which side people were on. They saw him and advanced like prefects to a deputy head.

'Ben, look at this!' Paul said, pushing a piece of paper at him. And at the first glance, Ben started coughing on ketchup. Because although he couldn't read Dutch, there was enough on the flyer to underline that *She-Pirate* was about more than a come-back for Flame. And his first thought was, what would Bunny Fortune have made of this? Because the heading – printed in a gothic font – said something like **FICTION INTO ACTION**! And buried in the text was the invitation to **Come to Paris.**

So what was all this about? Was it connected with the show? And where had Paul Filey found it?

'In the street,' Paul told him. 'Blew round the corner from where the barney went on...'

'What barney?' Ben hadn't known about the punch-up. That smallish fire had been dowsed before the crew had finished re-setting the stage. Now Paul filled him in.

'By the time we got out it was being sorted; a few police and people making statements. Old 'uns and some youth...'

'OK,' Ben said finally. 'Again, keep schtum! Eyes and ears! Mouths zipped. We *mustn't* show out. We'll only win on this if we don't react, keep our heads down for now.' He pocketed the paper before telling them, 'I'm going to get in touch with Sadie Baker's agent – find out what he does and doesn't know about all this. And then we wait...'

The others looked a bit disappointed; but he rallied them: 'This is always the hardest part of the game,' as if he were doing this all the time. 'Waiting. Being a mole. But it pays off in the end, believe me...'

And the looks on their faces said they did sort of believe him. Except, he wasn't even sure that he believed himself. Like playing hide-and-seek, there comes a time when you want to run out and say, 'I'm here! I'm here!' But *where* was he? – that was the question.

'FOUR CORNERS' HOTEL, APELDOORN

When he woke next morning Ben hung a scuffed and bent
DO NOT DISTURB notice outside his bedroom, locking
the door before keying B on his mobile phone Contacts
scroll. B for Bunny Fortune. Serendipity! He'd been going
to sound out Bunny, now Bunny had left a voicemail
message to be called – 'Urgent, Ben, if you would...' Ben
took a couple of deep breaths, set his phone to Record, and
pressed the dial key.

Bunny Fortune:
Rusel Hudson Management – Bunny's phone.

Ben Maddox:
Is that you, Bunny?

Bunny Fortune:
It is to you, Ben! Long time no hear! And long time no
splendiferous European exposure of my client! – so far as
I've seen.

Ben Maddox:
Bunny, is that what's urgent – getting up after a late finish
to a rollocking from you?

Bunny Fortune:-
Not at all! I'm sure you've got great plans for my client...

Ben Maddox:
I have, actually, Bunny. Because I'm off today to try to get
RTL or Nederland Three to do some filming for us – from
She-Pirate. Flame's got a very strong final scene I'd like to
push around the networks...

Bunny Fortune:
That'd be very good! But listen, there's a *News in Brief* item in the *Times* today – well hidden away, praise the Lord, some sort of a scuffle outside the theatre last night? Where was it, Apeldoorn?

Ben Maddox:
Oh, that didn't amount to much. A few local musicians bending their bows over the use of digital music. There was nothing about it on TV here. It was all finished before I'd cleared the building.

Bunny Fortune:
Well, that's a mercy. Can you play it down if anything *does* come of it?

Ben Maddox:
And we'll be in touch very soon over the TV shoot. It'll all seem to come from Zephon in London so I don't blow my cover. Probably Bloom Ramsaran; Flame won't know I've done it. But can Bloom liaise with you for filming permissions?

Bunny Fortune:
Certainly. Excellent! Now we're getting somewhere!

Ben Maddox:
OK, she'll be in touch. Cheers, then, Bunny.

Bunny Fortune:
Cheers, m'dear.

Ben clicked off the phone. So, word had got out about the fracas outside the theatre – and Bunny Fortune was worried about it. Then did that mean he knew what this tour was about, that he was in on some plot? It was hard to tell about so many things – what was what, who was who, and whether when it all shook down there really was anything going on beyond Allen Green sticking his racist head out of his closet.

Although there was one possible way of telling smoke from fire. Ben pulled out the flyer that Paul Filey had picked up from the pavement the night before; and from his bedside cupboard he pulled his laptop.

Quickly, through the hotel broadband router, he found a Dutch/English translation website – and sitting on his bed he typed in a few sentences from the FICTION INTO ACTION manifesto. And within moments he had his pidgin English version.

F X C M
Translation Service

You have looked our play.
We hope you enjoyed and know our message.

Our message is carrying all over Europe – mainly Paris September 24 at the Phoenix Theatre. This is a big theatre and we want all support on a momentous day.

Book tickets please at Phoenix Theatre direct or with your branch. Come to make a change in Europe!

Ben checked the tour schedule – and sure enough *She-Pirate* was due to play Le Phénix de Paris on the 24th of September. It was the last date in the tour, a single show at twelve noon – which seemed a strange time to be putting on a performance. But the venue's website showed just how big the Phénix was.

Grande jauge :	parterre debout 6 293 p
Grande jauge :	parterre assis 5 783 p
Petite jauge :	parterre debout 3 959 p
Petite jauge :	parterre assis 3 740 p
Mini jauge :	parterre debout 2 466 p
Mini jauge :	parterre assis 2 024 p

He quickly guessed what *jauge* was – from driving in France he knew it had to be something like 'capacity'. *Parterre* meant 'stalls', *debout* meant 'standing' while *assis* meant 'sitting': so the *grande* auditorium at its maximum for a seated audience would be nearly six thousand people: which put *She-Pirate's* twelve hundred seater venues into the shade. And the way the flyer sold it, the Paris thing was very important. So, what was the message being spread all over Europe? Could it possibly be anything like the message Roarin' James and *Supremacy!* was sending out every night?

Well, that was what he was now undercover to find out! But what he knew for sure was that the Zephon building would be a no-go area when he was in England next week for the Bolton shows.

KITCHENER ROAD, LONDON E7

It was a memorable homecoming for Paul. His mum had opened the door before he'd swung his sports bag through the front gate. He'd been away for a fortnight – less time than he spent away in the summer with his dad – but he was welcomed back like a soldier from the front. He looked up to check that there wasn't a banner strung across the street.

'Paul!' And his mum cried.

'Hold on! I'm a big boy! It's not a miracle I'm home…' But he was delighted to be there. The smell of his mum's coffee, a ready-to-cook loaf in the oven wafting from the kitchen on a Tchaikovsky waltz from Classic FM – the perfect coming-through-the-door. 'You all right?'

'I'm great! How are you?' Sylvie looked at him as if he might be carrying duelling scars, or love bites. 'You've lost a bit of weight in the face…'

'Have I?' Paul checked in the hall mirror – his sports bag still heavy in his hand.

'Give me that – come on, we'll sort your washing later… What time's your call tomorrow?'

'Half past eight. Company bus, outside Mile End tube. Four or five hours to Bolton.'

'It's marvellous you could pop in for a night. So, how's it going?' She led through into the kitchen. 'Cup of coffee? Then I've got a chicken to roast…'

'Great! Real food!'

But what did he tell her about the things going on? He'd thought it through, for nights he'd thought it through, when sleep was hard after the 'high' of a performance. But when it came to saying the words, would they be what he'd rehearsed?

They were. 'It's going OK. I'm getting the main Ardal shows, the other bloke's more a traditional alternate now. So far! Yeah, it's OK. Voice is holding out, I can still hit that top "F".' *But had she read anything about an audience punch-up in Apeldoorn?*

'Terrific!' she said. *She hadn't.* But there was something else in his mother's eyes on top of being pleased to see him; and it was poured out with the coffee.

'I've got a couple of days' work!'

'Brill! What is it?'

'Only a *Crimewatch*. But it's work, it's telly, it's the first for a while...'

'Sure. So what are you? A murder victim? A beautiful woman mugged in the park?'

Sylvie smiled. 'I'm a look-alike for a photo-fit drugs mule bringing cocaine into Stansted...'

'Starring role!'

'Well, it might get me onto *The Bill* or *Casualty*. I'm sending transmission details out to casting agents.' She turned to the sink to wash out some grouts. 'Who, sad to say, haven't bitten on your *She-Pirate* hook...'

'Don't worry!'

'But I've sent out to the Manchester brigade. Never know, they might come to see you in Bolton...'

'Cheers.'

Paul went up to his bedroom and put on his favourite tracksuit. The room hadn't changed, but it looked miles bigger than the hotel rooms he'd been staying in. And the great thing about it – it was his own. It had his own stuff in every drawer, it didn't smell of stale tobacco, and it had the West Ham football team on the wall: black and white: the 'kick-racism-out-of-football' official photograph. And he suddenly felt so at home again, that what was happening on the tour seemed some sort of other life. This was what he had to cling to; *his* existence – and a pirates' curse on the low-life who dealt in racial hate and envy. He was a Stratford East boy. He'd grown up, gone to school, lived his life around here with kids of every race. It was East London's pride through the years to be home to people fleeing from persecution, or wanting a chance of a better life; and those people, in their turn, had made London better. In their day, Paul's heroes, the great Joan Littlewood and her partner Gerry Raffles had put on people's theatre up the road at the Theatre Royal. To be an actor who walked those boards would be Paul's greatest ambition. His lips curled with disdain at Allen Green's crude stereotype of a West Indian. He'd like to see him try it on at Stratford East!

Well, perhaps he might yet get the chance to help show up that bigoted apology for a human being...

FORBANS RESTAURANT, VICTORIA, LONDON SW1

Meera wasn't best pleased, but before Ben went home to Leyton High Street he met Bloom Ramsaran in a small bar at the back of a crowded restaurant near Victoria Station. E-mails and texts were all very well, but a few sentences face-to-face could get a lot done without misunderstandings.

'Ben Maddox! Firm and fit!'

'Bloom Ramsaran – as gorgeous as ever!'

She was sitting up at the small bar, a white wine already poured. Unusually, Ben was late, but Channel ferries were always at the mercy of summer storms. He asked for a beer, and challenging the barman's pretensions added, 'Any *bitter.*' He'd drunk enough of the blond stuff in Holland to last him a lifetime.

'You want something, don't you, Maddox?' Bloom stated. 'Or are you finally proposing marriage to me?'

'I want something,' Ben confirmed, as prudent as a peacekeeper in a minefield. And he asked her if, in her showbiz role, she could fix up ten minutes' Dutch or German filming of *She-Pirate.*

'Shouldn't be too difficult,' Bloom said. 'But why Holland or Germany, why not Bolton, that's why you're back in the UK, isn't it? Zephon could do it ourselves…'

'Excellent!' But was it? Ben wondered. He wanted shots of Allen Green blacked-up as Roarin' James – but would he do it in England? He hadn't in London. 'Bunny Fortune will help do the business side of things.' He'd take a chance, Ben decided: and shots of Roarin' James played either way would be good to have up his sleeve. He'd get out his own camcorder in Germany, if necessary… 'You've got Bunny's number?'

295

'Etched, Maddox, etched!' Bloom fixed him a warning stare. 'But you'd better send something down the line to Kath Lewis or she'll pull you back home. Those eyes of yours are not so blue in the office right now!'

Ben hesitated for a moment. He hadn't been thinking drugs recently. 'I've sent her a text, how I'm deeply embedded in the company, being trusted more and more, but mustn't show out too soon or we'll blow a big story…'

'You *are* talking about drugs?'

'What else?' Ben had already decided not to trust even Bloom with what he really thought was going on. He changed tack. 'How did you know about Bolton next week?' he asked her.

'I've got the tour schedule. I am showbiz, Sunshine. And I like to picture you wherever you are, whatever you're doing…'

'Doesn't sound healthy! Note to self – remember to keep the blinds drawn.'

'Anyway,' Bloom went on, 'shall we meet in Paris in September? You and me. Seeing as we're there at the same time. I'll take you up the Eiffel Tower…'

'Sure,' Ben smiled. 'We've got a noon show at the Phoenix…' That Apeldoorn invitation flyer practically crinkled in his pocket.

'So, are you going to be digging around the place where the girls' school stayed?' asked Ben.

'Yeah, someone's supplying there…' said Bloom.

'Good for you.' So why did he feel jealous that Bloom was doing the sort of thing he did – he'd been doing the sort of thing she did!

'*And* I'm doing a piece from the anti-racist rally! Kath wants her money's-worth!' Now Bloom lowered her eyes. 'And you can't take me up the Eiffel Tower, Ben Maddox

– I'm also meeting up with a dishy black Canal Media camera operator. And we're getting it together at the biggest rally the Place de la Concorde has ever seen!'

'Yeah, you mentioned.' Ben looked her in the eye – as a sudden shaft of crystal clarity hit him. 'Oh, my God!' he said.

'"Oh, my God"?' Bloom queried.

'The time!' Ben pulled a guilty face, and rapped his nails on his watch. 'I'm on European time! I'm an hour later for Meera than I'd thought! She'll go bananas...!'

With some panic goodbyes and kisses on the cheek, Ben reminded Bloom to get the Bolton shoot organised – and raced out through a busy room of diners.

And not until he was on the Underground did he realise what nonsense he'd talked to get himself out of there. Europe was an hour ahead of Britain, he'd gained an hour, not lost one. He sincerely hoped that he hadn't just lost a good friend, instead.

But now things were falling into place. It couldn't just be coincidence that White Ensign wanted to play to a huge venue in Paris on the day of a big anti-racist rally.

This had to be what White Ensign had been working towards all along...

File 11

Nearly all the M's – M1, M6, M62, M60 – a long motorway slog in the company minibus; with Charlie the driver chirpy all the way because he was driving on 'the bleedin' proper side of the road' again.

Flame sat up front with Kent. I sat well to the back, on account of Mum's survival advice for planes, coaches and trains – she reckons most survivors are seated near the back. Which I don't get, because the *front* of something is going to smash into the *back* of something else, isn't it? Except a plane, I suppose...

It's weird, this being thrown together with other people for weeks at a time, because you hear all about their lives and their hang-ups: someone with a dying father, someone with a two-timing girlfriend, everyone with rotten agents, and a daughter up the duff. And by Christmas we'll probably walk past one another in the street and just say a quick 'Hi!' – strangers again. Leading men fall in love with chorus girls, leading ladies sleep with the director; then at the end of the run everyone goes back to life as before. Or so Tootie says. I'm too young to know! But it's weird.

What I *do* know at the end of the week, though, is that Bolton has turned out the same as Holland. First off, it's been me as Ardal on Tuesday, Wednesday, Friday and Saturday nights. Turner's Ardal on Wednesday and

Saturday matinees and Thursday night. Which seems to be the pattern – and am I not pissed-off with that! But two other crucial Bolton bits of the jigsaw are: Allen Green is a *black* Roarin' James again – and the audience at the Imperial is much the same sort of white shirt, black suit, shaved head brigade as we had coming to the Holland shows. And at Bolton, Friday night, they came forward in the stalls like at a rock concert to clap and sing along with *Supremacy*! It got your heart thumping and I had to sing my heart out – but I can't see how the race relations people don't shut this show down. For a start, the Imperial Theatre people must be well-in with the cause…

And something else. Something *big* else! Mum asked for a spare *She-Pirate* programme to take to the *Crimewatch* casting director. So I got one to post to her. And what was tucked inside it, here in Bolton?

This!

TRAVEL DETAILS FOR PARIS 24ᵗʰ SEPTEMBER

Eurostar *– dep. St Pancras 07:30; ret. Paris GDN 18:30*
Channel Tunnel Shuttle *(car, minibus) – dep. Ashford every 30 mins; 35 mins on Shuttle, allow 3 hours for Calais to Paris drive (A26/A1); for Phénix Theatre exit Paris ring road at porte Le Pré-Saint-Gervais. Last return Shuttle: 22:00 (Calais)*
Ferry *– sailings from Dover to Calais by Sea-France and P&O 90 mins crossing (see directly above for car details);*

or rail: travel day before - Friday 11:53 am London Charing Cross, arrive Paris GDN 21:20; return Sunday: Paris GDN 08:04, arrive London 16:07.

<u>Flights</u> – frequent flights to Paris Charles de Gaulle from all over UK (British Midland under £20 return) – see travel agents or online

BUT BE THERE!

As soon as I saw it I showed it to Ben Maddox, found him in the wings waiting for the show to go up, Saturday matinee; but he didn't want to know right then, someone else in the crew was lurking a bit close. But after the second show we met up in his room at the Holiday Inn, where we're staying. Weirdly, he wasn't surprised by what I showed him. It was like he knew! Or sort-of knew. And he swore me to keep it secret, even from Tootie and Jo: not because I'm special and different, of course, but because it was me who tripped over that slip of paper in the programme.

Then he told me. Or, showed me on his laptop. He went to Ben's Programmes where he'd got a transcript of something he'd seen on TV the night before...

(To be continued...)

ZEPHON TELEVISION
TRANSCRIPT SERVICE

Programme 11606
Europe News

Wednesday 24th August

Programme music, fading to voice-over against title shots of a European map that is getting closer and larger, homing in on Paris.

CONTINUITY ANNOUNCER:
Tonight, Paris – and in our studio Francis Edgars, who's talking to *Paris-Monde's* Félice Jacqueman.

Edgars and Mme Jacqueman are in black armchairs, a three-camera set-up, cutting between close-ups and two-shots, the third camera portable and moving behind the 'talking heads' participants for a variety of angles.

The banner head of Paris-Monde is on the bluescreen background.

FRANCIS EDGARS:
Felice Jacqueman, your newspaper has been running a series of pressing stories this week. Share with us what important issues are burning your government these days.

FÉLICE JACQUEMAN:

You choose the right verb. Burning. In Paris, and other big cities – Marseille, Lyons, Strasbourg, many others – we have the burning of cars in the poorer districts, we have what you call 'disaffected youth' who are upset by high unemployment in these zones, we have poor housing, no hope—

EDGARS:

The same 'hot summer' syndrome we've seen in recent years?

FÉLICE JACQUEMAN:

A little bit different. No, a huge bit different – very significantly different I think...

The background shows library footage of the urban estate riots of the year before.

EDGARS:

Which is...?

FÉLICE JACQUEMAN:

Racism. The racial dimension. It was there before with the deaths of some immigrant youths at police hands, when the police were regarded as being in the wrong. But now this situation is turned around. Now the immigrants are perceived to be the bad boys, the villains, and there is a campaign in France to put anti-immigration at the top of the political agenda.

EDGARS:
Was it ever *not*?

FÉLICE JACQUEMAN:
Not at presidential level. The campaign for the new president is started, and one of the candidates comes from the Far Right, the *France-Blanc* party...

EDGARS:
White France.

FÉLICE JACQUEMAN;
Of course.

The bluescreen cuts from the urban riots back to the Zephon 'Europe News' logo.

EDGARS:
So, how—?

FÉLICE JACQUEMAN:
I am going to say. As you know, the next presidency of the European Union will be in the hands of the French. It is the French turn to preside over debate and decisions in the Council of Europe for six months—

Edgars is nodding

FÉLICE JACQUEMAN:
And the new French president will ensure that our country promotes his or her policies in Europe, through the European Council presidency...

EDGARS:
The French Presidential elections. With election day on Sunday 25th September.

FÉLICE JACQUEMAN:
Exactly so. And who is the candidate I fear?

The bluescreen shows Bernadette Flute, a severe-looking woman of around fifty, blonde, with piercing dark eyes.

FÉLICE JACQUEMAN:
Bernadette Flute – a Far Right candidate from *France-*

Blanc. Because if she is elected she will help to steer the European ship in the direction the French Far Right wishes. With so much European immigration legislation to determine, there is a real danger that the face of Europe will resemble again Europe in the nineteen-thirties, before the war with Adolf Hitler.

EDGARS:
That's a chilling thought!

FÉLICE JACQUEMAN:
Yes, as you say, a chilling thought, and very realistic. The French people are poised as if they are on the fulcrum of a balance. One badly handled event, one big police or government mistake, anything like this could do so much more than cause rioting on the estates. It will drive the voters into the Far Right polling booths of *France-Blanc* and into the arms of Madam Flute.

Ben switched off his laptop and looked up at Paul. 'That's the bones of it,' he said.

Paul's eyes were still staring wide at the blank screen. *Yes!* He was starting to understand! 'So,' he said, '*She-Pirate* plays a part in getting a crowd of racists – perhaps thousands – into Paris on—'

'On the 24th of September. With a big anti-racist rally in the centre of the city, and presidential elections the next day, on the 25th...'

'And these racists get all fired up by the play; black Roarin' James gets made to look less than the shite under their shoes and everyone sings *Supremacy!*' Paul knew how that rock beat thumping out like an anthem could drug anyone up to believe they ruled the world.

'Also,' Ben put in, 'with the scene enhanced for the occasion, you bet – an extra speech for Meg Macroo, or new resonating verses to the song, perhaps the white pirate crew crowing harder than ever about being supreme over the likes of Roarin' James... And the hyped-up audience gets sent to march out of the venue and break up the rally!'

'Which they must know about! White Ensign has planned it for the same day!'

'The same day!'

'Blimey!'

'Right, "Blimey!"'

'So we tell the French police!' Paul said. 'We warn them what's going to happen—'

But Ben was shaking his head. 'That could be what they want. The police coming in heavy-handed to defend the black rally, pictures of the *gendarmerie* baton-charging the white contingent! Pictures like that will more or less tell France how to vote the next day. Because all they'll see is the white underdogs of society being prevented by force from counter-demonstrating against their country being taken over by Algerians and Africans...'

Paul sat on Ben's dressing table chair. 'Bloody Nora!' he said. 'You've got to say it's clever!'

Ben nodded. 'White Ensign has thought this through

to get the sympathy vote. They're setting up their own supporters to take a beating from the police. The big question is, how do we stop this happening?'

'Simple!' Paul got up again. 'We don't play Paris. We get stuck on the auto-route, or we all go down with swine-fever, or we pull out the fuses on the theatre electrics...'

'Yup. That's a nice take. But we've still got 6,000 racists on the rampage in Paris. Same result, don't you reckon?'

Paul shrugged. 'So? Short of blockading the Channel and closing the airports?' He snapped his fingers. 'Then *we* pull out. The cast. Early. No show, so the racists don't come.'

'*Some* cast pull out. Kent's got enough support to throw some sort of *She-Pirate* onto the stage.'

'Or we get the race relations people to kill the show for us. Stop it in its tracks...'

Ben had started walking the room like a tiger in a city zoo. This way, turn; that way, turn; this way again, turn... 'Wouldn't work, Paul, not in time. Kent would fight it tooth and nail, it would go to appeal, meanwhile we're back in Germany – and remember how those BNP speech-makers got off scot-free a year or so back? No...' He went on with his pacing, in the middle of which he stopped to stare at Paul. 'I've got it!' he said. 'But it's going to be bloody hard, and dangerous...'

'So?'

'I mean, *dangerous!* For you, Paul!'

'For me?'

'As Ardal.'

'Blimey!' Again.

Ben was nodding to himself, clenching his right fist

and thumping it in the air on an imaginary podium. '*Yes!*' he said.

Paul leant against the dressing table. '*What?*' he said, at last.

'THE FILEY FILES'

File 11 (continued)

...so that was it. Ben told me his plan.

And, brother – am I scared!!!

**U left in a
rush on Sunday!
Conscience?
We did the shoot
at Bolton & I've
seen it. It's out-
rageous. Up
the whites, down
the blacks. Wot
r u doing selling
this rubbish as yr
cover? Do u no
wot u're doing?
Bloom**

BEN MADDOX MEMO – DICTATED NOTES – SAT. 27/8 02:30

Paul Filey's a bright kid and a good actor, so far as I'm any judge. Could pull this off. That slip of paper in the programme makes everything very clear now – and no prizes for betting that similar slips are in the programme in Bristol. The question is, do I let Bloom in on this, or don't I?

I've left a message on Kath Lewis's voicemail telling her I'm getting some good stuff for a ground-breaking

310

programme. Well, events in Paris – if we can pull it off – will certainly get Zephon a few million viewers. Or not, of course, if we fall flat on our faces.

I've decided. I must e-mail Bloom to tell her not to show the Bolton package to Kath Lewis – and I must also tell Bloom that I know what I'm doing. And I'll meet her underneath the Eiffel Tower on 24th September at eight pm. I'll be wearing a red carnation – or a black eye! Things will have gone one way or the other by then.

Now for the big reason for these notes at this ungodly hour.

Deep breath, Ben!

Soon after Paul Filey had gone, Lee Conyers came knocking on my door. How about a drink? he asks. He and some of the chapter are meeting in a pub up the road. He's got a questioning look on his face, like, *I'm testing you out*, so I say 'yes' as enthusiastically as I can, and grab my wallet.

The crowd is in the Frog and Radiator – a murky place, festooned with England shields. And a right crowd they are. *Right, right, right!* They make Mosley's pre-war parading black shirts seem like Cub Scouts on a ramble. I'd like to say they haven't got a brain between them, but they have, they're sharp, this White Alliance, and the worrying thing is, apart from the young men with E-N-G-L-A-N-D tattoos on fingers and knuckles, and St George crosses on their white shirts and singlets, most of them seem so blooming *ordinary*.

Anyhow, as we go in it looks like they accept me as a mate of Lee Conyers – and suddenly it hits me what he'd been on about with his talk way back in the rehearsal room of laying some white around the clubs. It wasn't cocaine he was talking about at all – it was *him* – Conyers and his white friend picking on some black lad late at night and laying into him. That's what had got me to go under-cover, and now here I am – for a very different reason to the one I'd thought.

And who was sitting there, in the shadows? Squeezed in a booth together? Three of them – spiky little Martin Kent, fat Ronnie Hammond, and a pasty-faced Allen Green (he really is better-looking, black!). Conyers takes me over to them – and they slide along to squeeze me in. All the while, Kent is staring at me with his rat-like Hitler eyes, and Hammond is nodding as if some truth has just dawned: I'm not so much crew wished on him, more solid mate of Lee Conyers, there for the cause.

'You "belong", down south?' Hammond asks.

'Dagenham,' I tell him. And that seems enough said. But, 'We got a few councillors in down there,' I boast.

'Well,' says Martin Kent, folding his arms across his chest, 'we're after bigger fish than that!'

I want to ask him, *what?* But I daren't – I'm supposed to know, through Lee Conyers – who suddenly lays his arms across the table like a drowning man on a raft. 'Are we gunna get a drink, or wha?'

The others laugh, and Kent starts feeling in his pocket for some money. But, 'You do it, Ronnie,' he says. 'I'm bust.'

Ronnie Hammond makes himself a bit more room to go digging in his pockets, while Kent rants on – and I'm fizzing with this information now.

'I've spent every last penny putting *Pirate* on.' He looks me in the eye, like being stapled to the wall, 'But it's my life's quest to stand up to them. I'm driven! We must mortgage our houses, we must spend our savings, we must be prepared to bankrupt ourselves to rid Europe of its immigrant vermin.'

'An' use our talents to do it!' I soft-soap him. 'Martin, you couldn't do no more...'

Martin looks at me, the others shuffle, and then he smiles. I don't think I've ever seen Martin Kent smile.

'We can all do our best!' Allen Green puts in, his big eyes wide with actors' pride. And it's him who fixes me next. 'So, are you fed up with having the country filled with trash, Maddox?'

I don't nod too vigorously, I try with a bit of subtlety to out-act the man – which should never be too difficult – although the consequences for me right now could be dire. 'Blacks? Hate 'em?' I whisper. 'I loathe 'em! An' the rest...' I wave my arm at the windows as if I'm including all the Muslim streets of Bolton. 'England for the true English! That's my motto.'

'An' Europe for the true Europeans...' Hammond wheezes in.

'An' Newcastle f'r true Geordies!' says Lee Conyers, without laughing.

'Right!' Allen Green stands up. He fixes me again. 'Get up to the bar. You can get us all a drink. Stage crew, you're on better money than most of the cast!' At which he smiles at Martin Kent, who doesn't seem to be amused.

I get my wallet out and slide off the seat to head for the bar – Allen Green pushing through next to me when I get there.

'I know the round,' he says. But as I'm waiting to be served, he suddenly takes the wallet off me. 'You won't mind me having a little look at your credentials...'

I stare at him. 'Only we get MI5 and Special Branch and all sorts trying to get close to us.'

Now there's only one thing I can do. I take offence. I take the wallet back and throw it open in front of him – 'Go on, then! But you check my cred, Allen, an' you c'n buy your own pissin' drink!' I start pulling cards and a drivers' licence out of the wallet and slap them on the bar, then stand back. 'Go on! Have a good butcher's – and don' forget the lining!' I call Lee Conyers over. 'When your mate's finished with my wallet, Lee, fetch it back to the 'otel, will you?'

Lee Conyers slides through, frowning. But Allen Green has changed his mind. He laughs, and starts stuffing the cards back into the wallet. 'Don't get your party frock ruffled! Jesus, Conyers, our mate's touchy.' And he wipes the wallet on his sleeve where the leather has gone into the beer on the counter. Then he suddenly turns and gives me a big hug and shouts the round at the barmaid – 'With a bloody large Scotch for my friend!'

Meaning me.

After that, I'm in – and the talk back in the booth is all about how the whole white world is going to get kicked out of Europe, except as slaves, if we don't do something about it. Only not in those words – I'm not going to say the stuff that was said, it'll pollute the machine.

And after a couple of Scotches I come back to the hotel feeling as dirty as a paedophile – deeply filthy to the core.

I lock my door and sit on the bed – and take out my wallet, and remove my mug-shot Zephon Press Card out of the back compartment, which Allen Green hadn't quite reached when I threw a strop.

God... If he'd found it, I wouldn't have got out of that pub alive, I know it. And a big lesson has been learned by Benjamin Maddox about the under-cover life, I can tell you.

'THE FILEY FILES'

File 12

I bet most people wish some time or another that life could let you do what you can do on your computer – go back to a date before everything got cocked up: start again from a certain point. After taking the travel sheet to Ben Maddox that night and getting back to my own room, I suddenly wanted to be flashed back to the day I did my audition to get into Broadway – and fail it this time. I suddenly sided with my dad, this job *is* rubbish, and I thought how different things would be if I was going to college every day and only worrying about my 'AS' and 'A' level grades. I even started wondering what universities offered the best degrees in Sociology, and Politics, and Education. Because what Ben Maddox is planning to do in Paris is scaring the pants off me.

And we're not there yet. So the autobiography I'm supposed to be writing from these notes is likely to be read when I'm dead – something my mum and dad can go home to after they've seen me off in the East London Cemetery.

Thinking of what Ben Maddox is planning for me to do in Paris made the Germany leg of the tour a nightmare. The show ran OK, but those scary audiences, now we know who they are! Boy! Dresden, Regensburg, Munich, Göttingen – their new version of Hitler Youth all came out from under their stones. And Allen Green and Sadie Baker lapped it up. She's got to be in on it. She took the

317

standing ovations like Boudicca on her chariot, showing off her white cleavage, her fist clenched, her right foot down on Roarin' James's neck. And after the final curtain each time, Green was up off the stage and hugging her like they'd just won a couple of Baftas. It made me want to vomit – that and the 'high' I can't deny getting singing *Supremacy!* with that thumping rock.

Plus, Sadie Baker and Allen Green have been holding a few private rehearsals in Martin Kent's hotel rooms. Tootie saw them coming out one morning clutching new script pages – so Ben Maddox was right: they *are* planning some even bigger triumphant ending for Paris.

I didn't manage to get home before the Bristol week – we came directly here, and from Bristol it's Cardiff for three days, then on to Paris for the day I'm going to die. So there's no chance to get to Kitchener Road to sort my bedroom for Mum to sit in and weep. There's a couple of framed photos I'd like to put on the dressing table to give her a bit of comfort. But I've just had to get on with what I'm doing – and take comfort from knowing that if I *do* survive, I'll never walk on a stage again in my entire life. The city has turned out its sewers and gutters to come to see *She-Pirate*. So I've grown to hate audiences: and a greengrocer who hates fruit and veg isn't going to wheel his barrow very far. Which means Paris is going to be a final *something* for me, whichever way it cuts.

And this piece of Microsoft Word could be the final chapter of my sad little tale of a life in the theatre...

SHE-PIRATE – EXCERPT FROM 'THE BOOK'

For the duel, Captain Macroo and Captain James are each accompanied by a 'second'. Cap'n Macroo's is her son, Ardal.   The quartermaster from Roarin' James's ship *Hunter* officiates. He reminds the duellists of the rules. One pistol to be carried at belt, there are to be ten paces (for stage purposes) at which the duellists turn and fire one ball – the seconds to knock any further pistol attempt from the duellists' hands. It is then cutlasses, and the first to draw blood wins. That person shall be captain of the pirate band of two ships.

Roarin' James and Meg Macroo (still a man) duet: '*I shall be captain of the pirate band*'.

The duel begins. At ten paces both turn and fire. There is no hit – the quartermaster, throwing two pistol balls to the sand shouts, 'To cutlasses!' He had deliberately not loaded the firearms. (He is determined this should be a non-lethal contest).

Meg and Roarin' James fight with cutlasses, and it is clear that Meg does not see this as a token affair. She will not be cut, and therefore subservient to this man. She cries,

'I challenged to a duel, not a petty charade!'

Now they go to it in earnest. Good, exciting fight backed by a new *She-Pirate* arrangement of Flame's hit *Rock My Socks Off*. Roarin' James – seeing how serious this is – starts really fighting, and, through sheer masculine strength, is winning. Meg is retreating, beckoning him on over an exposed tree stump. Roarin' James stumbles, giving Meg a split second in which she tears her shirt open to reveal her female breasts. (Upstage!)

Roarin' James is shocked, aroused, giving Meg the chance to slash his neck and kill him.

Pirates gather from hiding places in the foliage around the beach and, led by Roarin' James's quartermaster, acknowledge Meg as their new captain. Ardal and other spared pirates from the *Smiling Rover* are among them.

MEG SINGS: *SUPREMACY (first line 'She rules the waves who waives the rules!')* – a song describing and celebrating supremacy.

ENTIRE COMPANY SINGS *SUPREMACY*.

CURTAIN

That was 'the book'. By the time *She-Pirate* had reached Bristol, Roarin' James was always being played as 'black' and Meg Macroo 'stamps' on his dead neck, celebrating his death. She was also adding a line not in the original script: 'Get to your eternal slavery! Such scum as you shall never taste freedom such as ours!' And, depending on the venue and the audience – never at a matinee – she would put the word 'black' in front of 'scum'.

Now, Ben Maddox knew, Martin Kent was writing even more explicit extra lines for the Paris performance – although the man was keeping it very close to those who needed to know. Allen Green was in on it, and Sadie Baker – they shut themselves into Kent's hotel rooms – but when Ben probed Lee Conyers he got the Geordie cold stare.

'They know wa' they're doin'. Why should ye be bothered?'

But Ben and Paul, Tootie and Jo were collaborating on an ending of their own, and when the show came back to England they all met up in Ben's room at the Bristol Airport Holiday Inn for a couple of sessions and a final polish.

And it turned out that it was all down to Ardal! Ardal is on the duelling beach as Captain Macroo's 'second'; and in Paris it would be Ardal who would turn the end of *She-Pirate* upside down. The winner would be the loser, and the loser would be the winner – and the audience wouldn't be left in the darkest doubt as to what they'd just seen. The whole idea was scary – with some surprise stage business and a rebel Ardal speech that called for real courage – an act that could get Paul Filey lynched.

That was the strategy; but like all strategies and schemes, nothing is guaranteed to go according to plan.

And the first devastating setback came as the cast met up for the minibus call at six o'clock in the morning on Friday the 23rd of September, the day before the final show-down.

And it was a real scything-off of the legs with a cutlass slash…

'THE FILEY FILES'

File 13!!!

I'm not down to play Ardal in Paris!

As we drive to the ferry at Dover, Martin Kent gives us some notes on the Cardiff performances; and as a sort of after-thought, he turns again and calls to the back of the bus, 'I've made up my mind, Brad, you'll be doing Ardal tomorrow.' He doesn't even look at me. And Bradley knows already. I know that Bradley knows.

Bombshell! Turner as Ardal for the final show! With what we've got planned!

So, what to do? Ben Maddox has been laying it on the line how vital it is to turn the tables on Flame and Michael Kent and Allen Green – our mission is to scotch any TV pictures of French riot police baton-charging whites – the story White Ensign wants the world to see: European whites not being allowed to be seen and heard in Europe.

But if I'm Frenchie Roche and not Ardal I'm dead and off the final scene – literally! If the dead Frenchie Roche walks onto that stage for the end of the play, Green and Baker will know something's going on and they'll stifle me, kill me again, shuffle me off; but as Ardal I'm on as a 'second' for the duel, on and active with a few lines, and everything will seem to be going their way – until I kick in with our new ending before the racists can get

323

to theirs. But not any more. Now the plan's ruined – and I wouldn't be honest if I don't say I feel a bit of relief at that! Would I be human if I didn't?

But the fact of things is as plain as the nose on my face: I've got to forget my relief and take out Bradley Turner. I've got to get rid of the kid in some way so that I get to play Ardal in Paris. Someone else can always come on as Frenchie Roche.

Easy to say, quickly! 'Take out Bradley Turner.' But what do I do? Maim him? Kidnap him? Or cut his throat and ruin his singing voice? Do I put him in hospital, push him under a train, or throw him overboard and leave him trying to swim the English Channel? OK, nothing as drastic as any of that – but *something's* got to happen to him. The trouble is, Ben Maddox isn't with us – the crew have gone on ahead for the get-in. So, it's down to Tootie, Jo, and me. But, what? *What's* down to us?

I look across at Tootie, who scorches her eyes back at me. This is a big-time shock! And scary. The look between us says only one thing: whatever is done to Bradley Turner is going to be dangerous, and physical, and drastic.

And all at once things are even more terrifying than they were before…

HOTEL IBIS, NORTH PARIS

**Hi Bloom! Urgent.
Can u get a camcorder into
the Phoenix show
@ 12 noon? Cd
have a real scoop. Say zero
to Kath but tell yr
guy he's working
for Zephon. Zephon
have got to get this,
exclusive.
I owe it. Ben**

**BEN – WOT R U
UP TO? IT'D
BETTER B GOOD.
CAMCORDER SORTED.
LUV BLOOM X**

So that was on! But the other news Ben got at the North
Paris hotel that Friday night was definitely not good. Paul
came to find him – to report the Martin Kent minibus
bombshell – that Bradley Turner was on as Ardal the next
day: their re-written final scene was going to be scuppered.
Ben's first suspicion was that Martin Kent had got wind that
something was being planned to counter the White Ensign
grand plan. But he dismissed that as unlikely.

'It was there from the start. Turner's got to be in on it with them!' he told Paul. 'He dresses with Allen Green. He's always with him over breakfast and in the bars. You can bet Ardal's got some crucial part to play in *their* grand finale in the same way he's key to ours.'

'So how do we get rid of him?' Paul asked, all white-faced apprehension. 'That's the million dollar question. Or couldn't we go to the French police and get the show cancelled?'

But Ben started on his tiger pacing again, different room, same route, before he suddenly stopped and clicked his fingers. 'Got it!' he said. 'Gaffer tape!' Listen – I've been under the stage at the Phoenix, poking around; no one's down there. No musicians have to go through to get to the orchestra pit, all they've got down there is our music stacks, a few racks of old costumes, and some props...'

'Yeah...?' Paul's apprehension showed on his face.

'But there's a space as big as the stage that they use for rehearsals...'

Paul cleared his throat.

'...So—' Ben was getting to it. 'You persuade Turner to do your warm-up down there. You tell him the fight arranger's come over from London and wants a final run-through for the big stage, somewhere private...' This was now Ben thinking aloud as much as telling, his eyes closed, the way a script editor comes up with a great idea. 'You get him down there – and I'll be somewhere behind the costume racks. I jump him, we bind him up with gaffer tape – arms, ankles, round his mouth – and you report to Fat Boy that Turner's run out of the theatre, too scared to do the big, final show...'

Paul breathed in now. 'Strewth!' he said. 'Muscle!'

'Minimal, if I jump him right. Then that gives you time to change as Ardal – and it's back to Plan A...'

Paul swallowed.

'Because we've got to do it, haven't we? We can't let these racist fanatics ruin the world's view of Europe's great march for equality...'

Paul was nodding; but slowly, very slowly and thoughtfully. 'What about after?' he asked. 'When we let Turner out?'

'We take care of after, after. We make sure someone knows where he is and we skidaddle out, lose ourselves in Paris. Have your passport with you. I'll get you home to London. But I'll make sure through Zephon TV that their scheme comes out for what it was – a racist plot – so no one in show business is going to look at Paul Filey as unreliable...'

Paul's scared stare said that that wasn't important any more.

'So – are you up for it?'

Paul nodded. 'The Turner bit's easy,' he said, 'with you being there. It's back to the new ending that's messing my trousers!'

Ben Maddox smiled, almost confidently. 'Don't forget the old theatrical saying,' he said. 'It'll be all right on the night!'

While the look on Paul's face said he only wished he could believe that...

THÉÂTRE LE PHÉNIX DE PARIS

Ben took his place off-stage right. Eleven o'clock and the rig was done, the show was ready, the cast was warming up. The house would open in half an hour, but the audience was milling in the foyer and out on the street, the theatre bars packed and busy. There was a tension about the whole building amounting to so much more than a last-performance high: there was the same sense of drama that wafted like a curling mist off the Thames into the Zephon studios on Election Night. It could be felt, touched – the clammy grip of excited fear.

From the darkness, Ben could see across into the stage-left wings, and beyond them to the door that opened onto the dressing room stairs. Onstage, Flame was warming up her voice: *'many men making much money in the moonshine...'* Allen Green – not yet 'blacked-up' – was tongue-twisting around *'red leather, yellow leather, red leather, yellow leather'*, and Bob Tremaine, as Felix Lawes, was running up to the high notes of his song, *Booty!*; but what Ben wanted to see was a 'thumbs-up' through that door from Paul Filey to say that he and Bradley Turner were on their way to the under-stage space. He could then take the stairs on his own side to get down fast behind the costume racks. In one hand he gripped the silver gaffer tape for Turner's limbs and mouth; and with the other he patted his pocket where his passport and wallet were ready for a quick get-away after the show.

But with a creak of leather, he was suddenly grabbed by a voice – and by a hard gripping hand on his shoulder.

'Maddox!' It was Lee Conyers.

'Wotcha, Lee. 'Ow's it goin'?'

'You tell me!'

'Eh?'

Conyers suddenly swung Ben Maddox to face him and held up something thin and shiny before his eyes. A phone. Ben's phone.

'Came over summat by a seat in the Green Room...'

Ben felt in his trouser pocket, where he kept his Motorola. To where it wasn't. 'Cheers! Slip out easy, them...'

Conyers was staring him in the face. 'Forgit *easy*! Who's this Zephon? What scoop's this ye're gettin'? An' who's feggin' Bloom?'

'Just contacts!' Ben tried desperately to think of something brilliant to put Conyers off the scent; but his mind had gone blank.

'Ye're piggin' undercover, en't ye? Aye, funny 'ow ye got in the show from no-bloody-where – na mittens, na contacts I've ever met. Ye're never one of us! Ye're telly *scum!*'

Ben tried to look innocent, but Ronnie Hammond had come up behind him, blocking him in with his size.

'Bastard! You're up to something!' Hammond pushed Ben hard against the rigging cleats like a stab in the back – and with the sudden point of a Stanley knife against his throat, Ben was pulled off and marched backwards to the scenery door. With one hand, Hammond pulled it open, and before Ben could put up any guard, Conyers hit him with a hard-knuckled punch to the side of his face. The pain exploded inside Ben's head. He couldn't hear. He tasted blood in his mouth. With a final kick in the crotch, Conyers and Hammond slung him into the street.

'We can cover for scum like you!' Hammond shouted.

'Ye're piggin' lucky ye're still breathin'!' Conyers spat after him. And the door was shut hard, and bolted tight against him.

'THE FILEY FILES'

File 14

I get him down under the stage. He's fallen like a patsy for the line about a warm-up with the fight arranger.

The space down there is big. Our show's sound control stacks are there, winking in the light from a working strip overhead. Straight off I can see the main rail of costumes over at the side – where Ben Maddox is hiding himself well, because you'd never know he was crouching there.

Turner stands in the middle of the space looking around. 'Where's the stunt man guy?' he asks. I flap my arms, sort of, *Beats me!* – but Turner goes looking for him, as if he might be sitting having a puff behind the costume rail. Which is perfect – right where Ben Maddox is. As soon as Turner swings round my way again, Ben can have him!

Which Turner does – and Ben Maddox doesn't. There's no move. Not a coat arm flaps. And it suddenly hits me like a stonking free-kick into the defending wall. Maddox isn't there! I'm down here on my own with Turner!

Something's gone wrong! So what do I do? I've got to do something. I've come this far, and, God, I hate the thought of Turner and his lot getting what they want out of life – preaching supremacy over loads of my friends.

'Who did you say wanted us down here?' Turner's asking.

'Kent. Martin Kent said...' But I must sound as feeble as I feel. I look around – and suddenly I see the table of props. And lying across it, pommels towards us, is a collection of swords: not our pirate cutlasses, more the straight, thin, duelling swords of Louis the Something.

I run across and grab up two; sling one across to Turner, who catches it like Robin Hood. Impressive.

'I'll fight you, Brad Turner!' I shout. 'I've got agents in today – I've got to do Ardal. I'll duel you for Ardal. First man to lose his sword does Frenchie Roche...'

I go *en-garde*, a straight arm in front of me but my sword head-height, threatening, above the fencing target area.

Will he? Won't he? He doesn't have to duel me for Ardal – he's down to play it. All he's got to do is walk away and up those stairs. But he stares at me, suddenly jumps his feet into the duelling position, immediately looks fearsome, like he's never looked on stage. And with a sudden roar like Roarin' James he comes swiping at me across the space. It's not fencing, it's not duelling, it's a killer attack like some yob with a butchers' knife. Town Centre stuff. I parry a cut at my left shoulder, go horizontal to block a downward slice to my throat, step back to gain some room to move, but he's on me with another slash across my chest – missing by a millimetre.

Fence! I tell myself. *Footwork! Think Broadway!* Superior skill should beat brute force. But as I turn my body to present less of a target, as I balance myself with my high left hand and start the toe-in-line footwork to advance myself towards him, he sweeps a great cutting scythe at my ankles – and like Ardal against Frenchie Roche I've got to jump. As I land he pushes me and I go sprawling on my back across the space, desperately trying to hold onto my weapon. But it's gone; and Turner's got the point of his sword at my throat.

Turner has won. No argument. He has fought me for the right to play Ardal – and he has won. Something has happened to Ben Maddox – and now I've lost this vital fight – the most important theatrical battle of my life.

So all there is left for me to do is pick myself up and go back to the dressing room to get ready as Frenchie Roche.

RUE RÉAUMUR, PARIS

Out in the street, Ben finally picked himself up as the sickening ache in his groin started to subside. He spat the blood from his mouth, and pulled tissues from his pocket to tidy himself up. The last of the audience had gone in, and he was left in the Rue Réaumur with a bright noon sun casting a full stop of shadow beneath him. He was hurt, and shaking, and angry: hurt from the attack, shaking over the Stanley knife that had been put to his throat, and angry at his stupidity at losing his phone from his trouser pocket.

But hurt and anger and the shakes weren't going to count for anything right now: now was for feeling nothing and doing something. What, though? He ran round to the stage door to get himself back into the theatre, but a security man stood like a boulder against him.

'I'm in the show!' Ben told him. 'Je suis stagehand – machiniste!' But the man's folded arms heard nothing, the eyes in his bouncers' face staring above Ben's head. 'Je suis "White Ensign"—' Ben went on – 'Drapeux Blanc!' Still nothing, not the merest shake of the head.

Ben backed off and ran around to the front of the theatre, into the huge foyer that served one of the biggest venues in Europe – where every door to the auditorium was firmly closed and guarded, while from inside Ben could hear the thumping overture of *She-Pirate*, and the shouts and cheers of the packed audience that within two hours would be marching clench-fisted to confront the French riot police at the Anti-Racist rally.

He ran to the man who looked like the front-of-house manager, coming down the wide stairs from the top audience entrances. Quickly, Ben flashed out his Zephon press I.D. card.

'Zephon!' he said. 'Nous avons un caméra de film en haute!' He pointed upwards to where he guessed the Canal Media man might be. But the manager shook his head.

'Desolée – mais impossible! Le spectacle a commencé.' He showed two apologetic palms. 'We cannot interrupt.'

But at least Ben wasn't being thrown out on his ear. So, now what...?

Then he saw the pay phone. Paul Filey had been right, he had to involve the French police. It had been stupid and egotistic of him, trying to foil this racist plot on his own. But who would listen to a pay phone caller right now, with everything that was going on in Paris today? He looked down at himself in his scruffy blacks – and there in his hand he was still clutching his Zephon press card. Yes! Quickly, he found some euros and tapped in the number of the duty controller at Zephon.

Rosie Plummer, Zephon duty controller:
Zephon, duty office.

Ben Maddox:
It's Ben Maddox here, on assignment from Kath Lewis – special operation.

Rosie Plummer (duty controller):
Ben Maddox... **(sounds of paper shuffling)** What's your assignment number, Ben?

Ben:
God knows! Listen, this is urgent. Get Kath Lewis, wherever she is, and tell her what you're doing. But, after! First, you've got to get onto the Paris police. There's a massive anti-racist rally in

Paris today. And right now there's an audience-full of White Alliance and European fascists in the Phoenix Theatre, bent on—

Rosie Newton:
The Phoenix in Charing Cross Road?

Ben:
No! The Phoenix Theatre in Paris! It's all going off in about an hour and a half. There's no time to waste! We've got 6,000 of them in here about to march on the rally. It's going to be mayhem and bloodshed...

At which moment, with all the wonders of modern technology, the phone went dead. And when Ben tried frantically again, all he got was the 'unobtainable' tone. The dead phone – a Maddox recurrent nightmare...

Then a lifeline came – Ben saw the front-of-house staff starting to prepare the counters for the sale of refreshments in the interval. The interval! Getting into the auditorium would be easy after the interval, no one re-checks tickets; Ben could just walk in and lie low somewhere.

It seemed like real time. It seemed as if the whole of the seven seas had been sailed in that dire show before the thump of *Dirty Work* came out from the theatre. Ben still didn't know what he could do to twist the ending – and Bradley Turner would be on as Ardal, so Paul Filey couldn't do anything. It seemed hopeless. What could one of him do against the 6,000 in there?

To roared applause the first act ended, and out they came: the strutting, crop-headed, shaven-pimpled Extreme

Right youth, white-shirted, black-shirted Aryan bigots –
British, Dutch, and German. Heads up as if they were all
celebrating some supreme victory, they swarmed for a
smoke, a pee, a can – milling like a Cup Final crowd. Of
course, they weren't exclusively the White Ensign dream
audience. Among them were people already heading for the
exit; heads down, frightened, getting themselves out of the
evil atmosphere.

Ben kept himself low-key against the foyer wall. He was
in his blacks, dressed for backstage – but it takes all sorts.
And after fifteen minutes, as they all trooped back, he
joined the queue and slunk in among them. He knew the
place was huge, but he had never felt so small and
outnumbered as in this fervent mob. There was
testosterone in the air to seed a riot, which was the aim.
And without any doubt, there was nothing he could do
here. Nothing this side of the curtain line would even be
seen, let alone heard – and who on God's earth would
think they could speak to this Nazi rally?

He thought of the plan they'd had – he thought of the
lines of the ending he and Paul and Tootie and Jo had
written; and he knew that it could only be something
played up there on the stage that could ever make any
difference: it was up there where doubt could be spread.

So could he dress himself as a pirate and go on to deliver
the new Ardal speech they'd written for Paul Filey?
Possible! Whatever, he needed to get backstage. He thought
about it – he didn't know the code to any pass doors; and
he couldn't just climb up onto the stage and crawl under
the curtain. The only other front of house and backstage
connection was the orchestra pit...

The orchestra pit!

Yes! Instantly, Ben slipped through men taking their seats and came to the front. His first thought was to unhitch his crew lanyard, a sturdy piece of leather, and throw it up towards the back of the grande parterre, to create a diversion. But from the way a couple in the audience were looking at him, he suddenly realised that he was in his blacks, with KREW! on the T-shirt.

''Scuse!' he said. 'Technical hitch.' He waved his lanyard and calmly clambered over the orchestra pit rail to drop to the floor beneath. Seconds later he was through the black curtain that separated the pit from the under-stage space, to drop further down onto the cement floor.

The sound stacks twinkled and flashed as he ran to the stairs – grabbing up a prop sword that was lying across his path. He paused at the top, awaited his moment, which was the Act Two intro when everyone backstage would be busy. Up came the stage lights, out went the 'tabs' – and Ben could quietly slide into the wings. Before him on the stage was the familiar scene of the opening of the second half: the *Smiling Rover*, with 'smoke' billowing in from the wings and booty being carried below decks by pirates and captured slaves. Keeping himself well in the shadows, Ben checked where Lee Conyers was – which was where he should be, over on the far side of the stage – with Neil Strong where Ben should be, bending over a smoke machine just a couple of metres away.

Should Ben go to find some pirate gear? Nice idea, but he knew he'd be yanked off the stage by Conyers and Strong before he could open his mouth. Once seen, he'd never get to deliver any speech...

So, what? He stood and desperately racked his brains as the second big scene change started to happen: everyone frantic in a few chords of rock music to change the stage from the *Smiling Rover* to the King of Dahomey's bamboo palace. And Tootie was a nubile in the king's court. Could he get to her and tell her to infiltrate the last scene, deliver Paul Filey's new lines? Meanwhile, he couldn't take any chance of being seen. Busy as Strong and Conyers were, it would only take a split second for a knife to come at his throat. He pulled himself further back behind a flat – twisting his head for some sort of view of the stage.

Up went the lights, where to derision from the audience the black King of Dahomey was being weighed against sacks of gold dust. On came the servant to warn him of attack – struck down by the pursuing Ron Quick, with Flame as Meg and Paul as Ardal running on, shouting and slashing close behind.

Paul as Ardal? Ben stared his eyes dry. *Paul as Ardal?*

So what had happened before the show? What had been going on while Ben was being kicked into the street?

And what would happen now at the end of the play?

File 14 (continued)

Bradley Turner has won and I'm just about to go back to the dressing room to get ready as Frenchie Roche, when, 'You do it!' he says. 'We didn't need to play pissin' games about it! You do Ardal. You're welcome to it!'

I can't believe what I'm hearing. 'What? Are you sure?' He has outfought me and well and truly earned himself the right to play Meg Macroo's fighting son tonight.

But he suddenly sits on the ground, cross-legged, like a schoolkid in circle-time. I pull myself forward to sit opposite him, same position. Because he's going to tell me something.

'I'll have a sore throat,' he says. 'I'll tell Martin I can't hit the top notes...' And all at once he opens up.

'They've made me Ardal today for a reason. Specially for something. Won't go into the ins an' outs, but it's a bloody long speech to have to learn.'

I'm staring at him with my mouth open, and he starts shuffling his bum as if he might change his mind and get up and go. But then he slumps, and tells me: 'Allen Green – he's my mother's boyfriend. It's a payback to her, getting me into this show. Only...today he wants me to do this special thing at the end.'

'Special thing?' I ask him.

'Nothing to do wi' you what it is, son, but I just don't want to do it. There's TV out front today, an' I've got mates where I live I don't want clocking what I'm supposed to say...'

'Black mates?' I come out with it. I have to. 'But you had a big go at the blacks at rehearsal...'

'Allen was around – it was for him. It's all right for Allen, he's hardly ever there, in and out of Europe for his firm, he's never about, nights...'

'Firm? He's an actor, isn't he?'

'Yeah, that's right.' Turner clams up. 'He's an actor.' Now he does get to his feet. 'Anyhow, I'm not an actor! Wouldn't be here if my mum's money wasn't in the show.' He pulls me up, too, as if he's doing all this before he changes his mind. 'So let's piss off upstairs and drop it on Sadie, you tart.' He punches me on the shoulder and laughs, suddenly Turd-face again. 'Filey can have the soddin' glory...'

Sadie Baker has to accept what Turner says. We knock on her door, her dresser's head peers round it, but we soon get in when Turner calls through with a husk in his voice. Nice bit of acting, I've got to say...

She's into her make-up. She swears. But it's not the end of the world to her. 'Tell Martin what's happening and say I'll cover it,' she tells Turner. 'I'll cover everything, OK?' And to me she gives one of her rare warm looks, the sort I haven't seen since rehearsals, just stops short of putting her arm around me. 'Keep on your toes in the final scene, Paul; I'm putting in a few extra words for the last show...'

I nod, and try to smile. *Not if I can help it!* I think. *It's going to be me, Mother dear...* And my stomach does a flip; no, a somersault; no, an earthquake of nerves hit it, Richter Scale Ten – and I go off to dress, wishing that I'd never in my life had a whiff of the greasepaint.

Ben stayed hidden where he was. Somehow Paul had won out, he was onstage as Ardal – and now they were on for playing the new ending themselves – unless someone had got at Paul and threatened him the way he'd been threatened – perhaps with the point of a knife? Was Paul Filey still up for it, or not? Well, he'd just have to wait and see. But, God, did the second act of that awful musical take a lifetime to play itself out! Like before, Ben looked at his watch every half minute – until finally, mercifully, the last scene of the last act of the last performance of *She-Pirate* started. And never in all his life, in a TV studio or out of it, had Ben taken a keener interest in every move and every word of what was going on out there under the glare of the stage lights.

For the rest of his life, he reckoned, he would remember Act Two, Scene Seven of that shameful, racist, play...

She-Pirate

Act Two

Scene Seven

An isolated beach, fringed with foliage

The quartermaster of the Hunter *marches onstage
leading Captain Macroo and Captain James;
Macroo with her son Ardal as 'second' and James
with Ames as his. Macroo is dressed as a man, with
no indication of her true sex.*

Quartermaster:	Ye knows the rules! It's one pistol at belt, an' at ten paces on my count, at the drop o' the duster, ye turns an' fires one ball! If both survive, it's cutlasses, gen'lemen, an' the first to draw blood is the winner. That man shall be the captain of the band, astride the *Hunter* and the *Smiling Rover*, both.
Meg Macroo:	Aye, man, we knows the rules o' duellin'!
Roarin' James:	*(Roars)* To it! Let's have at it!

Macroo and James stand back-to-back. Ardal and Ames stand aside.

Drum roll, music (off)

Meg Macroo (sings): I shall be captain of the
pirate band.

Roarin' James (joins in singing) – duet.

Quartermaster: Are you list'ning? (*Raises a duster*)
Uno –

Macroo and James take one pace.

Quartermaster: Dos –

They take another pace, and as the quartermaster counts on, Macroo and James pace to his count.

Quartermaster: Tres, cuatro, cinco, seis,
siete, ocho, nueve, diez!

Macroo and James, as one, pull their pistols from their belts, turn, take aim, and fire at their opponent.

There is no hit. Both are surprised.

Roarin' James: You're a lucky man, Macroo!

Meg Macroo:	No black man's shot is fit to lodge in this white flesh!
Quartermaster:	(*Tossing two pistol balls into the sand*) You were never loaded, gen'lemen! This ain't to be lethal – the Lords o' both crews has decided! The first to draw blood, is all! To cutlasses!
Ames:	Slice him, Cap'n!

Suddenly, Paul Filey as Ardal stepped in. 'Listen to sense, Macroo!' he shouted to Sadie Baker. 'Heed the words of the quartermaster! Not lethal!'

Sadie Baker looked at him with utter surprise. She twisted to stare into the prompt corner – this line wasn't in the script – she had to get on with the duel. With a curse at Paul, she turned and went into the sword fight, performing it as choreographed – up to the point where Allen Green, as he was supposed to, finally got her into her submissive position before she flashed her breasts at him.

'Submit, Macroo, you're no match for me!' Green crowed.

'Cower and whimper, you black slave!' Sadie Baker shouted back, all the depth and vibrancy of the famous Flame voice, her hands going to the Velcro on her blouse. 'All blacks are sl—'

At which moment Paul Filey suddenly leapt forward and snatched Sadie Baker's sword away from her. 'No! Sword up, Captain!' he commanded. The star of the show stared at him with angry, unbelieving eyes. Now even if she exposed herself, Roarin' James would be the winner – he was the only one with a weapon.

'Get your hands off me, you little fool!' she growled at Paul. 'Give that here!'

But instead of obeying the famous Flame, Paul pushed her backwards and ran downstage to sling her sword over into the orchestra pit: 'Give in – you're beaten!' he shouted, just as Tootie and Jo, dressed as two pirates, leapt from the wings and grabbed Flame by the arms and pinned her against an upstage flat. She cursed, she fought, but they had her held hard.

'Stay here, Macroo!' Tootie shouted. 'Your supremacy is over!'

'Never!' Allen Green roared, and rushed at Paul with his scimitar, a scowl on his face that said this would be no theatrical wounding, this would be for real.

There was confusion all around the stage, Sadie Baker was still kicking and struggling, the cast were shouting, the wings were thronging, as Paul had to leap to his guard – and go into the stage fight of his life, a final contest that covered the length and breadth of the set, Green stamping forward, sweating, swearing, slashing, stabbing – Paul fighting like a true son of Broadway, parrying and thrusting, jumping and ducking; until after a minute of it, upstage, downstage, left and right, both of them starting to tire, Green came leaping at him with a snort and a slaughtering slash – when Paul suddenly, inspirationally, threw in a maverick Bradley Turner twist to dive in under the man's arm and come up under his guard to neatly flick his own sword upwards, sending the scimitar skidding into the wings.

'Enough! Enough!' Paul shouted.

Chaos was running all ways in the wings. Some sort of new ending was being played, Ardal was going to change it. Flame shrieked and swore. Meg Macroo had been stopped from baring her breasts and winning the fight by surprise – breasts which today, to arouse and inflame, were going to be truly bared, painted with the red cross of St George. And the message she had been going to give, crowing over the defeated and dead body of a black man, wasn't going to be heard: her racist call to go out into the world and march – and fight – for white supremacy was being ruined.

Taking a quick chance to save the day, Lee Conyers lurched for the OP corner to grab at the handle that would pull the curtain down on the show before more damage was done. But in all this confusion Ben could act. He leapt from his hiding place and ran to grab at the same handle, throwing his free arm around Conyers's thick neck.

'Wha! Ye bastard!'

But with a jerking, choking move learned from crack troops in Lansana, Ben left Conyers slumped on the floor with the curtain only a part of the way down. He looked up to see Paul centre stage, jumping onto a 'ships' hatch' and staring out into the audience, his arms held wide and high. 'Supremacy?' he told them. 'There is none! There is difference – and difference is our strength.' He turned and pointed a straight arm at Allen Green. 'That black man is as good as these white men, my blood is no purer than my neighbour's, my brain no superior to my brothers' and sisters' around the world, nor to any of my earthly cousins...'

Seats started slamming up in the audience, someone clapped, stopped by the sound of a fight, murmurs turned to angry shouts, and Allen Green roared, 'Stop!' as he suddenly went lunging at Paul. But others were there. He was quickly grabbed by chorus and dance actors who must have been briefed by Tootie and Jo – holding him back despite his strength; dancers are as fit as any sportsmen.

Without losing his concentration, Paul went on. 'We must put up our swords, and unite in the strength of a thousand tongues, of countless cultures, of a history of heroes of every skin.'

From the look in the boy's eyes, Ben could see that he was enflamed, up there delivering the Ardal speech that they'd written in secret hotel rooms. He had rarely seen such fervour and belief in an actor's face.

'So, celebrate! If the future is to spin true there must be no race domination over race, not under God's heaven – but skin kinship with skin, living side by side on our small earth in racial harmony!'

It was word perfect, and a supreme and brave performance.

Inspired himself, Ben brought the curtain down to on-stage cheers from Tootie, Jo, and those who went along with Paul's speech. There were stunned faces, angry shouts, pushes, jostles, wild punches, and a sudden lunge by Allen Green to get to the tabs and through them – a man desperate to speak to the disoriented racist support. But he didn't get to pull the curtains apart. As he dived for the middle, Ron Quick took him crashing to the boards with a rugby tackle. He spat into Green's face.

'Wipe off your crap with that!' he said. 'Crawl back to your sewer!' And he cracked him with a righteous punch.

Neil Strong was heading for Ben Maddox; but Ben had already pushed the button to lower the fire-safety curtain, which came ponderously down. Nothing can stop 'the iron' once it has started to descend, hard as Strong tried – while Ben headed for the Prompt Corner – and to the audience address system.

Martin Kent was shouting his anger into Sadie Baker's face. 'How did you let that happen!? Do you know what all this has cost me?' His voice was falsetto with anger.

She shrieked back at him, telling him what to do and where to go. And while wild fighting spread over every metre of the stage, Ben's voice was amplified into the auditorium.

'*Mesdames et Messieurs!*' he began, with the accent of a Frenchman speaking English. 'The French police has can-celled the Paris rally today. You will please go to your transport peacefully and to your 'otels, and not to go to Le Place de la Concorde. It is not in occupation, it is empty, in control of the Polis Nationale. Everything is been can-celled. Thank you.' And with a great yank he destroyed any chance of the sound system being used again before a technician got to it.

There had definitely been something Ben Maddox could do.

Now, far from marching out to confront a rally, the audience was in discord and disarray. There was fighting where the racists took out their frustrations on normal members of the audience. In the void left by not having

Flame's instructions delivered from the stage some headed out of the exits into this street, others into that, some shouting 'left', some shouting 'right'. Heads yelled over heads about meeting up, but no one knew the geography well enough. From the stage the factions in the company went off to their dressing rooms. Fists and shouts still flew on the staircases; while Ben, Tootie, Jo and Paul – prepared – made their getaway as soon as they could change into street clothes.

'I didn't know the police had cancelled the rally!' Paul said to Ben as they strode the Rue Réaumur. 'That's a stroke!'

Ben waited for a spilt-out fight to clear from the road and headed towards the Le Parking de Carrefour before he stopped and put his hand on Paul's head, like a Pope with a blessing. 'I made that up,' he said. 'It's very much a live rally – the biggest ever in Europe. And you know what, we're going there! To celebrate how different we are from Green, and Kent, and Baker!'

And Paul swung into step with the others. All four marching like heroes.

ZEPHON TELEVISION
TRANSCRIPT SERVICE

Programme 12689
Zephon News

Saturday 24th August

End of package from Le Phénix Theatre, Paris, showing actor Paul Filey making an impassioned speech.

Live link from the Anti-Racist Rally, La Place de la Concorde, Paris. Banners, a band playing, shrill whistles blowing, people from all backgrounds waving at the camera, behind Ben.

BEN MADDOX (TO CAMERA – CLOSE UP):
So that's what happened in the Phoenix Theatre here, earlier today. An unpleasant and divisive attempt to sway French voters to the Far Right has failed. The white, racist elements of the audience have decomposed, thanks to that brave speech by a young actor, who undoubtedly took his life in his hands. Now we shall investigate White Ensign Productions, its accounts, and its undoubted murky doings.

Wide shot of the huge rally.

BEN MADDOX (OVER):
As for Flame, singer Sadie Baker – where will her career go from here? It's hard to think of her enjoying much of a comeback in the realities of a cosmopolitan world. There must be a few British and European theatres that even now are disinfecting their stages…

End of excerpt

Kath Lewis turned away from the monitor in her office. She leant to the drawer where she kept her claret and poured herself a glass. 'So,' she said to her secretary, 'Gary Fredericks and his trafficking wait for another day. Who knows – it may even have links with what Bloom's digging up on the drugs scene over there…'

'A sort of double undercover story, wasn't it? I thought Ben did very well…'

'Don't ever tell him so because he'll believe it – but our Ben Maddox is a star. A maverick Zephon star…'

And she drank to that, with a rare smile.

Paul saw the recording his mother had made of that Zephon News broadcast. He saw Ben Maddox's piece to camera from the midst of the peaceful, celebratory rally – and he saw the package from the theatre. It had shown the final scene in the Phoenix as it was played out – not shot on a pro-standard camera, but clear enough; a view from the audience of Ardal's speech, of the safety curtain coming down, and of the anger and confusion among the angry, baffled and disoriented audience who didn't know which way to turn, what to think, where to go. For every hard head that made for an exit, another seemed to be arguing with an organiser, or tearing up a programme, or just standing staring into space, like supporters of a football team that's just been relegated. And then there were the fights...

He had to say, though, Paul Filey as Ardal had done all right! There behind him on the stage had been Tootie and Jo with Sadie Baker in an armlock, and Ron Quick blocking Allen Green's light. They'd *all* done all right, Paul thought.

And as he watched it, he saw his mother crying across the room, and he began to cry himself. Holding the stage in such dramatic fashion, making that speech to a dropped-jaw house, saying something he so believed in saying – it had lifted him a sky higher than the singing of the finale had ever done. And so much stress and emotion has to have its release. He gave his mum a cuddle, made a cup of tea, then went upstairs to send an e-mail of congratulation to Ben Maddox. It was that man who had made sure that the racists didn't have their day.

But as Paul opened up his Outlook there was an unread message in his inbox. From his dad.

From: a.filey@gemstone.net
Sent: 25 Sep. 16.00
To: p.filey@tiscali.co.uk
Subject: future

Dear Paul

Was watching the news from the Paris Anti-Racist Rally – and who was on it but you! I watched your brave speech from in the theatre and was a v. proud father indeed. Brilliant!

It got me thinking about man's earliest history, his rehearsals for the hunt, and his cultural ideas. I thought about something Mum reminded me of on the phone last week, and I remembered a few Plays for Today that we saw together on TV as students; and some of the decent shows I've seen among the dross, like Samuel Becket, and Arthur Miller. The other night I saw a Ken Loach film – his stuff always moves me.

Your Ben Maddox explained what your break-away group in the cast was all about very well – and I've got to say that yesterday you made a difference. I suppose that racist singer thought it would be her making a difference, but it was you! What you did on that stage made a difference to the real world outside that theatre. Well done!

So... I think you should come over and see me very soon. I reckon we've got a few things to talk over, don't you?

With love
Dad x

Paul came off-line mouthing *Thank you, Mum* – and lay down on his bed, staring up at his West Ham poster. He started to wonder who the Irons were playing next weekend. But he suddenly jumped up and switched the computer on again, and got onto the world wide web – because more than West Ham he wanted to see what was on at the Theatre Royal, Stratford East, that week. That's where he'd spend his money, and his time.

For now, though, he set the e-mail to print his dad's hopeful words – and while the cartridge swiped, he threw himself on his bed again and let himself go, sobbing out his soul.

More **BEN MADDOX**
assignments

and other fantastic books by
Bernard Ashley

BERNARD ASHLEY

TEN DAYS
TO ZERO

£4.99

978 1 84362 649 7

BERNARD ASHLEY

When Ben Maddox is thurst into an investigation for
Zephon TV, he worries that he's in over his head. But as
he digs deeper into events, he realises that what's really
important is being prepared to fight for what you believe
in...and if that means taking risks, then that's exactly
what he'll have to do.

'Ten days to Zero is a brilliantly constructed thriller...
Hopping throught various formats, the reader is drawn
into a narrative web that is utterly absorbing.'
The Guardian

BERNARD ASHLEY

978 1 84616 059 2 £5.99

Ben Maddox is sent to find out what's really going on in Kutuliza, in Africa, and finds himself face-to-face with slick politicians, guerrilla fighters and a young boy who is the hope of football and his people. The situation is explosive – and Ben puts everything on the line...

'A powerful and exciting thriller'
Carousel

BERNARD ASHLEY

978 1 84121 306 4

£4.99

'Hold on tight!' Tom shouted at the girl. 'Grab hold of the side!'

Tom Welton's never done anything in his life that he's been proud of...really proud of. But a chance rescue of a girl off the Suffolk coast seems to offer him the opportunity to change all that, and soon Tom finds himself risking everything to save her.

BERNARD ASHLEY

£4.99

978 1 84362 204 8

Hard Stew always gets what he wants,
and he wants Davey's new bike.

But Hard Stew's not the only thing bothering
Davey, there's also the big family secret,
the one that everyone wants to keep from him.
A secret more frightening than a hundred Hard Stews.

The sort you've got to stare in the face.
If you've got the guts...

Shortlisted for the Sheffield Children's Book Award and
the Angus Award

'Bernard Ashley's great gift is to turn what seems
to be low-key realism into something much stronger
and more resonant.'
Philip Pullman

BERNARD ASHLEY

When Kaninda survives a brutal attack on his village in
East Africa, he joins the rebel army, where he's trained to
carry weapons, and use them.
But aid workers take him to London where he fetches
up in a comprehensive school. Clan and tribal conflicts
are everywhere, and on the streets it's estate versus estate,
urban tribe against urban tribe.
All Kaninda wants is to get back to his own war and
take revenge on his enemies. But together with Laura
Rose, the daughter of his new family, he is drawn into a
dangerous local conflict that is spiralling out of control.

Shortlisted for the Carnegie Medal and the Guardian
Children's Fiction Award

'So pacy that it is difficult to turn the pages fast enough.'
The School Librarian

'A gripping and compassionate tale.'
TES

MORE ORCHARD BLACK APPLES

Ten Days to Zero	**Bernard Ashley**	**978 1 84362 649 7**
Little Soldier	**Bernard Ashley**	**978 1 86039 879 7**
Tiger without Teeth	**Bernard Ashley**	**9781 84362 204 8**
Revenge House	**Bernard Ashley**	**978 1 84121 814 4**
Freedom Flight	**Bernard Ashley**	**978 1 84121 306 4**
Jacob's Ladder	**Brian Keaney**	**978 1 84362 721 0**
A Crack in the Line	**Michael Lawrence**	**978 1 84362 283 1**
Small Eternities	**Michael Lawrence**	**978 1 84362 870 5**
The Underwood See	**Michael Lawrence**	**978 1 84121 170 1**
Milkweed	**Jerry Spinelli**	**978 1 84362 485 1**
Stargirl	**Jerry Spinelli**	**978 1 84616 600 6**

All priced at £4.99 or £5.99

Orchard Black Apples are available from all good bookshops,
or can be ordered direct from the publisher:
Orchard Books, PO BOX 29, Douglas IM99 1BQ
Credit card orders please telephone 01624 836000
or fax 01624 837033 or visit our website: www.orchardbooks.co.uk
or e-mail: bookshop@enterprise.net for details.

To order please quote title, author and ISBN
and your full name and address.
Cheques and postal orders should be made payable to 'Bookpost plc.'
Postage and packing is FREE within the UK
(overseas customers should add £1.00 per book).

Prices and availability are subject to change.